Silence lay thick
and heavy between

It was Leslie who spoke first. "All this time," she whispered, "you acted as if you didn't care about Bonnie." She swallowed painfully. "But you do, don't you?"

When he said nothing, she regarded him pleadingly. "Tell me, Clint."

She saw his body stiffen. Then, just when she couldn't stand it anymore, he held out his hand. "Come here," he said softly.

She went, on shaky legs.

His fingers closed around hers, strong and warm. "Will you let me explain?"

His quiet entreaty made her ache inside. Suddenly she wished she had remained silent. "There's no need," she said unsteadily.

"I want to, Leslie. I think I need to—" the look he bestowed upon her was deep and intense "—for both of us."

ABOUT THE AUTHOR

Sandra James was inspired to set her eighth
Superromance novel in San Diego after
spending five days in that beautiful city on a
holiday with her husband. *Almost Heaven* was
begun shortly after their return from that visit,
Sandra recalls. The popular author lives
with her husband and three daughters in
Salem, Oregon.

Books by Sandra James

HARLEQUIN SUPERROMANCE

205–A FAMILY AFFAIR
249–BELONGING
277–STRONGER BY FAR
306–GUARDIAN ANGEL
335–SPRING THUNDER
352–SUMMER LIGHTNING
386–NORTH OF EDEN

Almost Heaven

SANDRA JAMES

Harlequin Books

TORONTO • NEW YORK • LONDON
AMSTERDAM • PARIS • SYDNEY • HAMBURG
STOCKHOLM • ATHENS • TOKYO • MILAN

Published January 1991

ISBN 0-373-70435-6

ALMOST HEAVEN

CHAPTER ONE

SAN DIEGO. Sunshine and palm trees. Fun and forget-fulness. At the time, it had sounded like such a great idea....

Now it was too late to change her mind.

Leslie Wilson was one of the last passengers off the flight from San Francisco. She stepped from the boarding tunnel, wishing she could share the bustle and excitement all around her. She watched as a fresh-faced girl with stardust in her eyes threw her arms around the young man who had sat in front of Leslie on the plane. All around, there were shouts of recognition, bursts of laughter, beaming grins and frantic waves.

She felt like a child—one who had strayed away from home and thought herself abandoned. No, she thought again, this hadn't been a good idea at all.

But Colleen's invitation had come at a time when her spirits needed a little boosting—as they had for quite some time, Leslie admitted reluctantly. Her best friend's call had come during the last week of classes. Golden Hills Academy was shutting down for the summer; most of the girls were going home. Some were headed for summer camp, or exotic vacations with parents or friends. Everyone had plans . . . everyone but her.

"You need a change," Colleen had stated in her typically blunt manner. "A change of pace, and a whole new change of scenery. Rob and I would love to have you come and visit. Why, you haven't seen our new house yet! Besides, since the divorce, every time I've talked to you, you've been down. I know when you're not at work you've just been sitting at home alone. And you already told me your last day of work at the school is Monday, and then you're free for the summer. So no excuses, Leslie."

Leslie hadn't been able to argue. Her time was divided between her job at Golden Hills and home. How she hated returning to an empty apartment! But getting out and socializing—which all her friends and acquaintances advised—was the one thing she couldn't do. She couldn't face the inevitable questions about her breakup with Dennis, for what could she say? The truth was simply too painful—worse, it was too humiliating. It was easier just to stay at home and try to forget....

It was impossible.

So she had hedged, and made excuses...until she'd picked up her mail later that week and found an envelope from her attorney.

Inside were her final divorce papers.

It was then she'd finally made up her mind to visit Colleen. She wasted no time phoning Colleen to let her know. But exactly one week later, almost the instant she left her apartment for the airport, her newfound determination began to waver. Naturally she hadn't booked with Dennis's airline. Still, one thought kept running through her mind. *What if I see him? What if he's there?* It had taken all the courage she possessed to walk into San Francisco International.

But she had, and here she was in San Diego. It was time, Leslie told herself staunchly, that she stopped looking over her shoulder. The seven years of her life she'd given to Dennis couldn't be wiped away as easily as chalk on a slate, but this visit with Colleen Stuart and her family was part of the healing process.

Nonetheless, Leslie's gaze was anxious as she scanned the milling throng for a pixie-faced blonde. She came to a stop just beyond the crowded waiting area.

There was no sign of Colleen. *You haven't changed since college, Colleen Stuart. As usual, you're late.* The thought cheered her for the first time since she had arrived in San Diego. But twenty minutes later, the feeling had vanished. She had collected her baggage, been to the ladies' room twice, and Colleen was still nowhere in sight.

Leslie fingered her shoulder tote and glanced around the baggage area. She felt rather conspicuous standing with her suitcase at her feet. Worse, it seemed she was the only one who was *alone*. Everywhere she looked, there were people in pairs, both young and old. An elderly couple stepped up to the luggage carousel. They stood waiting, hand in hand, scarcely aware of anyone else. It was really rather sweet—and sentimental. Another time, another place, and Leslie might have smiled. But right now all she wanted was to run home, curl up and cry—as she'd done countless times before.

She turned away, only to see a uniformed young man stop directly in front of her, smartly dressed in navy blues. Ruddy-cheeked and bright-eyed, he was flanked on each side by a woman. He smiled first at one, then the other.

There was a song—the thought swirled into her mind before she could stop it—something about a woman in every port....

Her breath caught painfully. She didn't need this. The tears which were never far away blurred her vision. She tore her gaze from the trio before she made a complete fool of herself.

The blood roared through her head, pounding in her ears. She reached for her luggage with trembling hands. Escape was uppermost in her mind. All she wanted was to put as much distance as possible between that young sailor and herself.

She began to walk—blindly, unthinkingly—concentrating only on putting one foot before the other. There was a corner just ahead. Her steps quickened. It was then that she saw him, a tall stranger standing directly in her path....

Dennis!

Her heart lurched. She couldn't breathe. For an instant all her mind was able to register was that he was tall and dark.

It took a moment before she was able to think clearly. Air seeped slowly into her lungs as she breathed a shaky sigh of relief.

The man before her was not Dennis. This man was broader in the shoulders, but leaner and rangier—and he braced himself on a wooden cane.

Nonetheless, the intensity of this man's look was enough to stop her cold. She paused uncertainly.

His scrutiny was disconcerting. A prickly sensation rippled along her spine as she saw that he had paused as well. Some twenty feet separated them, but Leslie felt as if she'd been singled out. And just for an instant, she could have sworn that he knew her secret.... Again, her impulse was to escape and retreat; she thought of whirling and going back the way she'd just come.

But the sailor might still be there.

She closed her eyes briefly, her grip tightening on the handle of her bag. *Stop it,* she admonished herself fiercely. She was being maudlin and paranoid, letting the whole sordid mess with Dennis control her life like this.

But was that so unusual? The thought reared up and snapped back at her, ringing with self-mockery. For seven years, her life—her whole world—had revolved around Dennis. All she'd ever wanted was to please him, to love and be loved in return, as desperately and wildly as she loved him.

What a fool she had been . . . and what a failure.

An impatient exclamation reached her ears. Someone jostled her, and Leslie relinquished the memory of Dennis almost gratefully. Murmuring a quick apology, she stepped back toward the wall. Her gaze veered automatically across the wide hallway once more.

The man was still watching her! She glanced quickly away, but his image remained—hair so dark it was almost black, features sharply angled and hawklike.

She eased her suitcase to the floor, battling a debilitating nervousness. Once more she stole a sidelong glance at the man.

He stared at her still.

Damn it, anyway! She tore her eyes away and fought a burst of hysterical laughter. She possessed neither the face nor figure that turned men's heads. What on earth was the dratted man trying to prove?

She hesitated, pretending to rummage around in her purse. Someone else might have walked straight up to him and confronted him outright. But her self-confidence had been badly bruised this past year, and it had never been like her to be so bold.

It seemed she had just one alternative. *Move!* Leslie commanded herself. He knows you saw him staring at you. Surely he won't follow. She picked up her bag, lifted her chin and walked forward again with a casualness she was far from feeling.

A moment later, she glanced back over her shoulder. The tall form at the corner was gone. She breathed a silent sigh of relief.

"Excuse me."

The voice at her ear nearly made her jump. Startled, Leslie looked up into eyes as dark as midnight.

He'd followed her! Leslie drew a sharp breath of dismay.

"Yes?" Her voice was clipped and rather abrupt. She thought he looked a little annoyed at her tone, but she paid no heed. She was too busy cataloging a face that was both handsome and arresting—bronzed skin drawn over ruggedly defined cheekbones, a sharp blade of a nose and thin sensuous lips. She experienced a vague nagging feeling. Had she seen him before?

Fast on the heels of that thought came the realization that he didn't look quite as fierce close up as he did from a distance, despite the almost arrogant arch of his eyebrows and the unyielding set of his mouth. In fact, he might be even more attractive if only he would smile....

Now *she* was the one who was openly staring, and a slight lift of those devilishly tilted dark brows told her she'd been caught. She despised the heated flush that rose to her cheeks.

"You know," she heard him say mildly, "another minute and you'd have lost me." He grimaced and shifted so that the right side of his body bore the brunt of his weight.

He was resting heavily on the cane, Leslie noticed, but she wasn't inclined to sympathy right now. She didn't know why he'd singled her out, but she wasn't about to indulge him.

"Lost me?" she inquired stiffly. "I'm afraid you've made a mistake. I can't think of a single reason why you'd want to find me." There. Now she'd told him and it wasn't so difficult after all.

But instead of looking properly chastised, he only seemed amused. "I can," he returned wryly. "I'm under strict orders to bring you home."

If he'd hoped to snag her attention, he'd succeeded. "Home?" she echoed. Her tone, as well as her expression, was wary. She squared her shoulders and looked him straight in the eye. "I'm meeting someone," she stated coolly. "So as I said before, you must be mistaken—"

He was shaking his head. "I don't think so. You are Leslie, aren't you?"

Leslie blinked. She gave a jerky nod before she had time to think better of it.

"Good. Because Colleen would shoot me if I left you here to get home on your own."

The relief in his voice was anything but reassuring. Her eyes roamed over him quickly. Again she experienced a glimmer of recognition. Her mind searched frantically, but she couldn't place him.

She wet her lips. "Do I know you?"

The question and her confusion seemed to amuse him. "Yes and no."

It was her turn to raise her brows. "That's quite an answer, Would you mind explaining it?"

He studied her a moment. "You really don't remember me?"

Leslie shook her head.

"No?" His lips curved slightly, a smile that wasn't quite a smile. "I'm Clint. Ring any bells yet?"

There was a small but expectant silence. Leslie stared at him blankly. Was he the father of one of the girls at Golden Hills?

"Obviously I made quite an impression." His tone turned dry as he added, "Clint Stuart."

Clint Stuart. It took a fraction of a second for the name to sink in. When it did, Leslie's hand flew to her mouth. "You're Rob's brother," she gasped, embarrassed that she hadn't recognized him. "I'm terribly sorry... I thought you looked familiar, but I just couldn't remember where... I—I honestly didn't mean to be so rude...."

"It's all right. After all, it's been a long time." Again, that smile that wasn't quite a smile. In some distant corner of her mind, she wondered what the real thing would look like.

And he was right, of course. She had retained little memory of Rob's brother, other than of a tall, dark man. They'd met only once, at Colleen and Rob's wedding nearly ten years ago.

Weddings. Leslie winced inside. Marriage and happily-ever-after was the last thing she wanted to think about right now. If she did, her fraying composure would come completely unraveled.

"Besides," she heard him add, "I'm the one who ought to apologize, I almost scared you off staring at you the way I did. You've changed from what I remember. Colleen showed me a picture of you, but you look so different it took me a minute to realize it was you." His dark gaze traveled leisurely over her, taking in her linen jacket and matching slacks.

Leslie's heart jumped. Judging from the appreciative glint in his eyes, Clint Stuart appeared to like what he saw. She'd given her appearance the seal of approval as well this morning. The pale yellow of her suit flattered her tall figure more than ever since she'd dropped ten pounds, and brought out the honey-gold highlights in her hair. It was odd, really. The worst year of her life and she'd never looked better.

But when she garnered the courage to meet his gaze, his features registered nothing more than polite detachment. Still, the diversion was just what she needed.

"Speaking of Colleen," she murmured, "I take it she got hung up somewhere and couldn't meet me."

From out of nowhere a smile appeared. Seeing it, Leslie caught her breath. It hit her in the pit of the stomach just how attractive Rob's brother was, and it was just as she'd suspected. When he smiled, he was nothing short of spectacular.

"Hung up," he echoed. Wry humor flickered in his eyes. "That's just a nice way of saying she's perpetually tardy."

Amazingly Leslie felt herself laugh, taken in by the warmth in his voice. "Then I guess Colleen hasn't changed at all, has she?"

"No," he affirmed dryly, "and I doubt she ever will. She did have a legitimate excuse though. Brian had a dental appointment at one this afternoon, but the dentist's office called at the last minute and changed it to the last one of the day. Colleen knew she'd never make it here in time, so she asked me to pick you up, instead." He reached for the suitcase at her side.

When she saw his intention, Leslie's eyes widened. She couldn't help but notice the way he favored his left leg. "Oh, please don't bother. I can manage myself, honestly. Besides, your leg—"

"Will be fine as long as we're not doing laps around the terminal." He lifted the suitcase and straightened. "I suppose we'd better be on our way," he said lightly. "Knowing Colleen, if we're not home soon she'll likely send out the marines."

This time, Leslie's smile was forced. Marines. Sailors. Men in uniform. All were reminders of the past she'd hoped to escape.

For the umpteenth time since her arrival, Leslie wondered if coming to San Diego hadn't been a big mistake.

CLINT KEPT HIS EYES trained on the ribbon of freeway stretched out ahead. He eased back against the comfortably worn leather of his seat, trying not to grimace. His leg was killing him; the jarring steps he'd taken with Leslie's luggage bouncing against his thigh hadn't helped. Yet he wouldn't have admitted it to her, though he didn't quite understand the reason himself.

Maybe it was because he was just as stubborn as Colleen and Rob always said he was. Or maybe it was because he suspected Leslie Wilson was a soft touch—and the last thing he needed was pity.

Or maybe it was his way of doing a little penance.

Colleen had told him several days ago that she and Rob were expecting a houseguest. According to Colleen, her friend was still recovering from her recent divorce.

Clint wasn't very proud of his initial reaction. His first thought was that Leslie Wilson was rather thin-skinned; after all, there were no kids, no messy custody suit to clutter the issue. A divorce was nothing compared to what he'd been through....

No, he hadn't been thrilled with the news, though he cared about his brother and sister-in-law far too much to let his true feelings show. When he'd left Florida, the doctor had told him he needed a big dose of R and R. Clint told himself this would be a good chance to relax and enjoy doing absolutely nothing for a change, other than checking in at the head office periodically to get a jump on his next assignment.

Relaxing and doing nothing were easy in theory, he reflected dourly. The problem was—he was too damn touchy these days. He didn't like being laid up. He liked to be busy. It kept his mind off... other things.

He also liked his privacy. Family was one thing—he loved Rob and Colleen and the kids. But the thought of a stranger in their midst annoyed him. He'd managed to conceal his irritation, though. He'd even managed to convince himself he didn't really care one way or another who Colleen's friend was or how long she stayed; hopefully it wouldn't be long and their paths would seldom cross.

But all that was before he'd seen her.

He couldn't forget her expression the moment she'd noticed him. He hadn't imagined her frozen features, the naked distress in her eyes....

Clint couldn't fathom her reaction. But more important, he didn't like knowing he was responsible for it.

His gaze was inevitably drawn to his passenger. They'd exchanged the usual small talk—the weather in San Francisco had been foggy this morning, her flight uneventful, and yes, she'd visited the L.A. area before but never San Diego.

She appeared to have completely recovered from whatever jolt he'd given her earlier. But Clint couldn't help thinking that despite her composure at the moment, the scared little girl he'd glimpsed earlier hadn't vanished into thin air.

He was right.

Leslie unconsciously gnawed her lower lip. Now, as when she'd arrived at Lindbergh Field, she felt completely out of the swing of things. She'd kept close to herself these past months, maybe too close.

She tried to content herself with watching the sweeping landscape outside the window. They'd left the glittering waters of San Diego Harbor and Mission Bay behind, passing crowds of roller skaters, cyclists and windsurfers. Now they were headed north along the coast. Every so often there was a glimpse of surf-pounded shoreline.

Her gaze touched on the profile of the man in the driver's seat. Clint Stuart looked strong, capable and confident, ready and able to take on the world. A pang of envy shot through Leslie. It had been a long time since she had felt that way—forever, it seemed.

She was almost glad to let her mind drift in his direction. She wasn't quite sure what to make of Clint Stuart. True, he was friendly enough, yet she sensed a kind of distance within him.

She was rather curious about him, as well. She had seen Colleen only occasionally in the past few years, though it was rare that even a month went by that they weren't on the phone together. It had been that way since college. But when they spoke over the phone, there was always such a flurry to catch up on personal things. Colleen seldom mentioned her brother-in-law.

Leslie took a deep breath and decided to strike up a conversation, no matter how inane. But then she noticed the tiny white lines etched around his mouth. As she watched, one lean hand slid beneath his thigh and adjusted the angle of his outstretched leg. For a fraction of a second, his lips tightened, as if he were in pain.

Compassion rose in her, sure and swift. She shouldn't have let him carry her suitcase, no matter how insistent he had been. "Are you okay?" she asked quickly.

Even his nod seemed a little strained.

Leslie watched him closely. "I can drive if you'd like. I'll need directions, of course, but I honestly don't mind."

Clint shook his head. "Thanks, anyway," he told her, "but there's really no need. Another ten minutes and we'll be home."

Leslie's eyes remained fixed on him. She hadn't stopped wondering about his cane and what had happened to his leg. The material of his pants stretched more tightly around his left thigh, leading her to believe there might be some kind of splint or perhaps a bandage beneath.

"I hope you don't think I'm being nosy," she said softly, "But do you mind if I ask what happened to your leg?"

Clint negotiated a sharp bend in the road before responding. "We had an accident at a construction site," he explained. "I was thrown from the car I was in, and a metal runner got the best of me. But don't worry," he added with a faint light in his eye. "I wasn't the one driving, so you're perfectly safe."

Leslie wasn't inclined to share his amusement. "How awful," she murmured.

"It's not exactly the vacation I'd have chosen," he commented dryly, "but Colleen keeps telling me it's a blessing in disguise."

"So you're off work for a while?"

"Another six weeks or so I'm told."

He sounded so much like a fidgety little boy that Leslie smiled. The next moment, however, she frowned.

Clint glanced over and saw it. His dark brows rose inquisitively. "What?" he asked.

Leslie bit her lip, more than a little embarrassed. "You're going to think I'm an absolute dunce, but I'm afraid I can't remember what it is you do." Her voice was small. "You mentioned a construction site, though, so you must be a builder."

His slow-growing smile was bewildering—and bewitching, as well. For the first time in what seemed like hours, Leslie felt herself relax.

"You're not a builder?" she asked with a half laugh.

He appeared to consider. "Yes... and no."

Leslie chuckled. She could like Clint Stuart, she realized, and she hoped this wouldn't be the last she'd see of him during her visit here. The thought kindled a warm glow of pleasure deep inside. "So we're back to that again, eh?"

Clint glanced over at her. He knew Colleen and Leslie had been bosom buddies since college, but he'd already deduced she was nothing like Colleen, who was bubbly and outgoing and just as outspoken. But Leslie's wide blue eyes were sparkling, full of an impish delight he wouldn't have suspected.

His gaze shifted back to the road, but the smile remained. "I'm a transportation engineer. I plan and design highway systems."

"That's right," Leslie exclaimed. Bits and pieces of memory were slowly returning. "I remember Colleen telling me once that you were in Central America. Is that where the accident happened?"

She wasn't prepared for the effect her innocent question had on Clint. Whatever softness she thought she'd seen in him vanished as if it had never existed.

His smile withered. His jaw tensed. His expression grew closed and tight.

"It happened in Florida," he replied curtly. "Central America was a long time ago."

Leslie stared at him. She tried not to let his abrupt change of mood bother her, but she couldn't help it. What had she said? She was confused and dismayed; she felt like a child whose hands had been slapped for no reason. Most of all, she was hurt, and with the hurt came humiliation. A cold hollowness filled her chest as her thoughts turned bitter. Thanks to Dennis, she'd had enough hurt and humiliation to last a lifetime.

More than ever, Leslie wished she'd stayed home in San Francisco.

CHAPTER TWO

THE REMAINDER OF THE DRIVE passed in awkward silence. Clint gave his undivided attention to his driving. Leslie sat with her head turned toward the window, her hands clasped tightly in her lap.

The landscape outside passed in a kaleidoscope of color—green palms, blue sky, golden sunlight skimming the ocean. But Leslie's world right now was confined to a dismal shade of gray. She scarcely noticed when they turned off the main road. It wasn't until the car began to slow that she sat up and took notice of her surroundings.

They passed through a small, quaint town and over the rise of a steep hill. Halfway down, Clint made another turn into a quiet residential neighborhood.

Leslie reached for her purse. Taking out her compact, she fluffed the wispy layer of bangs and pushed wavy strands of chestnut hair from her shoulders. She surveyed the result with a critical frown. Seeing her reflection in the mirror was still an eye-opener. Once she'd decided to take Colleen up on her offer, she'd changed her hairstyle and splurged on some new outfits. New image, new woman...with the same old fears.

She snapped the compact shut and shoved it in her purse. Moments later, the car rolled to a halt. Leslie found herself staring at a rambling multilevel house of whitewashed stucco. Late afternoon sunlight bounced off the gleaming red tile roof.

"Well," she heard Clint announce, "here we are. Safe and sound at last."

Thankfully there was no need for a reply. Leslie forced a tight little smile, opened the car door and stepped onto the sidewalk. In spite of her doubts about this visit, excitement was building within her. It was beautiful here, calm and serene. All at once she yearned to see Colleen again, to laugh and talk the way they had all those years ago in college.

And suddenly there she was, dear sweet Colleen. Seeing her flying across the yard, her round face alight with pleasure, was like coming home after years of exile.

"Les! Oh, Les, you finally made it!" Colleen's joyful voice rang through the air. Leslie found herself seized in a fierce embrace. "I'm so glad you're here. I can't tell you how good it is to see you again."

They alternately laughed and hugged. Colleen stepped back and ran a discerning eye over her. "My goodness, you look fantastic! You let your hair grow. I've never seen it so long, but I really like it! And you've lost weight, haven't you?"

Leslie laughed uneasily. Colleen had probably expected a pale little waif. But scars left on the inside were sometimes the worst. No one knew better than she.

"I'm really sorry I couldn't meet your plane," Colleen told her.

From the corner of her eye Leslie noticed Clint making his way around the front bumper of the car.

Colleen glanced at him with a mischievous toss of her head.

"But if nothing else, at least you've gotten reacquainted with my shifty-eyed brother-in-law."

Clint leaned against the hood of the car and playfully swung his cane at her feet. Colleen laughed and neatly sidestepped his aim. Leslie didn't miss the warm affection that glowed between them.

"Actually," she heard him say, "I don't think Leslie was pleased to discover I was her welcoming committee."

Colleen groaned. "Something tells me I don't want to know why."

"I think she suspected I was trying to pick her up."

Leslie felt the weight of his eyes on her. Was he poking fun at her? She wanted to snap her chin up and boldly challenge him, but something held her back.

"You?" Colleen laughed as if she found the idea totally outrageous.

Just then the front door opened and two small children raced across the yard. Blond ponytail bobbing furiously, the little girl skidded to a halt beside her mother and grinned up at the three adults. The little boy, older than his sister by several years, sought refuge next to his uncle.

Leslie's eyes widened. "That can't be Tess and Brian. Why, Brian's so tall! And Tess looks so grown up!"

Tess held up four fingers. "I'm four now," she disclosed happily. "I just had a birthday."

They all laughed while Colleen crooked a finger at her son. "Come here, young man."

Brian inched forward.

When he stood before her, Colleen glanced between the two youngsters. "Remember I told you we were going to have company for a while?"

Tess's ponytails wagged furiously, while Brian gave a barely discernible nod. Two pair of eyes swung expectantly toward Leslie.

"Well, this is Leslie, kids. Brian, do you remember her? We saw her two summers ago when we went to northern California to see the redwoods."

Brian silently shook his head. Tess proudly proclaimed, "I 'member her, Mommy."

Brian frowned at his sister. "No, you don't. You could hardly even talk then!"

"But she's making up for it now, isn't she?" Clint said in a low voice.

Colleen's laughter was carried away by a balmy breeze. Leslie's gaze flickered to Clint, but she couldn't appreciate his dry humor just now. She was still smarting from his earlier abruptness.

She eased down so that she was on the same level as the two children. Brian had inherited his mother's blondness, but his eyes were a warm toasty brown like his father's. Tess was the image of her mother—in looks and personality, Leslie suspected.

She smiled at Brian. "You know," she said softly, "there aren't any boys at the school where I work, so this is going to be a nice change for me."

Tess looked disgruntled. "Don't you like girls?"

"Of course I do!" Leslie hastened to assure her. "At my school we have big girls *and* little girls, but none as small as you. That's why I think the next few weeks will be so much fun for all of us."

That seemed to please Tess, who grinned broadly. Brian tipped his head to the side. "Are you a teacher?" he asked.

"I used to be. But now I help the woman who's in charge of the school. Do you have a principal at your school, Brian?"

"Yeah." He seemed to consider. "She's pretty nice—most of the time."

Leslie had difficulty keeping a straight face at his cautiousness. "Well, that's a lot like what I do. The principal at my school doesn't have time to take care of everything, so I help her."

"Do you like it?" he asked.

Now there was a question. During the last school year, her job as assistant headmistress had been less than satisfying. She suspected it was because of the upheaval in her life, but by May, she was more restless and dissatisfied than ever. She was seriously thinking of changing jobs.

"Yes," she said finally. But she'd hesitated a moment too long; she could see it in Colleen's face when she rose to her feet.

Colleen said nothing, however, Instead, she shooed the children into the house. "You two go inside and wash your hands. Dinner's ready, and Daddy will be home any minute now."

Beside them, Clint straightened. Leslie squared her shoulders and turned to him, determined to be gracious. "I may not see you again before I leave, but I'd like to thank you for picking me up."

The words seemed to surprise him, though for the life of her, Leslie couldn't think why. Nor did she understand the rueful half smile that followed.

"Colleen obviously didn't tell you you're not the only houseguest."

Leslie sucked in her breath. Houseguest? He was staying here, too? Wonderful, she thought gloomily. Just wonderful.

Colleen frowned at him with mock severity. "Listen up, brother-in-law. You may not be a permanent fixture around here, but you're hardly a guest."

"I know," he retorted. "You make me do my share when I'm here."

"Are you complaining?"

"Not at all. You're too good a cook, and I'd hate to starve."

Their good-natured banter had little effect on Leslie. All day long she'd been feeling rather lost and unwanted, and this latest revelation hadn't helped. She was silent while Colleen waved Clint off toward the house, telling him that Rob could bring Leslie's luggage up to the house later.

When he was gone, Colleen looked at her closely. "I apologize for not telling you about Clint earlier," she said quickly, "but when I asked you to come, we didn't know Clint would be here."

Leslie managed a smile. "It's all right. He told me about his leg. Besides, it sounds as if he's here quite often."

Colleen wrinkled her nose. "I don't know if I'd go that far," she said dryly. "Clint spends so much time away on one highway project or another that he's usually not home more than a couple of weekends a year."

They had begun to walk toward the house. Leslie pointed to a small building just behind the garage.

"That's Clint's place," she explained. "We figured it was originally meant for a mother-in-law arrangement, but it was only a shell when we moved in. We finished off the interior so it's completely self-sufficient and turned it over to Clint. Rob and I wouldn't have been able to buy this place if it weren't for Clint, so we figured giving him somewhere to stay when he's home was the least we could do. He's totally helpless in the kitchen, though," she finished with a laugh, "so he usually eats his meals with us."

She paused. The gaze she turned on Leslie was anxious. "You don't mind, do you? I was afraid if I called and told you Clint was here, you wouldn't come."

If I'd known, I probably wouldn't have, Leslie agreed silently. Though she smiled and squeezed Colleen's shoulder, her thoughts were on the tall masculine figure who'd just disappeared into the house.

She tried telling herself it was silly to be disturbed over Clint Stuart's presence, but her mental pep talk did little good. Perhaps he hadn't meant to upset her, but he had, and she wasn't inclined to forgiveness right now. Furthermore, it had been stupid of her to feel anything at all toward him. For just a little while she'd thought they could be friends; now she wasn't sure that was possible.

She had no idea what the next few weeks would bring. But here she was, and here *he* was, and she really had no choice but to make the best of it.

She only hoped they saw as little of each other as possible.

LESLIE NEVER KNEW how she happened to land directly across from Clint at the dinner table. But whatever dark cloud had come over him in the car seemed to have vanished. He was wonderful with the kids and teased Colleen unmercifully. If it hadn't been for that distressing episode in the car, Leslie might have fallen under his spell. As the meal wore on, however, she found herself softening in spite of herself. Perhaps he wasn't so bad after all . . . as long as Central America wasn't the topic of conversation.

She studied him covertly. There was no mistaking the physical resemblance between the two brothers. Both had the same sharply honed features and tall build, though Clint was much rangier and leaner. Rob, however, had a warm, friendly appearance with a gentle mouth that seemed to perpetually smile; Clint possessed a dark elegance as well as a hint of ruggedness. Oddly it was Clint who looked older. There was an underlying toughness in him that wasn't present in Rob, a hardness that both intrigued and repelled her.

With a start she realized Colleen had just asked if she wanted more coffee. She quickly placed her hand over her cup and shook her head. "Thanks, but I'm fine. Any more and I'm afraid I'll be awake all night."

"You probably will be, anyway," Rob said cheerfully. "Don't you think it's hard sleeping in a strange bed? Especially the first night away from home."

"She's a fine one to ask." Colleen replaced the coffeepot on the counter and moved back to the table. "That sounds like a question for the happy wanderer here." She nodded at Clint.

The happy wanderer. Leslie's smile froze as her thoughts veered directly to Dennis. As a flight navigator for a major airline, Dennis had spent more nights *away* from home than he had with her. . . .

Stop! screamed a voice in her head. Don't think about that . . . don't think about *him*!

"Hey," piped Tess in a cheery little voice. "Where's Leslie gonna sleep, anyway? With Uncle Clint at his house?"

For a moment there was absolute silence. Even Colleen was speechless. It was left to Rob to say hastily, "No, sweetheart."

"But she came with him."

"I know, Tess. But Leslie is taking the spare bedroom—the one next to yours."

"Which means you get to wake *her* up for a change." Clint's voice started out rather strangled, but there was no denying the undercurrent of amusement.

Leslie was too embarrassed to look at him. Summoning the last dregs of her dignity, she cleared her throat and stood. "Shall we get these cleared up, Colleen? Then when we're done, I think I'll unpack."

"Sure thing, Les." Colleen rose to her feet but made no move to gather up the dishes. "Before everybody scatters, Rob and I have something we'd like to tell you." Her expression was soft and radiant as she turned to her husband. "Would you like to tell them, Rob, or shall I?"

Rob grinned. "I know you're dying to, so I'll leave it up to you."

Colleen glanced around the table, her eyes shining. "We," she said proudly, "are pregnant!"

THE NEWS HAD A WRENCHING impact on Leslie. It was like being pushed off a swingset and hitting the ground with a bone-jarring thud. Yet somehow she managed to stay calm, cheerfully congratulating both Colleen and Rob. She even managed to still her trembling lips and force a parody of a smile.

But it was agony being there, witnessing the tender looks and beaming smiles exchanged between them. Leslie helped clear the table, then excused herself and escaped to her room. She started to unpack, but soon gave up. She sank onto the double bed angled in the corner and stared bleakly at the walls. The room was decorated in soothing blues and grays, but Leslie felt anything but calm.

After a while there was a scurry of footsteps outside in the hall and muffled voices. She guessed Colleen and Rob were putting Brian and Tess to bed. Somehow she wasn't surprised when a knock sounded at the door a short time later.

"Come in," she called.

The door opened a fraction. Colleen peeked inside. "Hi. Can I come in?"

Leslie waved her inside. Her throat was still tight from willing away her foolish tears, but she was glad she hadn't succumbed. The last thing she wanted was to make Colleen feel guilty.

But Colleen had known her too long—too well.

The bed dipped as she sat down. The look she gave Leslie was measured and intense. The concern in her eyes made Leslie want to cry all over again.

"You wish you hadn't come, don't you?" she said at last.

Leslie floundered helplessly. She didn't want to lie, yet what could she say? The truth would hurt Colleen.

"I won't be offended if you say yes. We've known each other too long, and there were never any secrets when we were in college."

No, Leslie thought numbly. *But that was then, and this is now, and there are things I can't tell even you....*

"It's . . . hard," she admitted haltingly. "You were right when you said I've been sitting around home moping. I—I haven't been out much since the divorce. And now I feel like a kid just learning how to ride a bike. I—I don't want to fall flat on my face, so maybe it's safer not to even try."

Colleen bit her lip. "I was hoping this visit would be good for you," she said quietly, "but I seem to have made things worse. You were fine until I blurted out that I was pregnant. I hit a sore spot, didn't I?"

"A little." Leslie swallowed painfully. "I'd wanted a baby for a long time," she admitted. Her gaze flickered up to Colleen's, then quickly away. "But Dennis always said—" to her horror her voice was quivering "—he always said he wanted to wait, that we had plenty of time to start a family."

Colleen reached out and hugged her fiercely. "Me and my big mouth," she whispered. "I'm so darned impulsive sometimes. I didn't even think about you and Dennis or how you might feel. I'm sorry, Les. I'm so sorry."

It had hurt to say the words aloud, more than Leslie had thought. But when she glimpsed the betraying moisture in Colleen's eyes, her heart went out to her. "Don't apologize," she said softly. "It's wonderful news. I'm very happy for you, Colleen."

They exchanged hugs again, and after a moment Colleen drew back. "I'm not trying to be nosy," she said slowly. "But you know we've never really talked much about Dennis and your divorce, and I was just thinking. Maybe you'd feel better about the whole thing if you did."

There was an expectant pause. Throughout this last year Colleen had never asked questions or pried into the whys and wherefores of her split from Dennis. But somehow the phone had always seemed to ring when Leslie was feeling her lowest, and sure enough, Colleen was there to pick up her sagging spirits, sensing her need to talk or simply to listen.

Yet a flurry of panic whirled inside Leslie at the thought of trying to explain. No one was closer than she and Colleen, yet she couldn't tell Colleen, she just couldn't! Oh, she was good at outward appearances—even her mother commented on how well she was coping. But this was Colleen, who knew her better than anyone else.

She shook her head. "Talking about it won't change what happened. When I married Dennis, I thought it was forever. Now—" her breath emerged on a deep, weary sigh "—it's over and I just want to forget."

"But you can't, can you?"

Leslie smiled sadly. "Am I that transparent?"

Colleen reached out and gripped Leslie's hands. "It still hurts to think of Dennis, doesn't it?"

No! It hurt to think of him with *her* . . . with *them*. But as much as Leslie wanted to deny the pain—swiftly and categorically—she said nothing.

"You don't have to tell me anything you don't want to," Colleen said softly. "I'll admit I was hurt when you didn't confide in me right away. And I was so surprised when you told me you'd filed for divorce. You never let on that anything was wrong—''

Because she hadn't known! She'd been so blind, so stupidly unaware. Eventually she'd begun to suspect something... but not what she found.

"Then I realized that some things are too painful to talk about, even between the best of friends. I started thinking about how lonely you must have been sometimes. I know Dennis's job took him away a lot....''

Bitterness choked Leslie. Dennis's job took him away, all right. It took him straight to *her*.

"There was another woman.'' Leslie's voice was low and barely audible; nonetheless, it startled her to hear herself speak.

She'd shocked Colleen—she could see it. Under other circumstances, Colleen's wide-eyed disbelief might have been comical. If Dennis's infidelity had shocked the usually unflappable Colleen, what would her reaction be if she knew that was only part of it? And not even the worst part.

"An affair,'' Colleen repeated numbly. "Dennis was having an affair?''

Another woman. An affair. A wrenching pain ripped through Leslie. If only it were that simple. What Dennis had done was worse—far worse.

Her nod was jerky. Tell it like it is, a voice inside prodded mercilessly. Tell her all of it.

She couldn't. She couldn't let anyone—even Colleen—know her secret shame. Only she and Dennis knew; Leslie didn't delude herself into believing Dennis had told *her*. Besides, the whole sordid truth was too outrageous for anyone to believe.

"Oh, Leslie." Colleen's expression brimmed with sympathy. "I'm so sorry. I know how hard this has been on you, but you can't let yourself feel that you've lost everything. You'll find someone else, and then you'll be on top of the world again."

Leslie's smile was half sad, half wistful. "And live happily ever after?"

"Yes! It may not happen tomorrow, or even the day after, but you have to keep telling yourself that things will be bigger and brighter than ever."

She sounded so fierce, so utterly confident and determined that Leslie could almost believe she was right. But happily-ever-after existed only in fairy tales.

She leaned forward and kissed Colleen on the cheek. "I'll try," she said softly. There was a brief pause while she studied her friend. "Thank you for inviting me here, Colleen. I really do appreciate it."

Colleen squeezed her hands. "Having you here means a lot to me, Les."

Colleen left her alone then. Leslie closed the door after her and began to prepare for bed. But her mind refused the balm of sleep; she was still awake at midnight.

Feeling suddenly restless and closed in, she slipped out of bed and pulled on a light robe. On impulse, she made her way through the darkened house and onto the terrace outside, quietly sliding the door closed behind her.

It was a beautiful night, clear and brilliant. Dozens of stars glittered against the backdrop of the night sky. The moon cast a pearly glow in the enveloping darkness. Leslie laced her hands together before her and lifted her face to the faint caress of the wind, praying the peaceful serenity of the night would ease the tumult in her heart.

It didn't happen.

Her conversation with Colleen—the awful reminder of what Dennis had done—was still too fresh in her mind. Her fingers strained against themselves as she fought the treacherous pull of the past.

Her eyes squeezed shut. She held fast against the misery that threatened to swallow her, but it was a losing battle. A scalding tear slipped from beneath closed eyelids, then another and another. Leslie despised her weakness, but she was powerless against the despair building inside. A sob escaped before she could stop it.

But all at once a prickly sense of awareness trickled up her spine. Startled, Leslie started to whirl around, only to freeze abruptly.

She wasn't alone after all.

CHAPTER THREE

CLINT TOSSED AND TURNED restlessly in bed for what seemed like hours. Finally he swept aside the sheet and rose awkwardly to his feet. He couldn't sleep, and there was no sense lying there any longer.

Pulling on a pair of jeans, he let himself outside and hobbled out to the flagstoned terrace. He eased himself down, stretching out on a chaise lounge. Folding his arms across his chest and leaning his head back, he held himself absolutely still, absorbing the peace and tranquillity of the night.

It took a while, but eventually he began to doze. Miraculously he found his mind drifting back to a happier time....

There was a smile of contentment on his lips, for he was back in the highland valleys of Central America. The winds that swept down the mountains were calm and peaceful. Rebellion had yet to brew its tempest. Life was slow and easy, simple and unhurried.

And she was there, laughing as only she could laugh... *Angelina.*

Clint saw her as if she were before him now; her hair sweeping her shoulders, black as a raven's wing; fiery and impetuous, brimming with vibrancy and life.

He'd been on loan to the government then, one of a group of engineers sent from the States. Planning and work on the cross-country highway system proved a long, arduous task, but Clint hadn't minded. He was doing what he'd always wanted—and so was Angelina. Their nights together were long and blissful. No one was happier than the two of them. No one was more in love. It had all been so perfect. Not once had he ever thought it was too good to be true...not once.

Deep in his dreamworld, images shifted and faded. He saw Angelina on their wedding day, her dark eyes as shining and radiant as her smile. And then later, smiling that beautiful, secret smile as she told him her news.

Not long after, rumors of discontent rumbled through the countryside. In the cities, there was open defiance and criticism of the government. Angelina had shrugged and laughed it off.

"It will pass," she told him. "I love you too much to let anything happen to the two of us." She snuggled close and patted her burgeoning tummy. "Besides, we are far from the city. What could happen here?"

What could happen here? Her words, spoken so long ago, burned into his soul like fire. Clint twitched and turned, as if in silent protest. He fought the shadowy hold on his consciousness and struggled toward wakefulness, dreading what was to come....

But he couldn't stop it. The scene continued to unfold; it was just like before. He could do nothing to change what would happen.... Not then. Not now.

In the blink of an eye, vivid pictures touched his mind and seared his soul. He remembered how he'd returned to the village that day, stunned to hear the distant ricochet of bullets; they cracked like thunder in the air. Then suddenly all was quiet.

The silence was horrible.

He leaped from the Jeep. He saw himself running, just as he had that day. Running and searching— praying as he'd never prayed before. An acrid odor burned his lungs, the scent of smoke...the scent of death.

His dream had become a nightmare. He knew even then that he'd lost her. He'd lost them both. The tinkling sound of laughter turned to anguished sobs that shattered endlessly through his mind, over and over....

Clint awoke with a start. He was trembling, his body beaded with sweat despite the coolness of the night.

He jerked upright. This was no dream, he suddenly realized. The sobs that pierced the air were all too real.

LESLIE DREW A SOFT GASP of surprise when a figure sat up. She wasn't sure who was more startled, she or Clint. They saw each other at the same time; for the longest moment neither of them appeared to know what to say.

It was Leslie who spoke first. "I—I'm sorry." She despised the quiver in her voice. "I didn't think anyone would be out here."

Clint watched her closely. Impatient at being caught in such a private moment, his first impulse was to snap at her. But there was something almost heartwrenching in the shaky breath she drew—in the betraying sheen of her eyes—and that awareness supplanted everything else.

"It's all right." Clint slid a hand through the rumpled strands of hair on his forehead. He peered up at her. "I thought everyone had gone to bed."

Leslie was embarrassed at having been caught. And in front of Clint, no less. She wouldn't have minded shedding a tear or two before Colleen, or even Rob. Rob was gentle and easygoing; he would understand. But his brother was a stranger...another story entirely.

"I guess Rob was right," she murmured. "My first night in a strange bed and I can't sleep after all."

She managed a wobbly smile and turned to retreat. Clint spoke without thinking. "You don't have to leave."

Leslie glanced back over her shoulder. "I don't want to intrude," she began with a shake of her head.

"You're not," he said quickly. "I only came out here because I couldn't sleep, either."

She drew her robe more tightly around her. She noticed that Clint's chest was bare, and she was suddenly grateful for the shadowy darkness. "But you weren't looking for company, either." The words were out before she could stop them.

A cloud passed over the moon. Lacy patterns of silver and ebony weaved all around them. Her directness surprised Clint. Through the darkness he caught a glimpse of the set of her shoulders, proud but stiff. Her wariness of him was almost tangible.

Was it any wonder?

He looked away. "No," he heard himself say. "No, I wasn't. At least not then."

When she said nothing, he forced his gaze back to her.

"Look," he said, his voice very low. "I owe you an apology. I snapped at you in the car today and I—I shouldn't have."

The words were inadequate. Clint knew it as soon as he spoke. Yet he couldn't say he'd been curt with her for no reason... because there *was* a reason.

Once again, Clint experienced a spurt of mingled frustration and irritation. She stared at him as if she expected him to explain. Yet he couldn't. Dammit, he just couldn't! Not to her or anyone else.

The silence that followed was nerve-scraping for both of them. His apology wasn't made grudgingly, yet all at once she sensed something hard and distant in him. Leslie felt ridiculously close to tears again. *What was it about Clint that made her feel so off balance?* she thought wildly. *And why did she let him get to her?*

"It's all right," she said stiffly. It wasn't, of course, but what could she say? Clearly she would get no more from him. She couldn't disguise the slight edge in her tone, and suddenly she didn't want to. "If you'll excuse me, I think I'll turn in now." She didn't bother with a good-night; she simply walked off without a backward glance.

Clint didn't stop her. Torn between a self-deprecating anger and a genuine feeling of regret, he watched her disappear into the shadows. Despite her show of bravado, he couldn't help thinking that he'd scared her away... again.

Oddly he wished she had stayed out here with him, yet he was just as relieved at not having to face her. He berated himself harshly. No doubt Leslie thought he was lower than a snake—and it was no more than he deserved.

He almost welcomed the arrowlike pain that shot through his leg as he struggled to his feet. That would heal, he thought vaguely. But the nightmare that haunted him, sleeping or awake, lurked within him still.

He wondered bleakly if the hurt would ever leave him.

THE KITCHEN HUMMED NOISILY when Leslie walked in the next morning. Tess's eyes lit up like light bulbs. Brian even bestowed a shy, impish smile. Rob immediately jumped up and grabbed a coffee cup from the counter. Colleen waved toward the stove and invited her to help herself.

"How's the expectant mother feeling this morning?" Leslie asked over her shoulder as she filled her plate.

"If her appetite is any indication, she's feeling fine." Rob grinned at his wife.

Colleen poked him in the ribs when he sat down. "No morning sickness yet," she said brightly. She raised a pair of crossed fingers high into the air.

Leslie's gaze had already scanned the table. It was almost a relief to note Clint's absence. But it was Tess who posed the question on Leslie's mind. "Where's Uncle Clint?" she asked her mother.

"He had to meet a friend this morning. He left a few minutes ago."

"Aha." One of Rob's eyebrows shot up. "Would this friend happen to be male or female?"

Colleen made a face. "Do you have to ask?"

Leslie wasn't sure how to interpret that. She told herself stoutly that she didn't care where Clint spent his morning, as long as it wasn't with her.

Rob's eyes lifted when she sat down. "Colleen tells me you've moved up in the world." His eyes were twinkling. "She said you're now the assistant head-mistress. The last I knew you were a lowly third-grade teacher."

Leslie laughed uneasily. "Yes, well . . . it's a living."

Colleen glanced over at her sharply. Leslie reached for the syrup, aware of her friend's perusal.

"Well, I'm impressed." Rob grinned. He hadn't noticed anything amiss. His gaze traveled between Leslie and his wife. "It's nice to know at least one of you got something out of your college education."

"And I got you," Colleen announced pertly, wrinkling her nose at him. She then promptly shooed him off to finish getting ready for work. Brian and Tess had wandered off to watch cartoons, leaving the two women alone. Colleen wasted no time turning to her.

"Les—" she peered at her friend across the top of her coffee cup "—I thought you were happy being headmistress at Golden Hills."

Happy! How could she be happy with anything after the nightmare Dennis had put her through? *Tell it like it is,* a grating little voice chided. Her job had become a drag . . . as she had become a drag? The thought made her cringe.

"I was," she said at last. She rose and carried her plate to the sink. Her eyes remained focused on the stream of water as she rinsed her utensils. "To tell you the truth, my job has been the last thing on my mind.

It's left me feeling rather restless, I guess. Even a little dissatisfied.''

Colleen began piling plates atop one another. "If you're not happy with your job, maybe it's time for a change.''

Leslie took the plates she handed her. "I've thought of that," she admitted. Her life had been in chaos ever since she'd learned of Dennis's betrayal. "In fact, I thought this trip would give me a chance to think about where I'm going from here.''

Colleen's eyes began to gleam. "Then let me give you something else to think about. Why don't you consider moving here?''

Leslie blinked. "To San Diego?''

"Why not? There's nothing holding you in San Francisco, is there?''

"No, but—''

"If you couldn't find a job at one of the local schools, you could always try something else. Why, the adoption agency Rob works for might even be able to use you, especially with your teaching background.''

Leslie could find nothing to challenge her friend's reasoning. Still, the thought of moving—of making such a complete change in her life—was rather daunting. Yet she couldn't discount it, either.

Colleen laughed at Leslie's confusion. "Hey, you don't have to decide this minute. You've got all summer. And you don't need to worry about finding a place to stay if you decide to look for another job, because you can stay right here. I wouldn't have it any other way.''

Leslie bit her lip. "You might not," she murmured, "but your brother-in-law might."

"Clint?" Colleen's eyes widened. "Why on earth would you think that?" She turned off the spray of water.

Leslie shifted uncomfortably beneath her scrutiny. "I just get the feeling that maybe—maybe he wishes I weren't here."

Colleen eyed her closely. "Clint has a shorter fuse than Rob," she said slowly, "but it's not like him to be deliberately rude."

"Oh, it's not because of anything he said," Leslie confirmed quickly. "You see, I...I couldn't sleep last night, so I went outside on the terrace. Clint was there and—and I'm afraid I was rather short with him." She gave a lopsided smile. "To tell you the truth, I don't think either of us was in the mood for company."

A network of tiny lines had appeared between Colleen's fine blond eyebrows. "I'm sorry, Les. Most of the time Clint is an absolute dear. But since he came back from Central America three years ago—" She sighed. It was almost as if she were talking to herself. "He may seem rather aloof sometimes, but he's really not. He's just had it tough lately."

Leslie's heart lurched. Central America. There it was again. She wanted to quiz Colleen further, but something held her back. Besides, it was really none of her business.

Saying nothing, she bent and began loading cups and cutlery into the dishwasher.

Behind her, Colleen said worriedly, "I don't want you to feel you're not welcome here, Les, because it's not true."

Leslie straightened. Seeing the concern in Colleen's eyes, she reached out and hugged her. "I know that, Colleen." She drew back so she could see her. "Don't think another thing about it. It's just that I don't know Clint like you do, and I guess I'm just being overly sensitive." Privately she doubted it, but she didn't want Colleen to feel she was ungrateful. And she certainly didn't want to create trouble for Colleen with her brother-in-law. After all, she was the outsider here.

Colleen squeezed her hands. "And you'll think about moving here? Seriously? I don't mind having a full house, Les. You know that. Rob and I will be glad to have you stay as long as you like—as long as you need."

She wasn't satisfied until she'd elicited Leslie's promise. Leslie then left to finish the unpacking she'd put off last night. Colleen's eyes followed her as she left, her expression pensive.

That was how Rob found her when he entered the kitchen again. He brushed her lips with his. "You look," he chided lightly, "like a woman with a heck of a lot on her mind."

"I was just thinking," she murmured.

Rob slipped his arms around her and tucked her bright gold head under his chin. "About what?"

"Clint." She closed her eyes and slipped her arms around his waist. "I wish he'd settle down and find someone to love. It's just what he needs. It's *all* he needs."

"He did once," Rob said quietly, so quietly she had to strain to hear. "But when Angelina died..." He shook his head. "He's changed—and yet he hasn't. There are times when he's the same old Clint he's always been. And there are other times when he's a million miles away. And I wonder if I even know him at all.''

"I know.'' Her troubled gaze sought his. "That's why I worry about him. And I'm worried about Leslie, too. Her divorce has been hard on her, harder than I realized.''

He slipped his hand under her chin. "Hey,'' he chided, "don't look so blue. It might be contagious.''

In spite of herself, Colleen smiled.

Rob kissed her forehead. "That's better. I was afraid you'd be slamming cupboard doors before long—the way you did the last time you were in this particular condition.''

He laughed when she tried to pull away, and suddenly Colleen was laughing, too. "You have the most amazing knack for cheering me up,'' she teased. "Does it work on broken hearts? If it does, maybe you'd like to try it on your brother and Leslie.''

He chuckled. "Oh, I think matters will take care of themselves before long.''

"I hope you're right. Because both Leslie and Clint have been through a lot. And all I want is for them to be as happy as we are.''

Rob smiled down at her. "They'll be fine.'' He pressed a kiss on her forehead. "By the way, I talked to Fran a few minutes ago, and she said there's no problem with us keeping that little Mexican girl. The latest from the orphanage is that they'll be transferring her here sometime in August.''

Fran was another social worker at the adoption agency. The agency planned to place the five-year-old orphan early in the fall. But first priority was surgery to correct a hip injury. The agency hadn't been able to locate a foster family who spoke Spanish, so she and Rob had offered to care for her in the interim. Even though they didn't speak Spanish, either, they felt they could manage.

Colleen nodded her satisfaction. "Looks like we're booked for the summer, doesn't it?"

"It sure does," he agreed.

Colleen slipped her hand in his as they walked to the car. "It's starting to look like we're dedicated to taking in stray cats," she said with a smile. "But you know—" her expression grew thoughtful "—I don't mind at all. Because I'd say where all of them are concerned—Leslie and Clint and that poor little Mexican girl—I think being here with us is the best medicine they could possible have."

CHAPTER FOUR

COLLEEN DECIDED TO CALL a day of play, so they spent the rest of the day lazily. In the morning, Colleen helped Brian put together a puzzle. Tess wanted Leslie to see her paper dolls; she soon found herself cross-legged on the floor, cutting out dozens of tiny paper outfits.

In the afternoon they headed for the beach, which was only a block away.

Around four o'clock Colleen began to gather up blankets and toys, stuffing them into her oversized beach bag. "I think I've played hooky long enough," she pronounced ruefully. "I'd better get back and start dinner or Rob will think I've decided to go on strike."

Leslie rolled over and started to rise, but Colleen quickly waved her back down. "No," she said firmly, "you stay here if you want. This is your vacation, remember?"

Leslie collapsed back on an elbow, shielding her eyes against the blinding glare of the sun. "I don't mind if I do," she said with an exaggerated groan. "The sun has made mush of my muscles. It'll take me an hour to climb all those steps back up the hillside."

Colleen laughed, rounded up her protesting children and left.

Leslie sat up, watching as a dog raced madly after a Frisbee thrown by its master. She thoroughly enjoyed the rush of the wind whipping her hair, the sting of salt spray on her skin, the distant chatter of children playing tag with the waves.

It seemed Colleen was right, she mused. She was hungry for moments like this. She needed to lap up the luxury of doing nothing—*thinking* about nothing at all. By the time she left a short time later, she felt fresh and invigorated. She even sprinted the entire length of the stairway that climbed the hillside.

She was still breathless when she rounded the corner of the garage. Then she came face-to-face with Clint, sitting on the steps of his bungalow. He glanced up when he saw her.

"Well, hello there. I was just thinking about you."

Leslie's footsteps slowed to a halt. She slid her fingers through her hair, conscious of her windblown appearance and bare feet. She'd pulled a pair of baggy cuffed shorts over her swimsuit, but she hadn't bothered to slip on her espadrilles.

"You were?" Her voice still carried a hint of breathlessness.

He nodded. "I was just wondering how you were doing today." There was a silent, deeper question in his eyes.

She paused, not sure whether advance or retreat was in order, and hoping neither would be necessary.

"I'm fine." Or at least she had been until this moment. She despaired of her fraying composure, half angry and half frustrated at the uncertainty that now plagued her.

His eyes searched her face. "No more tears?" he asked softly.

Leslie stood stock-still. So he had noticed! She felt suddenly awkward and exposed.

Her vision blurred. Through a haze of moisture, she watched him struggle to his feet and come nearer. But all at once her spine stiffened and her shoulders straightened. She wouldn't cry in front of him again—she wouldn't!

His gaze still hadn't left her. "Uh-oh," he said quietly. "I'm sorry, Leslie. I wasn't supposed to say that, was I?"

Why was he being so nice? His gentleness confused her. By now he'd reached her. Leslie was startled to see that his eyes were dark with compassion. His expression conveyed his regret.

"It's all right." She offered a slight smile. Oddly she found herself trying to adopt a light tone she was far from feeling. "I can just imagine what you must think. It's really not like me to—to break down like that."

He studied her for a moment. Leslie wasn't sure she wanted to speculate on what might be going through his mind. But he only said very softly, "I'd hardly call that breaking down. But I suspect your feeling so blue had something to do with Colleen's announcement at dinner last night."

His perception was startling. And suddenly it didn't seem strange at all to find herself confirming his suspicion. "I wouldn't be honest if I said it wasn't difficult finding out that Colleen is expecting another baby." She hesitated. "My first reaction was envy."

Clint experienced a pang. He'd felt exactly the same himself. "Colleen mentioned you were divorced." He paused a moment. "No kids?"

Her eyes clouded over. She shook her head wordlessly.

"But you wanted a family." It was more a statement than a question.

"More than anything."

Clint leaned slightly on his cane. His tone was very gentle as he asked, "How long were you married?"

"Seven years."

He let out a low whistle. "That's quite a while."

Her gaze slid away for a moment. It was disconcerting to find his dark eyes still riveted to her when she glanced at him again.

At her silence, Clint considered the faint shadow that flitted over her expressive features. He hadn't been prepared for the look of pain on her face at his questions. She looked a little hurt right now, rather young and very vulnerable. "You're still bitter, aren't you?"

Yes. God, yes! Leslie thought. But she only nodded and murmured, "A little."

"And you don't like to talk about your marriage."

There was an instant's silence while she summoned a wan smile. "It's not my favorite topic these days," she admitted. "But in spite of that, I am happy for Colleen and Rob. They're very lucky."

For just a moment, Clint's mind grew dark and bleak. Lucky. That was how he'd felt once. When he'd met Angelina, he'd never expected to find such happiness. . . .

But the woman in front of him looked so lonely and haunted that he felt some nameless emotion spear his heart. He couldn't stop himself from thinking that the scared little girl he'd first encountered yesterday hadn't completely vanished—she still lurked somewhere deep inside.

He reached out unconsciously and caught her hand. "You know," he said quietly, "it's a shame we got off on the wrong foot."

Leslie blinked. She didn't know what she'd expected him to say, but it definitely wasn't that.

Her lips quirked upward. "Actually," she said lightly, "we got started okay. But somewhere along the way we missed a step."

"Maybe we should remedy that."

To her surprise, the pressure on her hand increased. Leslie tried to pull away, but he tugged on her fingers and drew her nearer. Her eyes widened; her tongue darted out to moisten her lips.

"What did you have in mind?" She couldn't hide her sudden nervousness.

Clint smiled slightly. "Hey," he chided gently. "I'm really not the wolf you first thought I was. And all I had in mind was maybe going for a walk after dinner."

Leslie regarded him almost suspiciously. "Did Colleen put you up to this?"

"Colleen?" He frowned. "Of course not. Why should she?"

Why, indeed, Leslie mused. She tipped her head to the side consideringly. She wasn't proud of her behavior last night. She had acted like a child. *You hit me, so I'll hit you back*. But maybe it was just as she'd told Colleen. Maybe she *had* been overly touchy.

But so had he.

"Come on, Leslie." His tone was cajoling. "Even if I did try something, all you'd have to do is run." He glanced ruefully at his cane. "I'm obviously not going to catch up with you."

His words brought an unexpected smile to her lips. She felt herself relax. "It was you who told Colleen that. I never accused you of being a wolf," she said playfully. She paused and added more softly, "But I must admit you're right. Maybe we should give it another try. I doubt Colleen and Rob would be pleased if we made their house a war zone the entire time I'm here."

A war zone. He knew her choice of words was totally innocuous, but something twisted inside his chest.

This time when she pulled away he let her go. His expression was sober as she gave a tiny wave and headed toward the back door.

He couldn't stop the sudden emptiness that seeped into his heart. He knew he wasn't the only one to whom fate had dealt a cruel hand. He suspected that Leslie, too, had been hurt.

He didn't want to feel this strange compassion for her. But he couldn't help himself, either. Every instinct inside him warned him to stay away from her— to maintain a safe distance from her while she was here. For reasons he couldn't explain, she made him think of things that were best forgotten....

And that was his own private cross to bear.

CLINT PUSHED his empty plate away and stood. "Leslie and I will clean up in here while you two—" his gaze encompassed Rob and Colleen before he pointed toward the living room "—head for the hills."

Colleen and Rob looked at each other. Rob rose and pulled back his wife's chair. "Well, well," he teased, "I don't know what's behind this, but since it looks like we have a relief crew for the dishes, I'm not about to argue with my little brother." He turned his head and glanced at Clint. "Do you do windows, too?"

Clint managed to keep a poker face. "Not tonight," he assured Rob loftily. "When we're done, Leslie and I thought we'd go for a walk."

The startled look on Colleen's face was something to behold. Leslie might have burst out laughing, except Colleen cast a beaming sidelong glance her way. Her smug expression seemed to say, *See? I told you he wasn't so bad.*

Tess had already bounded from her chair. She jumped up and down in front of her uncle. "Can I go with you?"

Clint didn't have a chance to say yes or no. "Why don't you stay with us?" Colleen interrupted hurriedly. "We'll do something lots more exciting than going for a walk."

Tess didn't look convinced. "Like what?"

"Uh . . . I'm not sure. But we'll find something."

Tess wasn't budging. "But Leslie gets to go with Uncle Clint. Why can't I?"

"Because Daddy hasn't seen you all day long. He misses you, you know."

Colleen grabbed both the little girl's hand and Brian's. Clint crossed his arms over his chest and looked on. "Why don't you play some cards with them?" he suggested. "Tess likes concentration. Brian is partial to blackjack."

"Blackjack!" Leslie gasped. She twisted around in her chair. "Why, that's gambling!"

Clint shook his head. A half smile lurked on his lips. "Concentration hones memory skills. And blackjack sharpens addition skills." He gave an exaggerated sigh. "Unfortunately we have to bet with poker chips."

Colleen chuckled. "You're telling this to the wrong person, brother-in-law. Didn't I tell you Leslie was an elementary schoolteacher before she started climbing the ranks?"

Leslie could hold back her smile no longer. "Blackjack is one teaching method I hadn't considered," she chuckled. "But I doubt it's one that's ready for the classroom yet."

Colleen and Rob ushered the children from the kitchen.

When the doors had swung shut, Clint eyed Leslie quizzically. "You don't mind that I volunteered you, do you?"

"Not unless I end up doing the dishes myself," she retorted pertly.

The sound of his laughter was pleasing. It occurred to Leslie that he looked utterly transformed when he laughed. Watching his eyes light to a soft blaze of golden brown was like seeing the sun emerge after weeks of cloudy gray skies. She had the feeling he didn't laugh like that nearly enough...and all at once she wanted very much to hear him laugh like that again.

"Are you saying you're basically lazy?"

Leslie handed him the plate she'd just rinsed, watching as he dropped it into the dishwasher. "I'll admit to spending the afternoon lazing around on the beach—" her lashes lowered "—but what it really means is that I'm glad for the company."

Her words had an unexpected effect on Clint. They brought as much pain as pleasure, for there was a part of him that didn't want her to get too close. At the thought, a hand seemed to close around his heart and squeeze. Rob and Colleen were different—they were family. But it suddenly occurred to him that he had insulated himself since Angelina died....

Perhaps a little too well.

"We'll have to wash these pots and pans." Leslie's tone was absentminded. She began to run a stream of water into the sink. "Why don't you pull a stool up? You can sit there and dry while I wash."

Clint did as she asked. He was almost glad that she didn't seem to expect any kind of response from him. Yet he couldn't suppress a tiny stab of guilt.

He decided she seemed almost subdued over the next few minutes. Perhaps he'd hurt her feelings. "So you and Colleen played lazybones all day." He folded the dish towel, dropped it on the counter and eased off the stool. "I suppose that means you've decided you're not up to a walk, after all."

Did she hesitate? Or was it his imagination? But then she said softly, "I'm game if you are." She paused. Her eyes dropped down to linger on his leg. She added tentatively, "If you're sure it won't be too difficult for you."

He waved aside her concern. "Not to worry," he said dryly. "The doctor assures me that the more I use this leg, the quicker it'll heal."

She smiled then, a blindingly sweet smile that tugged at his heartstrings. "What are we waiting for then?"

When they were outside, he glanced over her head. "Where to? The beach?"

Leslie thought quickly. No matter what he said, she wasn't sure Clint was up to all those stairs leading down the embankment. "I've still got sand in my shoes from this afternoon. Let's just walk around the neighborhood, instead."

She stepped into place beside him, adjusting her stride to a slower pace so he wouldn't struggle to keep up with her. They ambled along the sidewalk in comfortable silence. Leslie enjoyed the laid-back charm of the broad tree-lined streets and the scent of freshly mowed grass. It was so quiet and peaceful here that she felt a measure of tranquility steal into her soul.

After a while, the street they were walking along ended in a small parking lot. She saw that beyond it was a small park. Several teenagers played paddleball in the center of a wide grassy strip that ran between two huge beds of primroses. Beyond was another small grassy area with a swing set and slide.

"Oh, look," she cried. "There's a playground. We should have brought Brian and Tess."

"If we had, you'd have gotten plenty of exercise, all right." Clint's tone was dry. "Tess flits around like a bee going from flower to flower, or hadn't you noticed?"

Leslie flipped back her hair with a low laugh. "Oh, I noticed, all right. I also noticed she's a big fan of yours. I had the feeling I was infringing on her territory by coming with you tonight."

She spied a wooden bench beneath a towering bay fig tree and pointed to it. "Do you mind if we stop for a few minutes? I guess I'm lazier than I thought," she said lightly. "All this exercise, and I need a rest."

Clint nodded his head. Leslie was glad she'd suggested it; the corners of his mouth looked a little pinched. She sat down and patted the spot beside her. He lowered himself slowly, letting out a long sigh when he was settled.

Leslie raised an eyebrow and sent him an arch look. "You," she announced primly, "are a very stubborn man."

He carefully stretched his legs out before him. "Now why would you say that?"

"If your leg was bothering you, we could have stopped earlier."

He had the grace to look sheepish.

"You see?" Leslie was amazed to find herself teasing. "I was right. You are stubborn—so stubborn you won't even admit it."

He propped the cane against the bench. "I can see you've got me pegged," he observed wryly. "Does that mean I get a crack at you, too?"

Oddly Leslie didn't mind at all. She'd grown rather defensive this past year whenever the subject grew personal. She hadn't always been so touchy, but she was a little surprised at how comfortable she felt with Clint right now.

"Why not?" she said with a shrug.

He turned his head to gaze at her. "First, you have to give me something to go on," he stated brashly.

"Hey!" she protested. "I guess I'll have to amend what I said before—you're stubborn *and* devious, because that's what I call cheating! I'm not going to give you the answers. You're supposed to come up with them on your own."

"Just a few questions," he pleaded. "A simple yes or no will suffice."

Leslie didn't quite succeed in holding back her smile. "Shoot."

"How old are you?"

Her lips still twitched. "My, you're forgetful tonight, aren't you? That happens to be something that can't be answered with a yes or no, dear sir."

"Damn!" He snapped his fingers and lowered his voice to a conspiratorial whisper. "I guess that means you're pretty sharp, since you're on to me already. But back to the question." He tapped a finger against his lower lip thoughtfully. "Are you under thirty?"

"No. But something tells me you're trying to charm me into revealing something I probably shouldn't."

"Aha," he murmured. "Over thirty but less than forty."

"Ouch!" She grinned. "I'm not an antique yet."

"Let me think then . . . you're thirty-one, right?"

Leslie wrinkled her nose at him. "That was a lucky guess."

He slanted her a triumphant glance from the corner of his eye. "Were you born and raised in the San Francisco area?"

Her eyes narrowed. "Yes. But how did you—"

"An only child, I'll bet."

Leslie tapped her foot and regarded him with a mock glare. "'Fess up, mister. You've got an inside source."

The merest hint of a smile played at the corner of his mouth. "My dear sister-in-law was just a bundle of information this morning."

He earned a playful nudge in the ribs for his efforts. Leslie liked seeing this easygoing side of him as much as she liked their banter. It was simple and low-key, nothing too deep or soul-searching.

And she was secretly pleased that he had asked Colleen about her.

He had turned slightly and propped his elbow on the back of the bench. The sleeves of his shirt were short, revealing tanned muscular forearms coated with a dense layer of silky looking dark hair. And he had such masculine hands, slender but strong-looking. Her gaze lingered for a breath-stealing moment on his fingers, long and lean and now clasped loosely together before him.

Leslie swallowed. Her mouth had gone dry. Her eyes skipped to his face, and she saw that the teasing laughter in his eyes had faded.

"You're certainly very different from Colleen." His lips quirked slightly. "I guess I always expected her best friend to be more like her."

Leslie frowned briefly. It was true she wasn't as open or vocal about her emotions as Colleen, but that didn't mean she felt them any less intensely.

"Oh, I don't know," she said lightly. "We're different in some ways—not so different in others."

"That may be true," he murmured. "But I'm curious about you. What were you like when you were younger?"

He studied her openly, his perusal just a little disturbing. She felt herself flush slightly, and passed it off with a shrug. "Oh, I don't know. I had a pretty typical childhood, I guess."

"Typical, eh? You weren't a problem child then. Or a rabble-rouser."

"A rabble-rouser?" That made her laugh outright. "That sounds more like Colleen than me."

He continued to regard her. "I'd lay odds you weren't a cheerleader."

Leslie wrinkled her nose. "Why, thank you. Does that mean you think I'm a klutz?"

Clint shook his head. "Of course not. You just strike me as the studious, dependable type. You," he mused thoughtfully, "were probably the class valedictorian."

She smiled. "Valedictorian? I'd have been terrified to get up in front of all those people. Even in college I was the kind of person who would walk into a class ten minutes early and still sit in the back row."

"But you ended up at the front of the room, instead."

She felt her smile freeze over. "That's because I—I love kids." She strived for a light tone, but wasn't sure she'd succeeded.

Apparently she had. Clint asked, in a voice laced with humor, "But you really haven't lost your shyness, have you?"

Leslie grew cold inside. She knew Clint didn't mean to be mean or spiteful with his observation, but it was a painful reminder nonetheless. . . . Her sweet shyness was one of the things Dennis had loved most about her.

Or was that just another of his lies?

She stared straight ahead. A wave of despair shot through her, so intense it bordered on pain. The last slanting rays of the sun made a dazzling display through lacy layers of clouds, but Leslie scarcely noticed.

Her throat was achingly tight. She thought of Dennis—and all he had done to her. Her voice, when it finally came, was carefully neutral. "It's amazing what a person can overcome when the need arises."

Clint's smile withered. Silence lay between them, dark and heavy. The only sound was that of the wind whispering through the tree branches. Her face was drawn, her hands clasped tightly in her lap. Her face was angled slightly away from him; he couldn't see the bleakness that plagued her, yet he could sense it.

"I didn't mean to hit a nerve," he said quietly.

But he had and they both knew it. Leslie said nothing, struggling for control and finally attaining it. She gave a tiny shake of her head. "I'm all right, really. It's silly to be so—so touchy."

Clint watched her solemnly. The smile she flashed was rather tremulous, but it was a smile nonetheless.

He touched her shoulder gently. "That's good," he murmured. "Because up until now I was thinking we'd gotten off to a pretty good start."

"Again," she added with a faint laugh. Strangely she felt no embarrassment. Instead, she experienced an odd kind of kinship with Clint. "But you know, I think you're right."

She smiled again, a tiny whimsical smile that caught him squarely between heaven and hell. He had no idea if Leslie was even aware of it, but he felt as if she were silently reaching out to him. And her vulnerability terrified him.

A faint bitterness crept into his thoughts. He was no knight in shining armor. He didn't want anyone depending on him—not ever again. Angelina had looked to him . . . and she had *died* because of it.

He glanced at his watch. "We'd better be getting back."

They were both quiet on the walk home, but the silence wasn't an uncomfortable one. Darkness had spread its veil by the time they arrived back at the house.

Leslie paused, one hand on the handle of the back screen door. "Are you coming in?"

Clint shook his head. He liked her, he realized suddenly. And he could like her a hell of a lot more.... But he wasn't sure that was wise—for either of them.

Leslie hesitated, strangely reluctant to leave him.

"I'm glad you asked me to come," she said quietly. A faint light began to dance in her eyes. "And you were right, after all. I didn't have to run away from you."

Her shoulders blotted out the light shining from within the house. The smooth clean lines of her profile were all he could see of her—the gentle slant of her cheek. The cute pertness of her nose. The gentle thrust of her lower lip...

Clint held himself very still. He had to fight the craziest urge to pull her into his arms, to ease whatever pain was locked up inside her. Equally strong and compelling was the urge to smother her lips with his.

"We could go again tomorrow night." God, he was out of his mind. What was he doing?

Her eyes were on his face. "I'd like that." She smiled. "Same time, same station," she quipped. "We could take Brian and Tess, and they could play on the swings."

That was probably a good idea, he thought hazily. Having the kids along would keep his mind from wandering where it had no business wandering.

She stepped back; Clint saw that she meant to go in. "Good night," she said softly. "I hope you sleep better tonight."

He wouldn't—she had just seen to that. He didn't say so, but his tone was almost somber. "Good night, Leslie."

He watched as she opened the screen door and carefully closed it, then disappeared into the house.

Only then did he whisper his thoughts aloud. "Oh, Leslie," he murmured. "You should be running. You should be running as far and as fast as you can."

Because something was happening inside him . . . something he suspected neither of them was ready for.

CHAPTER FIVE

LESLIE AWOKE SLOWLY the next morning, savoring the luxury of not having to wake to the blare of her clock radio. But when she rolled over in bed, she was stunned to discover that the bedside clock read nearly 10:00 a.m. She jumped out of bed and hurriedly showered and dressed.

Colleen had just sat down at the kitchen table. She glanced up when Leslie walked in. "Well, hello there!" she said brightly. "I was beginning to think you flew the coop with my brother-in-law last night. I haven't seen hide nor hair of him either this morning."

Leslie crossed to the cupboard and reached inside for a cup. "Well, if it isn't Mother Colleen. You are nosy this morning, aren't you?" She angled a glance over her shoulder, unable to resist teasing her friend. "Were you waiting inside with a broom in case your brother-in-law got fresh?"

"I think I was secretly hoping he would!"

Leslie blinked and turned around. "Colleen!" she gasped. "What are you saying?"

It was Colleen's turn to tease. "Oh, come on," she said brashly. "So what if something did happen? After all, you and Clint are two consenting adults."

Leslie's mind traveled fleetingly back to last night. Just thinking about it made her head spin and her pulse race wildly.

She had thought Clint was going to kiss her.

And she had wanted it . . . she had wanted it very much indeed. She remembered the breeze swirling around them; it seemed to pull them closer and closer. And she remembered the tight ache of sweet anticipation tingling in every part of her . . . and the crushing disappointment that seized her when he hadn't.

With a jolt she brought herself back to the present. "I didn't think Clint would be up to all those stairs leading down to the beach," she said, reaching for the coffeepot. "We just went down to the park—I'm sure you know which one I mean." She tried to pass it off with a laugh. "There's a playground there, too. You should have let Brian and Tess come along. They'd have had a great time."

"You just went down to the park," Colleen mimicked, pulling a face. "You sound like a prim old schoolmarm from a hundred years ago. Besides, I had a reason for keeping Brian and Tess home. They needed a bath." She rose and dumped her coffee in the sink.

Leslie tried very hard to keep a straight face. "That's certainly imperative."

Colleen just laughed and brought the cookie jar back to the table.

Leslie watched as her hand dipped into the jar. "That's probably going to go straight to your waistline."

"My waist is already a lost cause. I can't even get the zipper up on my jeans anymore." Colleen bemoaned her fate but she looked anything but forlorn. "In fact, I planned on digging out my maternity clothes this afternoon."

She fell quiet, then tipped her head to the side a moment later. "Tell me something, Les. You wouldn't be opposed to something developing between you and Clint, would you?"

Now there was a question—a very good question indeed.

Leslie heard herself laugh. "Oh, I wouldn't worry too much if I were you," she said lightly. "I doubt it'll ever happen."

THE REST OF THE MORNING was spent busily. Leslie helped Colleen with the laundry and making beds. Before they knew it, it was lunchtime. Clint made a brief appearance for a sandwich then disappeared again.

After lunch, Colleen put Tess down for a nap. She had no sooner descended the last stair than Leslie jumped up and blocked her way. "Oh, no, lady. You're going to take a nap, too." She glanced over where Brian was sitting at the dining room table coloring. The little boy was still rather shy around her, but his reserve was beginning to wear off. "Maybe," she added, "I can convince Brian to toss a few balls back and forth so he'll be all warmed up for his practice later."

Brian looked up eagerly. He was a member of a boys' summer baseball league; they hadn't begun their regular games yet, but Brian had high hopes of being chosen as a pitcher.

But suddenly he frowned. "Do you know how to play catch?" he asked worriedly. "Mom plays with me, but she never throws the ball even *close* to where I am."

Leslie struck a pose. "Do I know how to catch? Hey, I was the star player of the softball team in college. I had a curve ball that you wouldn't believe. And I was the top home run hitter."

His eyes lit up. "Gee," he breathed. "The star player. That's what I want to be."

"Well, then, let's go!"

He scraped his chair back and stood up. "Sure is. Let's go!"

Leslie pointed Colleen toward the stairs. "March, lady. Your son and I have a date." Colleen shook her head and held up both hands in a gesture of defeat.

Brian had quite an arm for a boy his age, and he was a good hitter, as well. But by the time an hour had gone by, Leslie was hot and puffing and Brian was just getting warmed up.

She lifted her hair off her neck and collapsed on the grass. "Definitely star material," she announced. "But you're wearing me out, kid."

Brian beamed. He dropped the ball in his mitt and moved toward her. "Can I go over and ask Tim if he wants to play for a while?"

Tim Mahoney was the little boy who lived directly across the street. Colleen had told Leslie that both Brian and Tess often played with Tim and his five-year-old sister Megan, sometimes here and sometimes at Tim's house.

"I don't see why not. You can practice that nifty fastball and see if he strikes out as much as I did." He was already off and running by the time Leslie picked herself up and dusted off her shorts. She was still chuckling when she walked through the back door.

To her surprise, Colleen was sitting at the kitchen table.

Leslie retrieved a glass from the cupboard and turned on the tap. "How come you're up already?"

"I guess I'm not used to taking a nap in the middle of the day. I heard the mail come so I decided I might as well get up."

Leslie plunked several ice cubes into her glass and sat down at the table, noting that Colleen held a handwritten letter. She drank thirstily, then laughingly began to tell Colleen how Brian had bested her. But she hadn't said more than two words before she realized that Colleen was staring blankly into space.

The letter lowered slowly to the table. Leslie was quick to notice her friend's hand wasn't entirely steady.

Her smile faded; she leaned forward. "Colleen? What is it?"

Colleen pressed her lips together. She stared at her through eyes gone dull and blank. Wordlessly she shook her head.

Leslie's gaze strayed to the letter. "Colleen, what's wrong? Who's the letter from?"

"My mother." Her voice was very low.

Leslie's heart jumped. She was almost afraid to say the thought aloud. "She's not sick, is she?"

Again her friend shook her head. The silence seemed endless before she finally whispered, "It's my father who's sick. And he won't see a doctor, so they don't know what's wrong with him."

Leslie's mind searched quickly backward. Colleen had grown up in a small town near the Oregon border. They'd met during their first year of college. But in all the time that had passed since then, she couldn't recall Colleen talking about her father. Her mother, yes, and her two brothers. She'd met the three of them when Colleen married Rob in San Francisco. Somehow she'd assumed that Colleen's parents were no longer married.

She spoke very quietly. "Your parents...they're divorced, aren't they?"

She was puzzled by the emotions that flashed across Colleen's eyes—hurt, anger, bitterness, frustration. "If only they were," she said wearily. "If only they were..."

Leslie took a deep breath. "I'm sorry," she ventured quietly. "But it's just that I've never heard you talk about your father."

Colleen's mouth twisted. "For good reason."

Leslie sat very still. Colleen was always full of such laughter and gaiety. It was strange to see her so dispirited.

She watched helplessly as Colleen rose and moved to stand before the window. The air was warm and balmy, but she clutched her arms around her body as if she were freezing.

After a long time, she finally turned. "You're my best friend, Leslie. I—I don't want you to feel hurt. But there's something I haven't told you—" her voice betrayed an uncharacteristic uncertainty "—about me."

Something seemed to grab hold of Leslie's heart. *There's something I haven't told you about me, too.*

She rose and guided Colleen back to her chair. Reaching out, she clasped Colleen's hand in her own. Her fingers were icy cold. "I won't feel hurt," she told her firmly.

Colleen swallowed. "Even if I told you that my father—" she stumbled haltingly "—is an alcoholic?"

"Is he?" Leslie's tone was very quiet.

Colleen's gaze slid away. She nodded. "I know everyone thinks I have a fairy-tale marriage." Her voice was very low. "But I didn't have that kind of childhood." She paused. "You've heard me talk about my brother Mike? The one who lives in Seattle? And Tom lives in Phoenix."

"I remember."

"Didn't you ever wonder why we're spread so far apart? Why none of us ever stayed in northern California?"

"To tell you the truth, no." Leslie smiled gently. "I really don't think it's all that unusual."

"But with us there was a reason!"

"Your father?"

"Yes."

"I remember you used to laugh and say you only went to college to get away from home," Leslie recalled slowly. "But it was no joke, was it?"

Colleen shook her head and closed her eyes for an instant. When she opened them, her features were strained and haunted.

Leslie squeezed her fingers encouragingly. If she wanted to talk, that was fine. If she didn't...well, that was okay, too.

"I can't remember a time when my father didn't drink." She summoned a wan smile. "He and I never got along because of it. And the older I got, the worse it got. Oh, there were times he'd be on the wagon, sometimes months. But sooner or later, he'd start up again." She was quiet a moment. "Mike and Tom felt the same way as I did. We all dreaded having him come home at night. We never knew if he'd be drunk or sober. We couldn't wait until we were eighteen and old enough to leave home."

Leslie's heart went out to her.

"He used to yell and scream at us ... I'd go to bed and pull my pillow over my head, and still I could hear him. And there was never any reasoning with him ... ever. He was never physically violent." Her laugh was a false and bitter sound. "But I used to think that would be better than the mental abuse we took ... You can't believe the dirty, filthy names he'd call us." She shuddered.

Leslie frowned. "But your mother stayed with him?"

"Yes." Her tone was bitter. "She loves him. She loves him no matter what. It's something I've never understood, because she deserves better."

She loves him no matter what. All at once Dennis's image flashed through Leslie's mind. When she had learned of Dennis's betrayal, she hadn't felt that way ... not at all. She had been too shocked. Too shattered.

And what Dennis had done was unforgivable.

She pushed the unwelcome memory aside and focused on Colleen. "Rob knows?" she asked quietly.

Colleen nodded, but her reply was a long time in coming. "I haven't been home since Rob and I got married," she confided. "My father wasn't at our wedding because he was on a binge at the time. Mom comes to visit every once in a while. But I refuse to go there and subject Rob and the kids to his drunken tantrums."

She faltered. "I hope you're not upset with me, Les. I know—I know I should have told you years ago. But I was ashamed. And I—I didn't want you to judge me."

But Leslie understood completely—perhaps more than Colleen could ever know. There were some secrets that were far too painful to reveal...like Dennis. Dennis and his—"

She touched Colleen's hand gently, unwilling—even now—to complete the thought. "I'm not upset," she told her softly. "You're my friend and that's what comes first."

Colleen brushed the dampness from her cheeks with the back of her hand. Leslie was relieved to note that some of the bleakness had left her features. "I don't know why I always dreaded this," she confessed breathlessly. "I should have known you wouldn't condemn me, because you're so...well, you're just you."

"I'll take that as a compliment," Leslie said dryly. They both laughed, at a time when they very much needed that release. Yet now it was Leslie who was filled with a wealth of shame and regret. For if ever there was a time to tell Colleen about Dennis, it was now.

But she couldn't. Dear God, she couldn't. And it hurt knowing that the humiliation she suffered was hers to bear alone...forever.

LESLIE TOOK A QUICK SHOWER and then joined Colleen in her bedroom, where she was rifling through closets and drawers looking for her maternity clothes. She was just a little quiet, but for the most part she was her normal cheery self. Tess was up from her nap and had a great time trying on shoes and clothes that were yards too big for her.

Suddenly Colleen clapped a hand to her forehead. "Darn!" she moaned. "All this time wasted! I just remembered I packed everything up in a box and stored it at Clint's. It's easier than climbing up and down the attic stairs, and since he's hardly ever home, he doesn't have as much junk as we have stuck in every nook and cranny." She wrinkled her nose. "That's one advantage to living out of a suitcase, I guess."

Leslie glanced up from the chair she'd settled in near the window. "I suppose all that travel is one of the reasons he's never been married," she murmured. Trying hard not to think of Dennis, she refocused on the magazine she'd been reading.

If she'd been looking up, she'd have seen the odd look that flitted across Colleen's face. "Les," she began.

Just down the hall a door slammed. The next second Tess flew into the room, nearly tripping over the folds of the dress she wore, which happened to be an old one of Colleen's.

"Mommy!" she wailed. "Brian won't let me in his room. He told me to knock before I came in and then he shoved the door in my face and I almost got my fingers caught!" She held up five stubby fingers.

Leslie and Colleen exchanged amused glances. Colleen lifted her and sat her on the bed. "I'll make sure he's more careful, sweetie, but if Brian has the door closed, you *should* knock before you go in."

Tess stuck her lip out. "But he wasn't changing clothes or anything."

"But he might have been," she reminded the little girl. "And boys Brian's age don't like it when their little sisters barge into their rooms."

"Why not?"

"Well, because they're..." Colleen stopped short, looking baffled.

Leslie smiled. "Modest," she finished. Colleen flashed a grateful smile.

Tess hopped off the bed, her attention now on Leslie. "What's modest?"

Something you're not, she nearly laughed aloud. Tess had yanked her dress off her shoulders and let it drop to the floor. Wearing only her underwear, she was busy rummaging through the discarded pile of clothes Colleen had told her she could play with. She paused long enough to throw Leslie another curious look.

"What's modest?" she insisted once more.

Leslie realized she'd just jumped from the frying pan into the fire. "It's...just the way some people are when they get older." She sent a pleading glance at Colleen, but Colleen's shoulders were shaking with silent mirth. "It's just like your mother said. You don't like it when someone comes into your room and doesn't knock," she finished lamely.

Tess appeared satisfied with her answer. Either that, or she'd forgotten all about it. Leslie strongly suspected the latter, since Tess had found a burgundy shirt dress and was busy yanking it over her head.

Colleen belatedly came to her rescue. "Les, how would you like to do me a favor? Would you mind going over to Clint's and asking him if he knows where he put that box of maternity clothes?"

By now Leslie was only too willing. She wasn't sure she wanted to be on the receiving end of another of Tess's sticky questions.

Tess's head popped through the neckline. "Can I go, too?"

Could anyone have resisted that eager tone? Leslie couldn't. She held out her hand. "Come on," she invited.

They headed over to Clint's bungalow, but not before Tess had slipped on a pair of her mother's heels. As she *clip-clopped* across the stones of the terrace, Leslie mused wryly that she could probably be heard miles away.

She raised her hand to rap on the door but Tess was there ahead of her. "Oh, we don't have to knock," she informed Leslie, twisting the handle and throwing open the door. "Uncle Clint's not modest like Brian." Tess tugged on her hand. Leslie had no choice but to step inside after her.

And indeed it appeared that Uncle Clint *wasn't* modest, Leslie thought fuzzily. He was directly across from the door, sprawled on the sofa, long legs angled out across the cushions. He wore nothing but a very brief pair of nylon running shorts.

Tess made a beeline for his side.

He put aside what looked like a blueprint and lifted her up next to him. "What are you doing wearing an outfit like that on such a hot day?"

Tess beamed. "It's Mommy's."

"Yes, I noticed." His eyes met Leslie's over the top of the little girl's head. They were dancing with amusement.

Leslie's tongue was glued to the roof of her mouth. She couldn't seem to stop staring at his chest. A thick, dense layer of crisp dark hair swirled over his chest and abdomen before dipping into the waistband of his shorts.

To make matters worse, Tess thrust her fingers into the dark thatch on his pectorals and tugged. Clint grunted. "Ouch! Didn't your father ever tell you not to do that?"

Tess giggled. "Daddy doesn't have hair on his chest like you do."

"A good point." Clint arched a brow and looked her up and down. "So you made off with your mother's clothes. How is it," he quizzed with a grin, "that you didn't manage to raid her makeup drawer, too?"

Tess's face brightened further. "Ooh," she squealed. "That sounds neat." She slid off the sofa, gathered the trailing folds of her dress in her hand and ran back out the door.

Clint looked after her. "Uh-oh," he murmured. "Why do I have the feeling Colleen won't thank me for that?"

Leslie finally found her voice. "It seems," she offered weakly, "to take some practical experience when it comes to learning what we should and shouldn't say around a child that age."

He chuckled. "Especially one like Tess."

Leslie silently agreed.

Clint's eyes lingered on her. She was dressed in a cool-looking sundress that left her arms bare and showed just a hint of her slim legs. The soft fringe of bangs on her forehead gave her a youthful look, but the rest of her hair was loose, falling in soft waves down to her shoulders. She looked pretty, he decided. She looked *very* pretty.

The observation surprised him, and so did the realization that he didn't have to look twice to recall the slender curves of her body hidden beneath the dress.

He tipped his head to the side, regarding her with a faint smile on his lips. "Did you come to see my etchings?" he found himself teasing.

The look on her face was precious. Her eyes widened, and she stuffed her hands into the oversized pockets of her dress. She quickly told him about the box of clothes Colleen thought was stored there.

He nodded. "I think it's in a corner of my closet." There was a brief pause. "How about if I show you around first?"

Her smile was warm. "Thanks," she said softly. "I think I'd like that."

Clint swung his legs to the floor. Leslie came closer, and it was then that her gaze fell on his leg. He steeled himself for her horrified reaction. But before he could draw a breath, the cushions beside him dipped and she was next to him.

"Oh, Clint." She drew a sharp breath of dismay. "I had no idea your leg was this bad." She reached out and indicated the mottled, dimpled area where the steel rod had ripped through his flesh.

Clint froze, acutely conscious of her nearness. As she leaned closer, a warm feminine fragrance, the lemony scent of shampoo and something else, reached his nostrils. Her fingers hovered above the jagged indentation of the scar that zigzagged across his thigh. Did he only imagine the cool healing touch of her hand, or was it merely wishful thinking?

He wanted her, he realized. Her hair looked soft and shiny, immensely touchable. He wanted to slide his fingers through it and pull her closer still.

Her voice reflected compassion, not pity. "Did you need surgery?"

He nodded. A halo of pain seemed to enshroud his heart. It hadn't occurred to him that he'd be so attracted to a woman again. It was jarring, after forcing himself for so long to feel nothing at all. But he wasn't entirely comfortable with it; he wasn't even sure he wanted—or if he was even capable—of feeling that intensely again.

She leaned back. Her eyes were on his face now, cloudy with distress. "It still must hurt terribly. No wonder you have to use a cane."

"It's not so bad now." Clint swallowed. Using the armrest for leverage, he hitched himself to his feet. "How about that tour now?"

Beside him, Leslie rose to her feet. "You don't have to, you know." She gestured vaguely. "I mean, I can come back later if you're working—"

"No," he interrupted her. "This is fine, really." His smile took her breath away. She thought again that he didn't smile like that nearly enough.

The bungalow was actually bigger than it looked outside. Besides the living room, there was a good-sized bedroom, both with wood-planked floors and desert-hued accents. Leslie's lips twitched when he led her into the kitchen. "Which you don't use?" she asked with a laugh.

"Which I don't use." Their eyes met. There was something warm in his, something that suddenly made her very glad she was there right now.

He moved away and quickly found the box of clothes for Colleen. In the living room, he dropped it on the cushions of the sofa.

When he returned, there was a heated rush of silence. Leslie sensed his eyes on her face and she hesitantly returned his gaze. Neither of them spoke.

Leslie noticed suddenly how tall he was, nearly a head taller than she, and the faint darkening of five o'clock shadow on his jaw. A shiver of awareness touched her spine; she wanted to tear her eyes away yet she couldn't. Her gaze slid helplessly downward.

His body was lean, not at all heavy. The muscles in his arms were sleek and tight. His skin looked like polished teak. Leslie stifled an insane urge to reach out and discover for herself if it was as smooth and taut as it looked. There was an air of virility about him right now that made her toes curl and her heart pound like a trip-hammer.

They were very close, so close that when he breathed, the bristly hairs on his chest brushed her arm. She wanted to turn and slide her fingers into the thick curls the way Tess had done; only she wanted it to bring pleasure to them both....

It was Clint who dragged his gaze away first. "Maybe I should take this over for you."

Disappointment flooded her senses. She had wanted him to kiss her—again. She had wanted it with a longing that stunned her.... But there was nothing reflected on his features except polite detachment.

She reached for the box. "I can manage," she said quickly. Avoiding his gaze, she hurried out the door, overcome with a burning shame.

She hadn't realized until that moment just how long it had been since she had been touched... with tenderness. With passion.

Her heart felt like a crushed blossom. Dennis hadn't wanted her. And neither did Clint.

Was she so desperate for approval that she sought it where none existed?

CHAPTER SIX

LESLIE WAS RELIEVED that the letter from Colleen's mother didn't seem to have any serious aftereffects. Leslie caught Colleen staring into space several times, but other than that, she appeared perfectly fine.

After dinner she helped Colleen sort through her maternity clothes. Because of the heat, she was anxious to locate a pair of shorts, but there was none to be found. Colleen held up a cute but rather faded smock top.

"Can you believe this is eight years old?" She wrinkled her nose in distaste. "I can." She stuffed it back into the box and sat back on her heels.

She wasn't disgruntled for long. Her eyes began to sparkle a second later. "Hey, I've got an idea. Why don't we go shopping tomorrow?"

Leslie thought of all the new clothes she'd bought before she had arrived. Still, the idea sounded fun. "Sounds okay by me," she chuckled. "After all, a woman can never have too many clothes."

"Good." Colleen smiled her satisfaction. "I'll see if Clint will keep an eye on Brian and Tess."

And as it turned out, it *was* fun. Clint didn't mind staying with Brian and Tess, but he had a doctor's appointment in the afternoon. Colleen phoned Tim's mother, Maryann Mahoney, to see if he could drop them off there when he left. Maryann didn't mind in the least.

They left around nine that morning to avoid the rush-hour traffic into San Diego. Colleen found most of what she wanted in two specialty shops at one of the malls in Mission Valley. At noon they drove the short distance to historic Old Town, where they laughed and chatted over Mexican food in an outdoor courtyard. Afterward they walked through flower-filled plazas and browsed through some of the shops. Leslie bought a pair of toy dune buggies for Brian to play with; for Tess she chose a matching necklace and bracelet, and some multicolored hair ribbons. For both she picked up a small basket of sea shells.

She had just finished paying for the items when Colleen glanced at her watch and yelped. "Uh-oh. Rob forgot a couple of files at home this morning. I told him we'd drop them off about one and it's almost one-thirty now."

They hurried back to the car. When they arrived at Rob's office twenty minutes later, Colleen insisted Leslie come in with her. "Who knows," she said brightly, "maybe you'll meet someone here who could help you land a job." She cast a meaningful look from the corner of her eye.

Leslie laughed uneasily. Since Colleen had suggested she think about moving to San Diego, her friend hadn't pressured her one way or the other. Leslie admitted to herself that the idea had more appeal than she had ever dreamed. But the thought of pulling up roots and starting over again was also rather scary.

Colleen knew the receptionist by name. She introduced Leslie, then asked if Rob was in. Rob chose that moment to come around the corner. His expression warmed when he saw the two of them.

"So this is where you are. I thought maybe you'd forgotten all about me."

"You? Not a chance," Colleen declared dramatically.

Rob glanced between them. "As a matter of fact," he said easily, "your timing couldn't be better." He gestured for both women to precede him down the hall.

In his office, Rob closed the door behind them. Leslie sat in one of the chairs across from him. Colleen perched on the corner of his desk. "My," she teased, "this sounds serious."

Rob smiled slightly. "Remember the little Mexican orphan girl? The one we expected later this summer?"

Colleen nodded.

"She's in with Fran right now. Fran's finishing up the final paperwork."

Colleen's feet hit the floor. "What! She's here now? Right now?"

Rob's mouth quirked. His gaze slid to Leslie. "Is it my imagination or is there an echo in here?"

"Rob, this isn't funny!" Colleen was practically wailing. "I wanted everything to be perfect when she came. I wanted her room to be just right—"

"Sweetheart," he put in gently, "I have no doubt that our house will seem like a palace to her."

His words gave her pause. "You're right," she admitted sheepishly. "It's just that after all she's been through, I wanted to make her feel special."

There was a small silence. Both of them appeared preoccupied. Leslie glanced at first one and then the other, then cleared her throat. "Can I ask what's going on here?"

For an instant they both looked at her as if they'd forgotten her existence. Then Colleen came over and perched on the chair next to her. "I guess it might help," she said with a rueful little laugh. "Rob and I are getting temporary foster custody of a five-year-old orphan from Mexico City." She frowned at her husband. "Do you know why she's here so early? I thought she wasn't coming until August."

"So did we," he said dryly. "It was hectic around here this morning, believe me. Fran got a call that she and Sister Carmen were waiting at the airport. Apparently they sent word a few weeks ago about the change in plans." He grimaced. "I don't know what happened, but the letter they sent never arrived here."

Colleen turned back to Leslie. "This little girl is going to be adopted here in the States, but first she needs surgery on her hip. Rob's agency and the orphanage in Mexico City raised enough money to send her here and pay for her medical costs. The agency couldn't find anyone who spoke Spanish and was willing to take care of her during the pre-op and post-op period, so Rob and I offered to do it. We'll have her until after she's recovered and someone decides to adopt her."

"Why does she need the surgery?" Leslie asked. "Because of a birth defect?"

Rob shook his head. "She's from a town in the mountains outside Mexico City. The house she was in collapsed during an earthquake there a couple of years ago and she was trapped in the rubble. Her hip was broken but never treated properly. Since it didn't heal correctly, she has a limp. The orthopedist on the team that first examined her said that the earlier the surgery is done, the better. Otherwise, the chances are greater that she'll never be able to walk normally."

"How awful," Leslie murmured. "And she's how old? Five?"

He nodded. "That's not the worst of it," he added quietly. "She lost both her parents and a brother in the quake. She was taken in by another family, but when the Mexican authorities found her a year ago they took her to the orphanage in Mexico City."

Leslie's heart twisted as she thought of a mere child losing all the family she had; getting used to another family and then being wrenched away and stuck somewhere else. Now it was happening all over again and this still wasn't the end. Nonetheless, with Colleen and Rob, the girl would be well off... at least for the time being.

"Colleen." She shifted and looked straight at her friend. "Since you didn't know this little girl was arriving now, maybe it would better if I went home—"

"Home! Les, you've only been here a few days. You can't leave yet!"

Colleen looked so hurt Leslie almost wished she hadn't mentioned it. Still, she had no intention of getting in the way.

"I could always come back later."

"But you won't and you know it!" Colleen jumped to her feet, visibly upset.

Leslie sighed. "I don't want to be in the way, Colleen."

"But you're not!" Her eyes turned pleading. "Oh, please don't go yet, Les. I want you to at least stay long enough to see if you like it. And you promised you'd seriously think about moving here! Besides, you could be a big help. With being pregnant and having three children in the house, I could use an extra pair of hands."

Leslie hesitated. Colleen had a valid point. But before she could say a word, Rob had joined the argument.

"That's right," he pointed out. "She hasn't been sick at all, but she's been a little on the tired side lately."

Leslie could feel herself weakening. The prospect of going home to her lonely apartment in San Francisco held little appeal; in fact, it held none at all. She was half afraid she'd fall back into the same old niche she'd been in before. And yet . . .

"But don't you think you have enough on your plate already? I mean, you were probably going to put this little girl in the guest room—"

"She can share Tess's room. That's better, anyway."

"But Clint is there and—"

"Clint is family, Les, and—and so are you!" She cast a beseeching look at Rob. "Rob, you tell her!"

Rob stood up and slid an arm around his wife's shoulders. "She's right, Leslie. We love having you, and we'd like you to stay. As long as you want."

Leslie bit her lip. "Tell you what," she said slowly. "Let's just play it by ear and—and let me think about it. Okay?"

"Okay." Colleen relented with a smile. "But you won't be in the way, you know." She caught Rob's eye. "When do we get to meet this little girl? And what is her name, by the way?"

"Her name's Bonita. Bonita Sanchez. By the way, honey, I understand she only speaks a smattering of English." He started for his desk. "I'll just give Fran a buzz and see if she's finish—"

But he never reached the phone. As if on cue, there was a knock on the door. A short, cuddly looking woman breezed in. "Okay, Rob, we're just about set—" She stopped when she saw Colleen. "Colleen! I guess I don't have to ask what brings you here." Her gaze fell on Leslie, so Rob quickly made the introductions.

Fran turned back to Colleen. "Rob gave you the news?"

Colleen nodded. "It's a good thing I stopped in after all."

"Your timing couldn't be better, that's for sure." Fran turned and gestured. "Guess who we have here?"

A plump middle-aged woman stepped into the room. Beside her, almost hidden behind the voluminous folds of her skirt, was a young child.

"Colleen, this is Sister Carmen. She's one of the nuns from the orphanage in Mexico City. And this—" Fran smiled broadly "—is Bonita." She beckoned to the girl.

The little girl stared back at all of them, her trepidation plainly evident. Recalling what Rob had said about her losing her family, Leslie felt her heart go out to the girl. It was no wonder she was terrified. The child had had no stability; no one to love and care for her the way a child deserved to be loved.

Sister Carmen bent and said something in Spanish. The little girl shuffled forward, but she refused to relinquish Sister Carmen's hand. She was very small and slight, with huge liquid eyes that dominated her tiny face. Her shoulders were narrow and thin beneath a faded red dress that was far too big for her. Her hair was rather clumsily braided in two long ropes that hung over her shoulders clear to her waist. The canvas shoes she wore were far too short; her toes pushed through a ragged tear in the left one.

Colleen had knelt down so that she was on the same level as the little girl. "Hello, Bonita. My name is Colleen." Her tone was as gentle as her smile. "We're glad you're going to be staying with us for a while."

Those wide, chocolate-colored eyes searched her face. A small hand crept out and made as if to touch Colleen's hair. But then the little girl jerked back as if she'd been burned.

Sister Carmen spoke in thickly accented English, "It is your hair, *señora*. She has never seen hair that color before." She shook her head. "And though she knows why she has come here, she is still afraid."

Colleen smiled at the child. "We expected that," she said softly. "Will you tell her that we're going to take good care of her? And we'll have lots and lots of fun once we get her home."

Sister Carmen broke into a stream of rapid-fire Spanish, but Bonita was having none of it. Her expression lost none of its fearful wariness. Not wanting to push her, Colleen smiled at her again, then straightened.

Everyone fell silent when Fran said it was time to take Sister Carmen to the airport. Sister Carmen bent and hugged the little girl. "God's blessing has fallen on you, *chiquita*. You will have a home and a family, and I know you will be very happy."

Bonita's thin arms went around her neck. She clung to the woman desperately. Sister Carmen shook her head and whispered in Spanish, hugged her again and then gently disengaged herself from the child's embrace. She left then, looking back once and giving a tiny wave.

Tears stood out in Bonita's eyes; her lips quivered pitifully.

Leslie felt a painful catch in her heart. *Poor little tyke,* she thought. Bonita had just watched her last link with security disappear.

Colleen cleared her throat. "Well," she said brightly. "Les, the three of us should be off, too."

Rob stepped forward and kissed her cheek. "See you in a little while," he murmured. He smiled at Bonita, then glanced back at his wife. "I'll bring a pizza home for dinner."

"Sounds great." She picked up the small shoddy bag that contained Bonita's few possessions. Slipping an arm around the girl's shoulders, she guided her gently toward the door.

Leslie moved ahead and opened the wide glass door for them. Her breath caught for a second as she followed them through. Bonita moved with a hitch in her gait, her progress stiff and awkward. *Poor baby,* she thought again.

In the car, Colleen decided to settle her between them in the front seat so she wouldn't be alone in the back.

Leslie ducked inside. "Hi," she said gaily. "Guess what, Bonita? I get to sit right here next to you."

Those huge black eyes roamed her face. The child's lips parted; for an instant Leslie was sure she would speak. But then her gaze fluttered slowly back to her lap.

Heaving a silent sigh, Leslie fastened the seat belt around Bonita's small body. She was careful not to move too quickly and startle the child.

The car angled out onto the street. Leslie decided to try a little experiment. She patted her chest. "Leslie," she said. She pointed to Bonita's chest. "Bonita." Then she pointed to Colleen. "Colleen."

Bonita said nothing. Her limpid gaze traveled between the two adults.

Colleen glanced over at Leslie. "This could prove rather interesting," she said with a grin. "I imagine my knowledge of Spanish is even more limited than her knowledge of English."

Leslie's eyes twinkled. "That's probably more of a handicap than anything else. A child can usually pick up a foreign language much quicker than an adult."

"Provided we can get her to talk," Colleen amended dryly.

Colleen was silent for a few seconds, but suddenly she looked like the cat who had swallowed the canary.

"All right." Leslie demanded good-naturedly. "What's behind that look."

"Well...I was just thinking this could turn out even better than expected. I mean, who better than a teacher to teach Bonita English—and especially one who majored in elementary education?"

"Aha." Leslie nodded knowingly. "This is just a roundabout way of saying I get to earn my keep then."

"So you've decided to stay?"

Leslie's gaze dropped to the little girl. Bonita's dark eyes were still fastened on her; she appeared to be watching her with more curiosity than anything else. And when Bonita saw that Leslie's attention was focused on her, the corners of her mouth curled ever so slightly. It was a tiny smile—only a hint of one actually—but it reached all the way to Leslie's heart.

"Yes," she said softly. "I guess it does."

TESS WAS THRILLED to discover that there was going to be another girl in the house to play with, even one she couldn't understand—and who had yet to speak to any of them.

Colleen had apparently told Brian and Tess earlier that Bonita would be staying with them sometime this summer. They immediately noticed the little girl's limp, so Colleen took them aside and explained to them about Bonita's hip, reiterating that they were not to laugh at her clumsy gait or make fun of her.

When Brian and Tess had loped into the house and exchanged hugs and kisses with their mother, Bonita's gaze skipped between the three of them, lingering on their hair. Seeing the three blond heads nestled together, Leslie could almost see her little mind make the connection between mother and children. Some of the fear seemed to drain from her then; she even smiled at Colleen once or twice.

As for Brian and Tess, she was a little shy but not afraid of them. She appeared fascinated by their fair coloring. More than once, Leslie saw her eye their hair and pick up one of her own fat braids and stare at it.

Oddly enough, it was Leslie she seemed to have chosen as her protector. In the living room, she sat down next to Leslie and stayed there. She stared in amazement when Brian switched on afternoon cartoons, but she didn't move, even when Tess dropped down in front of the television and crooked her finger at her. They knew she understood the gesture, because she shook her head no and eased closer to Leslie.

Tess came over with a frown. "How come she doesn't like me, Leslie?"

"It's not that she doesn't like you," Leslie tried to explain. "It's just that this is all very new to her. She's in a strange place, with strange people, and I'm sure she's a little scared."

"I don't want her to be scared of me," Tess said earnestly. The next second she grinned and asked in a stage whisper, "Did Mommy get me a surprise?"

Leslie laughed. "I don't know about Mommy, but I did. See that little pink bag over on the dining room table? If you'll get it and bring it over here, I'll show you."

Brian thought his dune buggies were great; Tess loved her bracelet and necklace. Leslie decided to save the seashells for later. She was very glad she'd also bought the ribbons. She didn't want Bonita to feel left out, so she presented the ribbons to her with a smile. The child accepted them gingerly, her expression rather puzzled.

"Ooh," Tess squealed. "Those are pretty. Hey, let's put one in Boni . . . Bon . . . let's put one in her hair!" she finished at last.

"I don't see why not." Leslie pulled out a yellow ribbon and gestured to Bonita's hair.

The youngster eyed it questioningly, so Leslie pulled it around her own hair, then gestured once more at Bonita's.

The hint of a smile appeared.

"See?" Tess jumped to her feet. "She wants it in, too. I'll go get a brush."

When she returned, Leslie began the task of un-braiding and brushing Bonita's hair. First she sepa-rated long silky strands with her fingertips, then began gently pulling the brush through. The child had beau-tiful hair, she marveled. It was wavy from the braids, but even so it reached well past her waist. Tess chat-tered beside them while she worked.

"I can't say Bon . . . Bonit . . . I can't say her name," she frowned. "Can't we just call her Bonnie?"

Brian piped up from across the room. "Yeah! Let's call her Bonnie. It's lots easier to say than Bonita."

Leslie slid the ribbon under Bonita's neck and brought it up toward her forehead. "Bonnie," she re-peated. "I like it. And you know, I think it fits her." She tied the ribbon with a flourish, then set her hands on her tiny shoulders. "There. All done."

Tess hopped to her feet. "Hey, she looks pretty! I bet she wants to see, too. I'll go get Mommy's mirror." She raced from the room, returning a few seconds later with Colleen's hand mirror.

Tess pressed the mirror into her hand, holding it up so she could view her reflection. Bonita's eyes widened; Tess grinned. "Pret-ty," she said slowly, reaching out a chubby hand to Bonita's shoulder. "Pret-ty Bonnie," she giggled.

Bonita reached up and touched the silky yellow ribbon, then turned to gaze at Leslie with shining eyes.

"See?" Tess crowed. "She likes it. Bonnie likes it!"

Colleen came in from the kitchen, wiping her hands on a dish towel. "How's our newest addition to the family doing?" she called out.

"Pretty good, actually." Leslie chuckled. "As quiet as ever, though."

Colleen's eyes fell on Bonita. "Well, well, what have we here?" She bent and tweaked one of Bonnie's long curls. "Pretty... pretty Bonita."

"Pretty Bonnie!" Tess corrected her mother. "We're going to call her Bonnie. See? She likes it."

And indeed, Bonita—or Bonnie—did seem to like her new nickname. Her head rose and she glanced around curiously whenever she heard someone say *Bonnie*. Rob laughed because she seemed more interested in looking at the pizza he brought home than eating it, but it seemed she was no different from so many other kids—she devoured every bit of the peanut butter and jelly sandwich she was offered instead.

Clint didn't return from his doctor's appointment until they'd finished. Apparently he'd told Brian to tell Colleen not to wait dinner for him; he'd get something on his way home. Rob was out in the garage, and Leslie was busy writing her mother at the dining room table. The three children were clustered around the table as well, each with a coloring book in front of them. But when Tess heard the sound of Clint's voice, she jumped and ran into the kitchen where her mother was greeting him. Leslie couldn't help but overhear part of the conversation through the doorway.

Colleen had just started to tell him the news when Tess burst in, babbling excitedly. "Guess what, Uncle Clint? I've got a new playmate—and she gets to sleep with me, too!"

He bent and picked her up. "Lucky you," he teased. "You get to have a friend spend the night, huh?"

"It's not just tonight. She gets to sleep with me every night, 'cause she's gonna live here with us!"

Keeping his skepticism to himself, Clint glanced at Colleen inquiringly.

"It's true," she laughed. "But I thought I'd told you that we were taking in a little girl later this summer. But later—" she grinned "—turns out to be now."

He lowered Tess and placed her on her feet, searching his memory. She had told him, but he'd forgotten all about it.

Tess tugged at his hand. "Come on, Uncle Clint. I want you to see her. We named her Bonnie!"

"Clint, wait!"

He glanced back at Colleen.

"You know," she said, starting after them, "it slipped my mind until just a little while ago, but with all that time you spent in Central America, you must have a pretty good working knowledge of the language. Didn't Angelina speak Spanish?"

Clint paused. His guard went up instantly. It was all he could do to prevent himself from stiffening. He nodded and forced a casual tone he was suddenly far from feeling. "Why the sudden interest in Spanish?"

"Because none of us speaks Spanish, and our little guest doesn't speak much English. In fact," she added dryly, "she doesn't seem to speak at all!"

But Colleen was about to be proved wrong.

They had reached the dining room doorway. Tess pulled away and ran across the floor. "See?" she cried. "This is Bonnie!"

At the sound of her name, Bonnie looked up curiously, as she had all evening. But then the strangest thing happened. For an instant Bonnie looked stunned, but then it was as if a glimmer of recognition flitted over her tiny features.

Her lips parted. *"Papá,"* she whispered. *"Papá..."*

CHAPTER SEVEN

CLINT STOOD HELPLESSLY as a shock wave ran through him. He couldn't tear his eyes from the yellow ribbon twined through shining black waves. It was as if he'd been locked into the moment—locked in torment and plunged back, deep within the nightmare that haunted him still.

Only now he was awake.

He sucked in a breath—it felt like fire in his lungs. He swallowed and blinked, praying he was dreaming...that she wasn't real; that she had been conjured up by some kind of twisted trick of his mind, this long-haired little sprite with eyes as dark as midnight, so much like Angelina's he wanted to scream.

From somewhere there was a childish titter—Tess. It all happened in a fraction of a second. For Clint, it was the longest moment of his life. He was only too glad when Tess claimed the spotlight.

"That's not *Papá*," Tess proclaimed, giggling. "He's Uncle Clint. See, Bonnie? Clint." She ran up to him and patted his arm, then thumped her own small chest. "Tess."

Bonnie's gaze followed her as she flitted around the room, happily reciting everyone's name. Bonnie remained silent throughout. Then once again, something amazing happened. Bonnie glanced up Leslie and leaned closer. "Lee," she whispered shyly, and then again: "Lee!"

Everyone laughed, everyone but Clint. He forced himself to feel nothing as Leslie reached out and impulsively hugged the child—Bonnie.

Clint harshly congratulated himself. He had fooled them, he realized, unable to prevent the sudden bitterness that seeped into his soul. They didn't know, any of them—not Rob, not Colleen, and certainly not Leslie—that the sight of that little girl penetrated his heart in one single, killing thrust.

Nor did he want their concern, their pity. He just wanted out, away from that tiny little figure that reminded him of all he'd once had—and all he'd lost. Yet he braced his body and took the nearest chair—the one furthest from where the child sat next to Leslie.

For everyone else, it was as if the incident had never happened. Everyone's attention was centered on the newcomer. And somehow he managed to gloss over the pain that knotted his insides every time his gaze fell upon the little girl.

He would never consciously hurt Colleen and Rob, and so he stayed for the sake of appearances. He even played interpreter a few times when the need arose. But he made his getaway as soon as he was able, glad for the household's usual uproar, thankful that no one had noticed anything amiss.

HE WAS WRONG.

The night was warm and still and silent. The moon spilled down from the sky in shining splendor. Leslie paused, one hand raised to knock on the door of Clint's bungalow. After Rob and Colleen had said good-night, she'd started over here half a dozen times, only to change her mind.

Clint had been . . . different tonight. It wasn't anything he'd said, or anything he'd done, yet he seemed a million miles away. Not precisely distant but—restrained. And so—so *alone*—despite the commotion going on around him.

She kept seeing it all again, that instant when Bonnie had whispered, "*Papá . . . Papá.*" For a heartbeat in time, Clint looked as if he'd seen a ghost. It happened so quickly she might have convinced herself it was her imagination. But all evening long, every so often his gaze came back to Bonnie. And always—always—he looked quickly away . . . as if he couldn't stand the sight of her.

It was an odd thought—and a disturbing one. She couldn't fathom why it came to mind so readily. But it lingered, like smoke in the air. . . .

Squaring her shoulders, she knocked on the screen.

There was no answer. The door was ajar, but not a single light burned inside the bungalow. She peered through the wire mesh of the screen, but the living room was dark and quiet. There was no sign of Clint.

She hesitated. Was he asleep? Somehow she didn't think so. She knew he was inside, and she had the strangest feeling that he'd chosen to shut himself away from the rest of them.

Her fingers closed around the handle of the screen door. She turned it tentatively and discovered it wasn't locked. She hovered uncertainly, thinking perhaps she should knock again. . . .

Clint hadn't heard her knock. He was lying on the sofa, carefully willing his mind to go blank. He had the notion that if he fell asleep, his horrible nightmare would return the way it had the other night.

The doctor's gentle but thorough poking and prodding had started his leg throbbing, and it continued throughout the evening. But right now Clint scarcely noticed the ache in his leg... because the ache in his heart was a thousand times bigger.

Tonight the window to the past was thrown wide open once more. Thoughts of Angelina had returned with a vengeance... and all because of a tiny Mexican orphan.

Everything rushed back with shattering clarity. He could almost see Angelina the day she'd found out she was pregnant, whirling around the room, her voice ringing with love and laughter.

"A baby—we have made a baby!" She flung her arms around his neck.

He couldn't remember when he'd felt so much pride... or so much love. "Are you making any predictions yet?" he teased. "Are we having a boy? Or a girl?"

"It is enough to have a baby—your baby! *Our* baby! But oh, I think I would love to have a girl!" She pressed her hands against his cheeks. Her eyes shone as brightly as a thousand suns. "A little girl, tiny and petite. She will have long black hair, and I will tie it back with a ribbon—a big, bright ribbon!" And she laughed delightedly, as only Angelina could laugh.

Clint's eyes squeezed shut. He screamed inwardly. They'd been so happy then, despite the smoldering political unrest. God! What a fool he'd been! Like Angelina, he never really dreamed they could be touched by it....

He relived the consequences of his mistake every time his eyes closed. The ground thundered with the sound of his footsteps. Once again he saw Angelina, only this time he held her lifeless body in his arms. He stared in horror at the flood of crimson staining her breast...at the bloodied fingertips curled protectively round her distended belly. A hoarse shout echoed in his ears, a cry of outrage...a cry of denial.

She's not dead. She's not...

But there were no shouts. There was only the sound of someone rapping at the door, softly calling his name.

His eyes flicked open. It was Leslie's voice he heard calling him. It took a moment to calm his churning stomach, but he sat up abruptly.

"Come in. The door's not locked." His voice sounded scratchy; he scarcely recognized it as his own.

The screen opened with a creak. "Hey," she chided lightly, "what is this? You're sitting all alone in the dark. Why didn't you turn on the lamp?"

Clint sat very still. Silvery moonbeams highlighted Leslie's slender frame. He silently followed her progress across the room.

There was a thump and a muffled exclamation. He reached over and switched on the lamp.

Rubbing her shin, Leslie stumbled for the chair across from him. "Ouch. Thank you." She sat down and glanced over at him. "You weren't sleeping, were you?"

He shook his head.

Leslie bit her lip. Other than his hoarse mutter telling her to come in, he still hadn't spoken. "I...I was worried about you. I didn't hear you say how your visit to the doctor went.''

"Everything's fine," he said curtly.

"Did he say when you can go back to work?''

"About a month. Till then, all I can do is paperwork.''

"A month! That's earlier than you expected, isn't it?''

Again he nodded.

She frowned, surveying him tentatively. "That's good news, isn't it?''

"I suppose so." He should be glad, he realized. If he were back on the job, he wouldn't be haunted by visions of a certain black-haired little girl.... But the truth was, he couldn't seem to summon much feeling for anything just now.

The silence spun out. Leslie paused, at a loss for what to say next. It didn't help that he appeared to be avoiding her gaze.

She studied him covertly. His legs were sprawled out in front of him. His eyes were still shielded from her, but she sensed the tension inside him. He looked tired, she thought with a pang. She yearned to reach out to him, to smooth the faint lines from his forehead.

She spoke hesitantly. "I didn't mean to disturb you.''

"You didn't.''

Again there was that stifling silence. She gathered her courage and spoke his name softly. "Clint. Can I ask you something?''

"Sure.''

She paused. "Are you okay?''

"I just said I was.''

She bit back the frustration that tore at her. He had chosen to deliberately misunderstand—and they both knew it.

She took a deep breath and shook her head. "You're not," she said clearly. "I'm not a fool, Clint. I know there's something wrong."

Her observation drew his eyes to her in a flash, but he said nothing.

She leaned forward. "I may be way off base here," she said slowly. "But you seemed to be okay until..."

His eyes narrowed. "Until what?"

She watched him closely. "Until you saw Bonnie."

"Why would you think that?" There was no denying the harshness in his tone.

Why? Because you're a dead giveaway, whether you know it or not. Because you get defensive every time Central America is mentioned... Because you went pale at the mere sight of a black-haired little girl...

And then there was the name Colleen had mentioned... Angelina. There was a connection; she was almost certain of it. But what? And who was Angelina?

Leslie longed to shout all of this—all of this and more. She wanted to tell him to stop hiding... because wasn't that what he was doing?

But she couldn't say a word, because all at once the tables had been turned. It was no longer her confronting him, it was Clint confronting her. His expression, his eyes, betrayed little emotion as the tension in the room mounted. Leslie grew uncomfortable beneath his stare, for somehow his lack of emotion served as a warning.

"Bonnie," he pointed out very deliberately, "is just a child. I've never seen her before in my life. What could I possibly have against her?" Deep inside he knew it wasn't only Leslie he was trying to convince, it was himself.

"I didn't say you had anything against her." Leslie floundered, "It's just that I—I saw your face. And I thought . . . maybe you felt a little the way I did when I found out Colleen was pregnant."

She lifted her hands, then dropped them back to her lap. This whole exchange was taking a direction she hadn't expected. She'd only wanted to help him, to lessen the strain of whatever was on his mind. But the set look on his face warned her any effort was futile.

It didn't stop her from wanting to try.

"Look," she began awkwardly, "I think I know how you feel."

"You don't."

His flat denial wounded her, but she forged ahead anyway. "Oh, but I think I do—"

He didn't give her a chance to finish. He shoved himself to his feet, his jaw knotted and tight.

"Do you?" A strange cold note crept into his voice. "I wonder. Oh, I know all about your divorce. I know you thought it was the end of the world. But these days people fall out of love as quickly as they fall *in* love. And it makes me wonder if you know what it's like to feel real pain. If you know what it's like to lose someone you loved so much it feels like your heart's been ripped out? Well, you're not the only one who can hurt, Leslie. In fact, it seems to me you're just feeling sorry for yourself!"

Leslie blanched. For a moment she sat stunned, unable to move. His last words were fairly flung at her; in fact, the whole speech was.

Or maybe it was his voice. It sliced through her like a whip; she had the awful sensation that if she gave him the chance he'd cut her to ribbons. His taunt echoed through her brain until she wanted to scream and cover her ears. *These days people fall out of love as quickly as they fall in love.* God! she thought wildly. It would have been so much simpler if that was what had happened to her and Dennis. Only Dennis hadn't fallen out of love with her. He'd just fallen in love a second time, and he'd thought he could have them both....

Dimly she heard herself make a small sound, a sound that might have been a cry of pain. She suddenly wanted out, away from this bitter, lonely man who refused to let anyone close.

She surged forward and would have torn past him, but despite being hampered by his leg, he was too quick for her. He grabbed her before she could get by.

Clint told himself it was instinct that made him reach for her. But he knew he was wrong the instant he touched her.

Her eyes were huge and wide and glistening; she looked as if he'd struck her. All at once he hated himself for putting that stricken look on her face.

"Leslie." There was a rough catch in his voice. "Leslie, wait. I—I'm sorry."

Hot tears pricked at her eyelids. She told herself they were tears of anger.

"Are you?" It was her turn to strike out blindly. "You think you know so much, don't you? Well, you don't, damn you! You don't know about my marriage. You don't know anything about me . . . about Dennis . . . or—or what he did!''

Her accusation made him flinch. He glanced away, disgusted at the way he had lashed out at her. It wasn't like him to be so cruel.

"You're right. It was a stupid, hurtful thing to say."

"Yes, it was!" she choked out. "Especially when I just wanted to help!''

"I know." Clint knew he should say more. He knew he should explain. Yet how could he explain what he didn't understand himself?

He didn't know what demon had seized him. He didn't mean to hurt her, yet he couldn't help it. Because here she was, reminding him of things he didn't want to feel, things he wanted to forget. He found himself torn by the urge to push her away and forget she'd ever come here tonight.

But just as compelling was the need to pull her close and drive away her pain, to stroke the honeyed silk from her forehead and bury his face in her hair.

His features were bleak and taut, as if he were fighting some fierce inner battle. Leslie sensed the conflict in him, just as she felt the two-way tug in her own heart. She was consumed with an inexplicable yearning to reach out and cradle his dark head to her breast, much as she might have done with Tess or one of the younger children at school, but something held her back. Clint wasn't thrusting her away . . . but he wasn't letting her close, either.

And close was where she wanted to be. She wanted to be near him, shielded and protected. She wanted to slip inside him and get as close as she could possibly get, her mouth under his, skin against skin...heart to heart.

He was man to her woman, and Leslie was suddenly—achingly—conscious of the differences between them. He'd unbuttoned his shirt against the heat; it hung completely open. The ribbon of flesh exposed by the open fabric was dark and matted with hair. The sight of his bare torso made her pulse leap out of control.

All at once her thoughts were a crazy mixture of hope and fear. She wasn't afraid of *him*. She wanted him to kiss her. She craved all the things she'd missed so much in the empty months since she'd learned of Dennis's betrayal, the deep intimacy that only a man's touch could bring. But she was also afraid of those longings, for more than anything, she feared being hurt again.

Her lips parted. When she spoke, there was a tiny break in her voice. "Clint, please," she said desperately. "Maybe it's best if...if neither one of us says any more. Maybe I should just leave...."

She tried to step back, but his grip on her shoulders tightened, reminding her she wasn't free. His touch was both comforting and disturbing.

She stood as if paralyzed. The air between them was suddenly alive and pulsing. She felt his tension in the hands that gripped her shoulders.

Lean fingers slid down her bare arms, pressing into the flesh just above her elbows.

She would have pulled away, if it hadn't been for the look in his eyes. He was staring at her intently; reflected on his tightly drawn features was the same shattering awareness that held her spellbound.

"Leslie..." There was such torment, such desperation in the way he whispered her name that she wanted to cry out for both of them. But before she could utter a sound his mouth came down on hers.

But the conflict in his heart didn't lessen. Leslie felt it as keenly as she felt her own. He kissed her as if he were starved for the taste of her, his lips stark and sensual, hungry but sweet. Her hands lifted, as if to push him away, but suddenly her fingers were on his shoulders, curling tightly into his flesh.

Her action caught him off guard, and sent him off balance, as well. He braced himself as they dropped back onto the sofa, catching her weight as she fell against him.

He eased to the side so that she was wedged between the length of his body and the back of the sofa. Even then their lips never parted. His mouth was fused against hers, taking what he sought, seeking with gentle demand all she had to give.

She fought to keep her hands where they were, but they displayed a shocking tendency of their own to wander where they would. Her fingers slid down his chest, twining in the silky jungle she discovered there. Her thumb brushed a flat male nipple nestled in crisp dark hair; she heard his sharp intake of air and reveled in it.

She had told herself she'd come out of concern for him—as a friend. And she *had* been concerned. But now her heart was thundering wildly in her breast. In some faraway corner of her mind, she wondered if perhaps this wasn't what she wanted after all....

She nearly moaned when his hands slid under her blouse. Her body burst into exquisite life with sensations long denied but not forgotten. For the first time she felt the pleasantly rough caress of his fingertips on her bare skin. She melted against him, grateful that they weren't standing, for surely her knees would have given way.

She wanted to die with pleasure when his fingers stole around to parallel the narrow indentations of her rib cage. His hand hovered just above the ripe fullness of her breast. Her breath quickened. Her nipples grew tight and tingling and aching for his touch.

It was a touch that never came.

Every nerve in her body was screaming in anticipation, crying out in frustrated expectation, when the next thing she knew Clint tore his mouth from hers. He rolled away and pushed himself to his feet. Stunned, Leslie gazed at him blankly.

She sat up slowly, watching as he shoved his fingers through his hair. He didn't look at her when he spoke. His tone was low but rough. "Maybe you're right, Leslie. Maybe you should leave."

Shame washed over her. She stood shakily, only half-conscious of what she was doing. She was halfway to the door when something made her look back.

He stood watching her. For a fraction of a second she thought she saw a lingering ember of desire in his eyes. But the look was compounded with...what? Confusion? Regret?

He appeared to hesitate. "I'm sorry," he said again. "This shouldn't have happened."

Leslie caught her breath. That hurt—more than it should have—more than anything else he had said tonight. Because until that very moment . . .

She hadn't been sorry at all.

CHAPTER EIGHT

BY THE TIME morning rolled around, Leslie was determined to put Clint Stuart out of her mind once and for all. Unfortunately she couldn't avoid him while she was there, so she would be civil and polite, but no more.

Lying in bed, she released her breath slowly, staring up at the ceiling. She wasn't going to set herself up the way she had last night, she vowed again. In fact, maybe it was better if there was a wedge between herself and Clint. Thinking of last night made her cringe all over again. Only once before had she felt so awkward, so...*exposed*.

That was when she had discovered the shocking extent of Dennis's betrayal.

Dennis. She nearly moaned, fighting the twisting surge of emotion that ripped through her. After all this time, she still felt so many things when she thought of him. Anger. Despair. But she would never ever forgive him—nor could she forget—the degradation she'd suffered when she learned the truth. How many times, she agonized, had she thought it would have been easier if he simply hadn't wanted her? A hand seemed to close around her heart and squeeze. If only he hadn't claimed to still love her. *Damn him, anyway!*

she raged silently. It wasn't possible for a man to love two women at the same time!

Leslie remembered the night she'd told Colleen there was another woman. *Another woman.* If only it were that simple! What would Colleen have said if she had told her that not only was there another woman in Dennis's life, but there was also another wi—

Oh, God. God! She clamped the brake on the thought just in time. To this day, she could scarcely admit the truth. Not once had she ever said the words aloud...*not once.* Was it any wonder no one knew her secret?

At least Clint hadn't deluded her, she acknowledged, hardening her heart. Oh, he hadn't come right out and said the words—but then there was no need. He didn't want her, and it was simple as that.

With a heavy sigh she slid from the bed. She quickly showered and dressed, then headed for the kitchen. She breathed a silent sigh of relief when she saw that Colleen and the three children were at the table. Tess called out a cheery greeting, while Bonnie's thin face lit up like a tree at Christmas. "Lee," she cried brightly.

Leslie knew she didn't imagine the pleasure in the little girl's eyes. Something melted inside her. Her spirits lifted, like a kite taking flight and soaring with the wind. She took the empty chair next to Bonnie.

Both girls were dressed in shorts and T-shirts. Tess's had a picture of Minnie Mouse, while Bonnie's sported Mickey. Leslie recognized Bonnie's as belonging to Tess, and she sent a silent glance of approval toward Colleen. Both women silently shook their heads over Bonnie's clothes last night as they readied the girls for bed. The few dresses they'd unpacked looked either far too big or much too small for Bonnie's thin frame; they were clean but ragged and threadbare in places, which was why Colleen had decided to meet Rob after work later so they could do some shopping for her.

She looked from one small face to the other, then tapped a finger in the center of Bonnie's chest.

"Well, well," she said lightly. "Who do we have here?"

Bonnie's mouth opened. "Mickey," she said clearly. "Mickey Mouse."

Leslie blinked. "Why, that's good, Bonnie. Very good!" Impulsively she reached out and gave the little girl a hug.

Bonnie fairly beamed.

Colleen drew a hand over her forehead, a gesture of feigned relief. "Hey, maybe she knows more English than we thought. The only problem," she laughed, "is that we don't know any Spanish."

Brian grabbed the cereal box from the center of the table. "Then it's a good thing Uncle Clint's here."

"Why," said a voice from behind them, "is that?"

Clint! Leslie knew by the prickle of the hair on her neck that he was almost directly behind her. He was the last person she wanted to see right now. God, how she dreaded facing him again! But the thought dropped off abruptly when Bonnie spoke. *"Papá!"* she said excitedly, slipping from her chair. She stopped near Clint, her liquid eyes traveling upward. Her expression was adoring.

Leslie held her breath, gauging every nuance of his reaction. She didn't know precisely what she was looking for, but whatever it was, she prayed she wouldn't find it. There was the slightest of hesitations—or did she only imagine it? Then Clint smiled slightly, his gaze drawn to Bonnie's upturned face. His smile seemed a trifle forced; while his expression wasn't warm, neither was it cold.

He'd claimed last night that Bonnie was just a child—that he had nothing against her. Leslie suddenly wanted very much to believe him, but there was a part of her that reserved judgment.

Watching Bonnie's clumsy efforts to reach him, Clint experienced a painful twist of his heart. As much as he'd tried to prepare himself for this very meeting, every muscle in his body tightened when she stopped directly in front of him. Her little hand stretched out.... His fragile control began to slip. *Don't,* he prayed silently. *Oh, God, please don't...*

She was only after the plastic cookie cutter he held in his free hand, a small gingerbread man. He forced back the tightness in his chest and offered it to her, somehow managing a smile. *"Buenos días,"* he murmured. "Is this what you're after?" He glanced over at Colleen. "Tess must have brought it over and forgotten it."

Colleen chuckled. "I have the feeling," she commented dryly, "that you may have another frequent visitor, as well." She nodded at Bonnie. "She seems to have taken quite a shine to you and Leslie."

"She's quite a charmer herself," Leslie said lightly. "I don't know how anyone could look into those huge brown eyes and not fall for her, lock, stock and barrel." She rose, intending to excuse herself, but before she had a chance, the phone rang.

Colleen reached for it. "That was Maryann," she stated briskly a moment later. "She's putting up wallpaper in her bathroom and said she desperately needs another pair of hands for a few minutes."

Brian scrambled up. "Can I come along and play with Tim?"

"And me and Bonnie, too," Tess chimed in. "We can play with Megan!"

Colleen was already hustling the trio out the back door. "As long as you stay out of the way. Brian, you and Tim can keep an eye on the girls...."

The sound of her voice drifted away. The room grew abnormally quiet. Leslie sensed Clint's eyes on her, but she couldn't find it in her to meet his gaze. Her pleasure in the morning had dimmed, and it was all because of him. She wanted to run, but there was nowhere to hide. Conversely she wanted to vent her simmering resentment and see him flinch.

Before she knew it, she was on her feet. Head down, she started blindly for the doorway. "I think I'll give them a hand," she muttered.

She didn't get more than three steps. Long fingers closed around her upper arm. "Please don't go."

Oddly it was his quiet plea—not his touch—that stopped her cold. There was a note in it that caused a huge lump to lodge in her throat.

She stared at his hand. She didn't want to feel so—so hurt all over again. And she didn't want to feel this strange compassion for Clint—she didn't want to feel anything for him!

His hand deserted her arm, only to slide up her shoulder. Gentle fingers lifted her chin, silently demanding that she look at him.

She swallowed. All she had to do was pull away and run. He would never catch her, not with his leg.

His gaze searched hers. "We need to talk, Leslie. We're alone now, and this is the perfect chance to do it."

Bitterness choked her. She spoke without thinking. "You didn't want to be alone with me last night." To her horror, her voice wobbled traitorously.

For the longest time he said nothing. After a moment, she heard his low murmur.

"I'm sorry, Leslie."

A burning shame washed over her. "You said that last night." It took several seconds before she was able to arm herself against him and her own treacherous emotions.

She raised her chin and looked him straight in the eye. "But it doesn't matter," she said evenly. "After all, I'm a big girl now. And it was just a kiss—"

"No." His voice sounded oddly strangled. "Not about that. I'm not sorry I kissed you."

Shock held her motionless. "You're not?"

"No. I'm sorry about what happened *before* I kissed you."

The air between them suddenly grew quiet and still. Clint appeared to hesitate. Something in his expression made Leslie think that this time he was the one treading on uneven ground. Still, she regarded him warily.

"I know you're angry. I know you have every right to be. But I want to explain, Leslie." His hand slid down to grip hers. "Please," he said quietly.

She stared at him. Part of her wanted to thank him for trying to make the awkward moment more comfortable for her. Another part of her longed to slap his hand away, because the anguish in her heart was still just a little too piercing.

And she couldn't forget that he was the cause of it.

She gestured vaguely. "I don't know what you want from me, Clint. I—I just don't understand you. After last night I didn't think you'd be any more anxious to see me than I was to see you."

Time marched slowly by. A part of Leslie wanted to be angry. That same part longed to lash out and make him bleed the way she had bled last night. But far stronger was her need to know that he had not meant to deliberately hurt her.

Clint hesitated, wishing he knew what to say. He was handling this badly, he was certain. He sensed her wariness toward him, and he knew he had no one to blame but himself. He desperately wanted to reassure her, but he was making his way rather carefully himself right now. It was a little like walking a tightrope without a net.

"I don't know what came over me last night," he said finally. "I guess I wasn't myself." And wasn't that the truth, he thought, deriding himself bitterly. He wasn't the same man he'd once been. Face it, a scathing voice resounded in his head. He hadn't been the same since Angelina was killed.

He'd been so certain that losing Angelina and their unborn baby had stripped him of everything. He'd thought he was empty inside, that he had nothing left to give. But that was before he'd met Leslie...and before last night.

Did she have any idea how hard he had struggled for control last night? She had such hauntingly gentle eyes. He'd wanted to lose the dark fringes of his soul in her warmth; seek forgetfulness in the tender touch of her hands on his body. He had wanted it so much that the force of his feelings scared him a little.

But there was something about Leslie that made him think that maybe he could find a measure of peace again. That perhaps he could forget his heartache and start anew.

Unconsciously his fingers weaved through hers.

"What can I say?" He shook his head, venting his thoughts aloud. "I accused you of feeling sorry for yourself, but I think . . . I think that's what I was feeling."

He fell silent. Leslie watched and waited, sensing how difficult this was for him.

"I took it out on you," he said finally. "I know it's no excuse, but sometimes there are things that are like . . . like a sliver under your skin. You don't know it's there until it starts to hurt."

His voice was even, but she thought she detected a rough note of strain in his tone. "I like you," he said slowly. "I like you a lot. And I want you to know I'd never intentionally do anything to hurt you."

"I see." And suddenly she did. Dammit, he'd just told her what she wanted to hear, hadn't he? *Hadn't he?* Disappointment sliced through her, but she swallowed bravely and forced a lightness she was far from feeling.

"So. Let's just keep it at that? Is that what you're trying to say?"

"No." His tone was guarded. "I'm saying that maybe it won't hurt to see where it takes us."

Her eyes darkened. She gazed up at him, her expression both troubled and searching. She suspected he might not like what she was about to say, but it was something that had to be said.

"Won't it?" she asked quietly. "I'm not made of steel, Clint, and I'm not invincible. I won't pretend it doesn't bother me when one minute you're sweeter than sugar, and the next minute you're pushing me away."

The pressure on her fingers tightened. Very gently he tugged her closer, his tone low but intense. "I'm not pushing you away now. It's true I haven't wanted to let anyone close lately, but maybe it's time that changed."

But Leslie wasn't about to play the fool twice. "And maybe we don't need . . . complications."

The merest hint of a smile lifted his lips. "What if it's too late?"

"Is that what you think?" The question was scarcely more than a breath of air.

His eyes searched her face. "Yeah," he said softly. "I do. In fact, I was just thinking we could have dinner somewhere, just the two of us. Then maybe you'd like to see some of San Diego."

The invitation surprised her—but it pleased her far more. "That would work out just fine, since Colleen's meeting Rob later and going shopping from there, and the kids will be over at Maryann's. Besides—" her smile was just a little tremulous "—how could I turn down a chance for my own personal tour guide?"

He glanced ruefully at his cane. "As long as you don't mind one with a little wear and tear."

"Oh, I'm not complaining, at least not yet." Her laugh was rather shaky, but all at once she was looking forward to the day with an enthusiasm she hadn't felt an hour earlier.

IT COULD HAVE been awkward. It *should* have been, Leslie reflected hours later, especially after last night. But it wasn't. Exactly why, Leslie didn't know. Maybe it was because she sensed that, in a different way, perhaps, Clint was just as lonely as she. But she did know that she didn't regret being with him—quite the contrary.

Rather than a sit-down dinner, they decided on hot dogs from an outdoor vendor at the Embarcadero. From there they took the Bay ferry across to Coronado. Leslie fell in love with the gingerbread domes of the Hotel del Coronado. Fascinated by the photos that dated back to when the hotel was first built in the late 1800s, she wished they could have spent more time exploring. But she had the feeling Clint's leg was beginning to bother him. She sensed he was relieved when she suggested they take the trolley back to the landing to await the ferry.

There they rested on one of the wooden benches facing the waterfront. Brightly colored sailboats bobbed gently in the water. Across the harbor, the waning sunlight glistened off the high rises of downtown San Diego.

Clint turned slightly and gently grazed the back of his fingers across the bare skin of her upper arm. "You look very pretty tonight," he said huskily.

His touch elicited tiny feathers of sensation all along her arm. Leslie was suddenly glad she'd chosen her clothing so carefully. The pale peach of the peasant-style blouse and full skirt she wore set off the light tan she'd acquired over the last few days. The wide neckline was slightly off the shoulder; while it wasn't overtly sultry or sexy, it was still faintly suggestive. She had eyed her bare shoulders uncertainly, but when she murmured her misgivings aloud, Colleen had laughed and told her she'd never looked better.

"Thank you," she murmured. But even while she flushed with pleasure, her heart twisted. The admiring light in Clint's eyes would have been perfect. Just the balm her tattered soul needed...if only she weren't suddenly besieged with doubt. Dennis had told her often enough how pretty she was; how fresh and natural he found her; how he loved her.

A feeling of burning betrayal crept through her. She hadn't been everything Dennis wanted. He wanted... what? Mystery and allure? Veiled excitement and thrills? Maybe that was why he'd done what he had. Because he wanted to challenge the odds. Because he couldn't resist chancing the risk of discovery...

But Dennis hadn't wanted to be caught, an unwelcome voice reminded her. He had wanted them both. Two homes. Two families. Two...

The touch on her arm made her start. She looked up at Clint almost guiltily. There was a frown wedged between his heavy brows. "I didn't mean to offend you," he said quietly. Slowly, as if he feared her rejection, he reached for her hand, gently weaving their fingers together.

Leslie shook her head. "You didn't," she denied. Oddly the awkwardness she feared still didn't come. "Only it's been a while since—"

"Since any man told you that."

She stared at their clasped hands, grateful for his perception. "After my divorce from Dennis the last thing I wanted was to rush back into a relationship, even one that was only skin-deep."

There was a long silence. "I can understand that," he said at last.

She might have doubted him, if she hadn't chosen that moment to lift her eyes. All at once she saw in him a torment that matched her own. The late evening sunshine had no mercy. She had no trouble reading the tautness of his shoulders, the starkness of his profile as he stared out at the harbor. His grip on her hand had grown tight and unyielding; she wondered if he were even aware of it.

Her heart caught painfully. She remembered the name Colleen had mentioned to him last night—Angelina.

A dozen unanswered questions spun through her mind. Was she the reason why Clint was so touchy about the subject of Central America? There was a connection. She was sure of it, just as she was sure that Clint had been hurt as much as she had...by the mysterious Angelina?

Who was she? she cried wordlessly. *Who was Angelina and what part did she play in your life?*

After a moment, his grip on her hand relaxed. She heard his voice. "Colleen mentioned you're thinking of moving. Is it because of your divorce?"

It was almost a relief to talk about herself once more. "Maybe," she admitted. She was suddenly echoing Colleen's rationalizations. "At any rate, I'm giving it serious thought. My job at Golden Hills hasn't offered anything new for a long time, so there's really nothing to keep me in San Francisco. Besides, maybe a change is exactly what I need.'' She glanced up to find him smiling. ''What? You don't agree?''

He shook his head. ''As a matter of fact, I rather like the idea,'' he told her softly.

''But you won't be here.'' The words slipped out before she could stop them.

''True,'' he allowed. ''As soon as my leg is healed, I'll be heading for Alaska.'' He lifted a hand and brushed a stray curl from her cheek. ''But this is still home, and if you were here, I'd make sure I came home as often as I could.''

He was teasing, of course. Still, Leslie couldn't prevent the shadow that crept over her. With Dennis she'd felt as if she were a weekend wife and no more. If something developed between her and Clint—and she admitted that was a very big *if*—the situation would be no different.

It was a sobering thought—and one she suddenly didn't want to think about. Yet she heard herself ask, ''How long will you be in Alaska?''

''It's hard to say,'' he shrugged. ''A lot depends on the weather up there, but if I had to guess, I'd say close to a year.''

She strived for an even tone and miraculously succeeded. ''And then where to?''

''Wherever good old Uncle Sam decides to send me.''

The dock had been alive with the sounds of voices, the distant call of sea gulls, but all of a sudden Leslie felt very alone. Clint's nonchalance said it all, yet she knew she had to ask. "Doesn't it bother you—traveling so much? Living out of a suitcase?"

It was more than just an idle question. Clint sensed it instantly. There was something in her tone—a kind of hurt vulnerability perhaps—that put him on red alert.

"It's my job, and I've been doing it so long I hardly think twice about it. Besides," he added, "some people thrive on travel. They find it glamorous. Exciting."

She was suddenly on guard again. The muscles in her face felt stiff. It was a monumental effort to even attempt a smile. She tried to summon the courage to meet Clint's eyes, but that failed her, as well.

"Some people might." Her voice came out tight and dry, exactly the way she felt inside.

"But not you?"

She shivered. "No. I'm afraid I'm very much a homebody."

Clint studied her quietly. He didn't like the way she had abruptly withdrawn from him any more than he liked the pinched look around her lovely mouth. Until then, he hadn't realized just how much he liked the ease that had marked their evening. The last thing he wanted was to jeopardize it. He'd said something wrong . . . but what?

He decided to do a little digging of his own. "Why not? Are you afraid of flying?" He remembered how shaken she had been the day of her arrival.

"No." She stared out at the array of brightly colored sailboats bobbing in the bay.

He probed very gently. "What then? Are you a bad traveler?"

She flinched when she discovered his gaze fixed on her in silent speculation. He had an unnerving knack of hiding his thoughts so that she had no idea what he was thinking... while *she* was thinking the worst.

"Dennis was a flight navigator for one of the domestic airlines," she explained, her voice very low. "It seemed as if he was never home, and I—I hated all the traveling he did. Sometimes I used to feel as if I'd been... abandoned."

There was more, he was certain of it. He'd felt the deep, shuddering breath she took. What, Clint wondered grimly, had that bastard ex-husband done to her? But she looked so anxious, so distressed, that he decided not to press any further.

They were both quiet on the way home. Clint walked with her to the back door.

Hundreds of glittering stars sprinkled the night sky. The back porch light centered their figures in a hazy pool of light. Leslie paused, battling a sudden feeling of inadequacy. It didn't help that, despite his cane, Clint looked so tall, strong and invincible. Why couldn't she be the same? she despaired silently. Just those few minutes of talking about Dennis had done this to her. She could never forgive him for what he had done.

And she was beginning to wonder if she could ever forget.

She despised the way she wanted to turn and flee into the house, but Clint didn't give her the chance. He reached out and caught her fingers lightly in his.

"You don't regret coming tonight, do you?"

She shook her head. Despite the disturbing turn of their conversation—despite everything—Leslie could think of nowhere she'd rather be right now than with Clint.

"Are you sure?" His voice was curiously husky.

"Very sure," she said shakily, then startled herself by asking, "Do you?"

In answer he tugged her closer. "Not a chance," he whispered.

His gaze dropped to her mouth; all at once she was breathless. She stared at the hollow of his throat, but that was even more disturbing than looking at his face. A wiry tangle of bristly hairs grew thick and dark there, and suddenly she remembered the pleasure she'd experienced last night when she explored his naked chest.

She nearly jumped when he slid his knuckles beneath her chin and guided her eyes to his.

"Would you mind," he asked very softly, "if I kissed you?"

She spoke without thinking. "You didn't ask last night."

He studied her wordlessly. "No," he allowed. "But I'm asking now."

Leslie glanced away in confusion. She didn't know how it had happened, but they stood only a breath apart. She was quiveringly aware of their closeness, the slight roughness of his palm lying warm and hard against hers.

She spoke in hushed, hurried tones, before she lost her nerve. "Clint, you don't have to. I mean, I don't want you to think you have to make up for what happened last night—"

His thumb sliding over her lower lip stopped the flow of words. "I know," he said softly. "But I want to. I want to... very much."

Even as he spoke, his head had begun its slow descent. Leslie nervously awaited the touch of his lips on hers.

It was a healing sort of kiss for both of them, both tender and gentle, a soothing balm to smooth the ragged edges of her emotions. The feel of his mouth clinging to hers, warm and sweet, coaxed forth a tiny sigh of pleasure. It was easy to respond, to give in to the need building within her, for she hadn't known how starved she was. And it felt wonderful to be held again...

His hand slid up to cup her nape, drawing her nearer. He kissed her again, deeper and longer this time. Leslie's arms slid around his waist. She clung to him, hungry for more of the sweet sensation his kiss aroused.

He lifted his mouth from hers slowly. Smiling crookedly he touched her cheek. "I'm glad you came tonight," he said softly. His fingers lingered along the fragile line of her jaw.

His expression, as much as the words themselves, made her heart sing. Leslie wanted to snatch his palm to her cheek and savor the moment, but she settled for a golden smile. "So am I," she whispered. "So am I."

CHAPTER NINE

THE NEXT COUPLE OF WEEKS fell into a pattern. In the morning she and Colleen usually took the kids to the beach. Colleen's pregnancy was beginning to make itself known; by noon her lids were usually drooping. While she and Tess napped, Leslie worked with Bonnie on her English.

But while Leslie was thrilled with the way Bonnie took to her like a duck to water, she remained baffled over the child's choice of Clint as her male champion. Because of the language barrier, Bonnie often relied on Clint for clarification. More often than not, she called him *"Papá."* Leslie speculated that perhaps this was because of his swarthy coloring. She knew that Bonnie was too young to have retained any active memory of her parents, but maybe a faraway corner of her mind connected Clint with the father she had lost. But whatever the reason, the little girl clearly idolized Clint. She looked for him when he wasn't around. Her eyes lit up like hundred-watt light bulbs whenever he entered the room.

Early one evening, Leslie sat in the living room, leafing through a magazine. Colleen and Rob had gone out to dinner with friends, and Brian was spending the night at Tim's. From her place on the couch, she could see Tess and Bonnie on the floor in

the dining room, absorbed in counting seashells. At
first Tess had slowly spoken each number, with Bonnie echoing each one. Now they chanted them together. A feeling of warmth unfolded inside her; Leslie
was feeling immensely proud of her newest pupil.

"... Twenty-three, twenty-four, twenty-five!" The
two girls clapped their hands.

Clint chose that moment to enter the room. Leslie
glanced up in time to see him blink. His startled gaze
slid beyond the two girls to where she sat on the couch.
"She's counting that well already?" he asked in surprise.

Leslie was feeling rather smug. "She and Tess can
also count to one hundred by fives and tens."

His eyes sought hers. "Then I'd say they have a
great teacher."

His praise warmed her, but far stronger was her
feeling of pride in Bonnie's accomplishment. "I'm
afraid I can't take all the credit," she demurred lightly.
"They're both smart as a whip. And Bonnie has
picked up so much just from being around Tess and
Brian."

Clint walked slowly toward the two girls. Tess
scrambled up to him. Bonnie levered herself to her feet
as well. Both girls stood in front of him, and Leslie
found herself holding her breath. Even with the width
of a room between them, she had no trouble deci-
phering Bonnie's expression. She gazed at him adoringly, then tugged at his sleeve and whispered
something. Clint bent slightly; he said something
briefly in return.

She exhaled slowly. Clint appeared to have relaxed
around the little girl—outwardly, at least. His first

glimpse of Bonnie was the one exception. Yet the thought kept thrumming through her mind that whenever he was around Bonnie, he was just a little restrained and controlled . . . too controlled?

As much as she wanted to, she couldn't dismiss the notion. Where Clint and Bonnie were concerned, she had more questions than answers. She also suspected the mysterious Angelina was the key to the puzzle.

The thought never failed to elicit a painful knot in her chest. Clint seemed so empty sometimes. Was Angelina the reason why? And was she jealous? A part of her refused to even consider it. How could she be jealous of someone she didn't even know?

But it didn't stop her from wondering who she was—and what she had been to Clint. Her mind conjured up all sorts of possibilities. An ex-lover. Someone who jilted him, perhaps . . .

She watched him cross to the chair across from her, the two girls on either side of him. He had scarcely seated himself when Bonnie tugged on his sleeve. She leaned close and whispered something in Spanish. She pointed at Leslie and giggled, but all Leslie caught was the word *bonita*.

Clint looked over at Leslie, a subtle softening in his eyes as he followed the little girl's gaze.

Leslie's brows shot up. "What did she say?"

His slow smile made her heart turn over. "She said you look pretty."

"*Bonita* means pretty?"

He nodded.

Leslie glanced at Bonnie. "Come here, Bonnie."

The little girl hobbled over and stood before her. Leslie touched the tip of her nose with her forefinger. *"Bonita,"* she said again. "Pretty. Pret-ty Bonnie."

Bonnie beamed and reached up to touch Leslie's cheek. "Pret-ty," she repeated. "Pret-ty Lee."

The rush of emotion that swept through Leslie was unlike anything she'd ever known before—yet she'd felt it many times these past few weeks. It had been like this almost from the moment she first laid eyes on Bonnie. When Bonnie looked at her with those melting brown eyes, Leslie wanted nothing more than to reach out and snatch her to her breast.

And that was exactly what she did. She hugged her as tightly as Bonnie's thin body would allow, silently rejoicing when Bonnie flung her arms around her neck just as fiercely.

"Come on, Bonnie, let's go get our nighties on!" Bonnie pulled away when she heard Tess, but not before her shining eyes sought Leslie's once more. But Leslie's heart wrenched at Bonnie's clumsy efforts to keep up with Tess as they climbed the stairs.

"Slow down, girls," she called after them. "You don't want to fall."

Clint's dark head was averted when she glanced over at him. For an instant she went absolutely still. Had he seen her hug Bonnie? Of course he had. Had it made him uncomfortable? Leslie was suddenly very certain that it had—yet why should it?

She rose and deposited her magazine in the wicker basket under the end table. She straightened and started toward him. "Bonnie saw her orthopedist this afternoon."

His eyes flickered toward her. "How did it go?"

"Her blood count is low. He's also a little concerned about her diet. She's still a bit weak."

"What about the surgery?"

Leslie watched him closely. Whatever she was looking for she didn't find. He seemed perfectly fine now, and genuinely interested.

"He's going to run some tests and X rays next week. He'll know more about what degree of correction can be achieved after he's reviewed the X rays, though he won't know for certain until after he's done the surgery. In the meantime, he'd like to see her physical condition built up as much as possible."

She didn't have a chance to say more. Tess bounced into the room, with Bonnie several steps behind her. Both girls wore pretty blue nightgowns. In one small hand Bonnie clutched the ribbon Leslie had given her that first night. The little girl limped toward her. Leslie chuckled. "You want the ribbon in your hair, don't you?"

But at the last minute the child stopped before Clint. Her face bright and eager, she gazed up at him. *"Por favor, Papá . . . por favor."* She held out the ribbon.

Time stood still.

"She wants you to tie her hair back," Leslie said quietly.

Clint froze. Bonnie was waiting, her expression so pure and innocent he wanted to scream aloud in pain. Oh, God, she was trampling all over his heart. He thought he'd been doing so well, but this was more than he could handle... Bonnie's pixie features swam before him, but suddenly all he could see was Angelina, and the little girl they'd never had . . .

Leslie instinctively stepped close to Bonnie. Something was very wrong. Leslie could feel it where it counted the most... in her heart.

The air was suddenly pulsing. For the second time in just a few short moments, she held her breath and waited. For the longest time she thought Clint intended to refuse. Then, slowly, as if he were trying to stop himself, he extended a hand toward the little girl.

His hand dropped to his side; he said something in Spanish to Bonnie, then glanced at Leslie. "I'm afraid this is a rather delicate task for my clumsy fingers. I'm sure you're much better at this than I am." His tone was rueful; he was even smiling. But he wouldn't meet her eyes, and that told the story only too well.

Bonnie had already turned to her. Leslie's heart went out to her as she glimpsed her disappointment. But she smiled and hugged her tightly and kissed her cheek, then turned her around and pulled the ribbon under her hair.

But all the while she battled a helpless frustration. Was he aware of how distant he seemed around Bonnie? They had all gone out of their way to make Bonnie feel at home, Rob included. Clint's behavior just now only raised more questions. Leslie wanted desperately to ask him why he acted the way he did.

She didn't. Because she had seen the pained tightness around Clint's mouth, and she couldn't be angry. Instead she was baffled. Bonnie was so sweet and loving. How could anyone not fall under her spell?

It was then that the oddest thought flitted into her mind. Not once had she ever seen Clint touch the little girl... not once.

And that made her heart ache for Bonnie...as much as for Clint.

IN THE DAYS following their evening in Coronado, Colleen didn't waste any opportunity to throw her and Clint together. Leslie didn't know whether to laugh or cry.

Despite Clint's reticence toward Bonnie, Leslie liked him. She suspected she liked him far too much for her own good. The thread of closeness between them was still tentative and exploring, but it was building. She could feel it, and she knew that Clint could, too. This awareness pleased her as much as it disturbed her.

It would be so easy to fall for him—too easy. But did she dare? Her future was in limbo. She still hadn't decided to take the plunge—to make the move to San Diego. Yet more and more, she was leaning in that direction.

But she wasn't the type of woman who could handle a casual affair. Somehow she sensed that Clint wasn't the kind of man to *indulge* in a casual affair. But as soon as his leg healed, Clint would be leaving for Alaska.... It was like a pebble in her shoe knowing that he had no real home—no roots or no sentimental attachment. The bungalow was simply the place where he slept and ate when he wasn't off on his job somewhere.

The realization never failed to kindle a twinge of bitterness in Leslie. Never again would she trust as blindly as she had with Dennis, for unless her feelings were returned in full measure, they meant nothing. Marriage to Dennis had taught her that, if nothing else.

It hurt knowing that Dennis had robbed her of something vital—her confidence in her womanhood. If only she were more like Clint! So strong, so sure of himself and his sexuality that he simply took it for granted.

For Leslie, it was a bitter pill to swallow. She despised her weakness, her feelings of inadequacy. Yet she couldn't banish the secret fear that Clint—or any other man, for that matter—might soon grow tired of her. She didn't like what she had become...what Dennis had made her.

Where Clint was concerned, perhaps it would be better to simply let things stand as they were right now—light and easy, no demands or expectations on either side.

She was pondering that very choice late Friday afternoon. The day had been a busy one for Colleen. Her obstetrician had phoned and asked if she could come in that morning instead of Monday, and Bonnie had another appointment with the orthopedist, Dr. King. Since hers was one of the last appointments of the day, Leslie volunteered to fix dinner.

She had just slid a tray of baking powder biscuits in the oven when she felt the weight of another pair of eyes upon her. She knew, even before she turned around, that Clint was there.

He was leaning against the doorjamb, his dark hair appealingly tousled over his forehead and only adding to his heart-stopping appeal. His pale yellow shirt set off his tan. Crisp khaki slacks completed the picture.

Even if she'd wanted to, she couldn't have stopped the sweet rush of pleasure that flooded her veins...and she didn't want to. It felt warm. It felt *good*. More, it felt so very right.

She watched almost hungrily as lean, almost impossibly long fingers slid into the pockets of his slacks. "Well, well," he teased, "Aren't you the picture of domesticity."

His dark eyes were alight with humor. Leslie felt as if her heart had sprouted a pair of wings. How, she marveled silently, could she have ever thought his eyes were cold.

"Aha," she said lightly, "you've come to help the cook."

The sound of his laughter made her go warmer still inside.

"Maybe I've come to kiss the cook." And he pointed to the apron looped around her neck. Leslie followed his gaze and smiled weakly. She'd slipped it on so the flour from the biscuits wouldn't dust her dark blue slacks, but she hadn't noticed until now the cross-stitched red lettering emblazoned across the front—Kiss The Cook.

She grabbed the nearest dish towel and playfully swatted him. "You haven't come to do either," she laughingly accused. "You've come to *harass* the cook."

"That, too." Clint's expression was all innocence. But he quickly proceeded to shred lettuce and slice the rest of the salad fixings she had set out. Leslie peeked absently at the wooden bowl he set in the center of the table, then did an abrupt double take.

"Hey," she cried. "You've been holding out on me, Clint Stuart. I thought you said you were totally helpless in the kitchen." She indicated the perfectly pared cucumber slices and radish rosettes artfully arranged across the top of the lettuce. He had also laid out a small relish tray.

She found his throaty chuckle immensely pleasing. "Colleen must have said that, not me. Though I'll admit I don't mind having her *think* I'm totally helpless. Salads are my one and only claim to fame. That and my celery sticks stuffed with peanut butter."

"Peanut butter!" Leslie blinked. A hasty glance revealed that he had indeed stuffed the celery with peanut butter. "That sounds...interesting."

He laughed at her tentative expression. "You'll have to try it. It's a Stuart specialty."

"So now the truth comes out," she commented dryly. "What other secrets are you hiding from me, Mr. Stuart?" She turned away just long enough to pull off her oven mitt and drop it on the counter.

She didn't see the fleeting shadow that flickered across his face.

When she glanced over her shoulder, he splayed his hands high in a gesture of mock defeat. The merest hint of laughter sparked his eyes as he adopted a contrite pose. "I'm afraid you've caught me again, Leslie. I have to admit, I do make a mean turkey sandwich."

"Oh, you do, do you—" she began. She stopped short and frowned. Something about his stance wasn't right; it was almost as if he were off kilter.... For an instant she simply stared. Comprehension dawned in a flash and she blinked. "You-you're not using your cane!"

Without stopping to consider, she rushed across the floor and threw her arms around him.

Her gesture quite literally put him off balance. Clint slid his arms around Leslie out of necessity, but they remained there for a different reason entirely. Only a few days ago he'd have rationalized the action to himself. But right now he didn't delude himself that he needed an excuse to touch her. It felt good—damned good—to simply hold her, to enjoy the warmth of her body flush against his, the way her sweet feminine curves fit so neatly against his angular hardness.

"I thought I'd try it and see how I got along." God, she was pretty. He liked the way a wayward strand of honey-gold curled softly against her cheek; he especially liked the way she didn't hide the pleasure she felt for him. She made no effort to pull away when his arms tightened . . . and that he liked best of all.

Leslie tipped her head back. His features possessed a harsh masculine beauty that was uniquely his own. His mouth, sometimes hard, sometimes wonderfully sensual, smiled ever so slightly just above hers. All she had to do was lever herself up on tiptoe and their lips would touch. . . .

The yearning inside her was so intense it was almost painful. But with a wordless sigh of regret, she reminded herself that this growing bond between them was still too fragile—too tentative—for her to be so bold just yet.

And deep inside, she was very much aware that she had yet to conquer the secret fear of rejection.

It was enough, for now, to be able to enjoy their banter. Her tone was deliberately light as she murmured, "You seem to be getting along pretty well."

An unholy gleam entered his eyes. "Oh, I'm not quite ready to chase you around the table," he drawled. "But if you keep looking at me like that, I may be tempted to give it my best try."

Leslie's heart fluttered. She absorbed both the words and the unspoken promise in his eyes like sunshine after months of darkness.

Her eyes sparkled impishly. "Oh, come on," she invited brashly. "I dare you."

"If my brother were here, he'd tell you I never could resist a dare." His grin was downright wicked. "Name the stakes and you're on, lady."

"What else? You get to kiss the cook!"

His laugh was husky. "That's a bet no man in his right mind would refuse."

Leslie's pulse set up a wild clamor when his gaze dropped to her mouth. She held her breath, every nerve within her tingling with the most delicious sense of anticipation as his dark head began a slow descent.

The back door burst open. Leslie's head whipped around in time to see Colleen breeze inside, holding Bonnie in her arms. The pixie-faced blonde stopped dead in her tracks.

Her startled expression was comical. Leslie's eyes widened and so did Colleen's. Colleen's mouth opened, then closed. Leslie might have appreciated her friend's speechless state far more if she hadn't been so embarrassed.

Colleen's loss for words didn't last long. She lowered Bonnie gently to the floor, her eyes on the pair across the room. "Hey," she snickered. She laid a hand on Bonnie's head and wagged a finger at them. "Not," she quoted primly, "in front of the kiddies!"

Leslie wondered if it were possible to die of embarrassment. She took a hurried step away from Clint, smiling weakly. She was immensely thankful that Tess chose that moment to race into the kitchen. "Hi, Mommy!" she cried. "Did the doctor fix Bonnie's leg? Is it all better now?"

Colleen exchanged a glance of subtle amusement with Leslie, then dropped to her knees. One arm slid around Bonnie and drew her close. "I hope it will be soon, Tess. Remember I told you and Brian that Bonnie has to have an operation on her hip? Well, Bonnie's doctor did some tests today. We have to take her back next week to see how they turned out. And what we need to do right now is make sure that Bonnie keeps eating lots of good things to help her get ready for her operation."

"Ice cream!" Tess cried happily. "Can we go out for hot fudge sundaes after dinner?"

Colleen bit her lip, struggling to hold back her laughter. "We'll see when Daddy comes home," she told her daughter. She nodded toward the counter. "You and Bonnie can have a carrot right now if you want."

Clint reached around and slid the small tray to the edge of the counter.

"There's salary, too," Tess cried delightedly. "And Uncle Clint fixed it with peanut butter, too, just the way I like it." Her hand shot out and grabbed two of the celery sticks, generously slathered with peanut butter. She offered one to Bonnie. "Here, Bonnie. See? This is a salary stick. Sal...a...ry stick."

Bonnie's fingers closed around the celery. "Sal...a...ry stick," she repeated dutifully.

Colleen shook her head and rose to her feet. "Salary sticks," she groaned. "She's a fine one for Bonnie to be hanging around. Whoever adopts her will need Tess as an interpreter!''

Leslie laughed, but there was a painful catch in her chest. The surgery on the little girl's hip was only one of the reasons she'd been brought here; locating a set of adoptive parents was the other. Yet the thought of Bonnie living with strangers seemed wholly unacceptable.

Trying not to think about it, she focused on Colleen. ''Did the doctor have anything else to say?''

Colleen shook her head. ''Only that he's going to schedule her surgery after all the lab reports are in. In the meantime, he still wants her to gain a few more pounds.''

Leslie nodded. ''She could certainly stand to, that's for sure.''

Her friend chuckled. ''If she's around Tess long enough, she will. Tess could eat ice cream morning, noon and night.'' She started for the door then stopped and turned. ''I'm going to change, and Clint, you'd better stay out of Leslie's way.'' She wagged her finger playfully. ''I'd hate to see our dinner burned to a crisp.''

But the dinner was perfect. Leslie found herself glowing with pleasure at the compliments showered on her. She had always loved to cook, but cooking for only herself wasn't very satisfying; during her marriage, she had eaten more dinners alone than she had with Dennis. . . .

She willed away the demon thought and smiled brightly at something Rob had said. The three children immediately ran off outside. Leslie rose and automatically reached for her plate and Bonnie's. But

Colleen had already scooted around the table and gently swatted away her hands. She bodily turned her around and pointed toward the living room.

"March," she ordered firmly. "You fixed dinner, so Rob and I will clean up."

Leslie protested, to no avail.

Clint rose as well, a silly grin on his face. Colleen whirled on him, hands on her hips, her eyes dancing merrily. "Running off so soon, Mr. Stuart?"

"I helped with dinner, too." His tone was all innocence.

Colleen snorted. "From what I saw, you were hindering, not helping," she retorted.

"I did, I swear! Ask Leslie, if you don't believe me."

Leslie's lips twitched. "He did fix the salad. And the relish tray with those yummy celery sticks." She caught Clint's eye and smiled.

"I suppose I'll have to let you off the hook this time. Though I do hope you didn't overtax yourself." His sister-in-law rolled her eyes and motioned him away from the table.

"To tell you the truth," he said mildly, "I'm afraid that's exactly what Leslie and I have done. So if you'll excuse us, we'll be out on the terrace."

Colleen chuckled. "Watching the sun go down?"

Clint stepped up to Leslie. "Watching each other," he tossed back over his shoulder.

Leslie had been listening to the exchange, sharing an occasional look of subtle amusement with Rob. But when Clint extended his hand, the low flame in his eyes made her think he wasn't kidding at all!

Her pulse was suddenly thundering in her veins. The way he said *Leslie and I*, and *we* ... so naturally and easily, as if the two of them had been paired together for ages. It pleased her, but the thought never evolved beyond that.

Beside her, the phone rang. Leslie nearly jumped. Colleen and Rob had their hands full of dishes. Colleen cast her a pleading look. "Les, will you get that?"

"Sure thing." Leslie picked up the receiver and gave a cheery "hello."

"Colleen, is that you? It's me, honey, and I..." The quavery female voice trailed off. There was a muffled sound, like a tearing sob being smothered by a hand.

Leslie's heart lurched. Her smile was wiped clean. She motioned hurriedly and held out the receiver to Colleen. "I think it's your mother," she said quickly.

Something must have shown in her face. The plates slammed noisily on the counter. Colleen grabbed the receiver and jammed the phone to her ear. "Mom? Mom, what is it?"

She got no further. The room grew deathly quiet as Colleen listened to the voice on the other end of the line. Rob moved to stand next to his wife. She clutched his hand almost frantically, occasionally murmuring a word or two to her mother. Finally she said, "I'll see what I can do, Mom. Let me talk to Rob and I'll call you back as soon as I can."

The minute the receiver was dropped into the wall cradle, Rob slipped his arm around his wife. "What is it, sweetheart? Your father?"

Her nod was jerky, her green eyes were the only color on her pale face. Leslie stood helplessly. She could see her grappling for control.

She let out a long shuddering sigh. "He's been pretty sick this last week, so weak he could hardly get out of bed. Yesterday morning Mom had a hard time waking him up. She noticed his skin was a funny color...she took him to Emergency and they hospitalized him."

Leslie's gaze flickered to Clint. As their eyes met, she could see the same thought running through his mind. Should they leave Rob and Colleen alone?

Clint cleared his throat. At the sound, Rob looked over at him. Apparently he read their intention, because he shook his head and spoke. "You don't have to leave. Besides, we may need you."

Colleen silently echoed the sentiment. She offered a tremulous smile, then turned her attention back to Rob once more.

"Apparently he has severe liver damage," she stated quietly. "It was never caught because he would never go in to the doctor. And now—" her voice cracked "—now it's too late. He...he's not expected to live longer than a few weeks at the most."

Rob pulled her against his body. He gently tucked her head beneath his chin. "I'm sorry, babe. I'm so sorry."

Her voice was choked. "He asked to see me, Rob, me and Mike and Tom. Mom has already talked to Mike and Tom. They're both leaving tonight." She clutched his shirtfront. "I—I know I should go, too, for Mom's sake if for no other reason. She said he looks awful—he's got a million tubes going in and coming out of him. Oh, God, but I feel like such a hypocrite! I'm afraid to see him again after all these years. Yet I know if I don't go, I'll never forgive myself!''

"Then go." Rob's voice was very gentle, his touch gentler yet as he tipped her chin up. "I'll come with you if you want. I've got over a month's vacation due. Besides, under the circumstances, I know there won't be a problem with getting the time off." His lips lifted in a ghost of a smile. "Much as I'd like to think so, I'm not indispensable."

"Oh, yes, you are." Colleen's shaky smile was as fleeting as his. "Of course I want you with me, but what about Brian and Tess? Maybe it's selfish and overprotective but I—I'm not sure I want Brian and Tess to see my father like that . . . it's better that they have no memory of him at all. And there's Bonnie, too! I hate the thought of dropping her on yet another doorstep—she's just starting to feel at home here." She bit her lip, clearly in a dilemma.

But Leslie's mind was already off and running. She stepped forward unconsciously. "Wait," she said breathlessly. "You and Rob go ahead and go. Bonnie can stay here—and so can Brian and Tess."

Three heads swiveled in her direction. Rob frowned. "What are you saying, Les? They can't stay here alone, you know—"

"But they won't be alone!" Leslie interrupted excitedly. "I'd be more than happy to stay here with them—and Bonnie, too, if the agency doesn't mind—for as long as you need me. Besides, Clint's here, too, and surely between the two of us, we should be able to manage." Her glance bounced between Rob and Colleen.

It was Colleen who spoke first. "You'd do that for me?" she asked slowly. "Without thinking twice about it, you'd offer to take over a household with three children?"

Leslie smiled slightly. "As you repeatedly pointed out when you invited me down, I don't have anything else to do with my summer." Her eyes softened. She crossed the few paces between them and hugged her friend warmly. "You're my best friend, Colleen," she said softly. "I want to help you any way I can, and if staying here with the kids will help you, then I don't need to think twice about it."

Colleen looked at Rob. "Bonnie has another appointment with the orthopedist Friday," she murmured thoughtfully.

"If you give us directions, I don't think we'll have any trouble finding his office," Clint said.

Colleen tipped her head to the side. "What do you think, Rob?"

Rob's smile encompassed Clint and Leslie. "I think we'd better call your mother and Fran and then start packing."

CHAPTER TEN

LESLIE WAS RELIEVED that Colleen didn't have to make the trip alone. Rob phoned his supervisor at the agency and had no trouble securing the needed time off. He was also able to clear the way for Bonnie to continue staying at their home, under Leslie and Clint's supervision.

The first pale fingers of dawn streaked the horizon when Leslie awoke the next morning. Down the hall she heard a door ease shut. She jumped out of bed and dressed hurriedly, anxious to see Colleen and Rob before they left.

Rob was just loading the suitcases into the trunk when Leslie slipped outside. Clint was there as well, standing beside his sister-in-law.

Rob was the first to spot her. He slanted a rueful grin at his wife. "Uh-oh. I guess we weren't as quiet as we thought—" He broke off and stared past her shoulder. Leslie heard the screen door slam behind her and turned to see three small pajama-clad figures scurrying toward them.

Tess was the first to arrive. She promptly lifted her arms to her mother. Colleen scooped her up, shaking her head ruefully. "What are you three doing up already?" she scolded good-naturedly. "We said good-bye last night, remember?"

The child's lower lip thrust out. "I want to go with you."

Colleen smoothed rumpled blond curls. "Sweetie, I explained why you couldn't come with us last night."

Brian looked as if he were trying very hard to be brave and failing miserably. "How long will you be gone?"

Rob's face softened. "We'll be back as soon as we can, son. I promise."

There was a small tug on Leslie's blouse. She looked down into Bonnie's sleep-flushed features. Reacting instinctively, she lifted the little girl high in her arms.

Brian's shoulders slumped. "I wish you didn't have to go. Tonight's our first real baseball game, and it won't be the same with no one there to watch."

"Whoa! Hold it right there." Leslie stepped up to him. "This is one game I wouldn't miss for the world. You'll be the shining star, just wait and see. After all—" she winked at him "—I taught you all my secrets."

"And your mom and dad won't really miss it at all." Clint jumped into the conversation. "Maybe I can tape it on your dad's new video recorder. It'll give me a chance to play around with it and decide if I want one." He ruffled his nephew's hair.

Brian's dark mood vanished. "Gee," he breathed, "that'd be neat to watch it over and over again."

"It sure would." Colleen hugged her daughter then handed her over to Rob. "And we'll bring all of you back a little present."

Tess's face brightened. "A bike with training wheels! And one for Bonnie, too!" Bonnie loved standing on the back of Tess's trike while the younger girl wheeled her around.

Rob chuckled. "I don't know about a bike, but we'll find something you'll like, I promise."

Farewell kisses came next, with last-minute instructions from Colleen. "There's food enough for at least a week, but if you need gas for the car or more groceries, there's money in the jewelry box in our room. And Les, please think about what I mentioned when you first came, okay?"

She meant the move. Leslie hugged her. "I will," she promised. "And don't worry, the kids will be fine. Call and let us know how you're doing when you have a chance."

Colleen nodded and turned to Clint, slender brows raised high in mock severity. "I'm trusting you with my dearest friend, brother-in-law. She's like one of the family, so you'd better take good care of her or you'll have me to contend with when we get back."

"I'll keep that in mind," Clint murmured dryly.

Leslie smiled at the fierce loyalty in Colleen's tone. She didn't dare look at Clint, afraid of what she might find on his face.

Brian and Tess waved frantically once Rob started the engine. Bonnie squirmed. "Down, Lee." Leslie set her on her feet, and the three children scampered toward the back door, happy-go-lucky as always.

She had dreaded this moment ever since last night. Throughout their last-minute planning session, Clint had been rather quiet. Leslie glanced at him a dozen times, but his expression revealed nothing.

It was then that she began to wonder...had she made a big mistake by volunteering to stay here with the three children? She didn't regret her offer one bit. What she wasn't sure of was her arbitrary inclusion of Clint. Had she somehow ruined things between them? Smashed the fledgling feelings inside both of them?

She started at the fleeting touch on her arm. Clint stood beside her, his look deep and penetrating.

"Are you okay?" he asked softly. "I wouldn't worry if I were you. Brian and Tess will miss Colleen and Rob, but they won't give us any trouble. They'll be fine, just wait and see."

"It's not them I'm worried about," she blurted.

He frowned. "Who then?"

"You."

He laughed softly. "Me? Why on earth would you be worried about me? Are you afraid what will happen now that we're alone?" He held up both hands in a gesture of defeat. "I'll keep my hands to myself at all times, I promise. I must admit, though, a few laps around the table might prove to be the miracle cure for my leg."

Leslie's throat tightened. He was doing his best to make her laugh when suddenly all she wanted to do was cry.

She linked her hands together to keep them from shaking. Like it or not—wanted or unwanted—her jumbled thoughts came out in a rush.

"I didn't mean to make you angry or upset last night. It didn't even occur to me until it was too late that I practically volunteered you to stay here and help me with the kids. I didn't mean to be so presumptuous, honestly, or put you on the spot.... It just seemed that leaving the kids behind was the logical thing to do.

But you needn't feel obligated to lend a hand or anything...."

Clint's smile faded. *Nice going,* he chided himself harshly. He hadn't realized he'd been so transparent. The truth was, he *had* been thinking of himself last night, and he'd been feeling guilty as hell ever since. It wasn't that he resented stepping in for Rob and Colleen. Indeed, his feelings of reluctance, if that's what this vague nagging inside him could be called, had nothing to do with Leslie, or even Brian and Tess ... and everything to do with Bonnie.

Bonnie. He couldn't say her name—he couldn't even think of her—without experiencing a crushing sensation in his chest.

He looked at her and he saw Angelina, lying broken and bloodied. He looked at her and he saw the dark-eyed little girl who could have been his.

The mere sight of her hurt unbearably, every bit as much as that first night when she had whispered *Papá.* And it was simply easier to look away than to be touched....

It was silly to be afraid of a mere child. At least with Colleen and Rob there, he'd felt there was some kind of buffer between them. But now that barrier was gone, and he was very much afraid his past had finally caught up with him.

He had no choice but to lay his ghosts to rest. But it wasn't as easy as snapping his fingers and closing the door on that part of his life. He would have to deal with it in his own way, and in his own time.

Yet he couldn't stand the thought that Leslie blamed herself for his damnable moodiness, and it was readily apparent that she did.

His fingers on her lips stalled the flow of words. "Don't," he commanded softly. "You did the right thing. To tell you the truth—" his smile held a twinge of regret "—I'm a little ashamed that I didn't think of it myself."

Her features remained troubled. "But I don't want you to think I was too forward, although maybe I was. I didn't mean to be, though."

"You weren't," he said swiftly. Right now his own feelings didn't matter. What mattered was driving away that worried frown from between her brows.

"Besides," he added softly, "with Rob and Colleen gone, I've got you all to myself."

The ploy worked, far better than he'd hoped. He stood stock-still, absorbing her slow-growing smile like warm hazy sunshine after days of torrential rain.

"You're forgetting," she pointed out dryly, "that there are three very impressionable young minds in the house as well."

His dark eyes flickered with amusement. "Then I guess I get to play knight in shining armor."

If he was, he was a reluctant knight indeed. The observation slipped into her mind unbidden, but Leslie refused to let it ruin the moment.

"I see," she said lightly. "What does that make me, then? A damsel in distress?"

She loved the teasing light that filled his eyes. "That depends," he murmured. "Are you in need of rescuing?"

Yes, she thought. God, yes. But only by you...

He seemed to sense her sudden insecurity, for he ran a pleasantly rough fingertip down the curve of her cheek. Slipping his knuckles under her chin, he guided her eyes to his.

"You know," he said softly, "we're going to be okay, all of us."

Leslie didn't know who he was trying to reassure, her or himself. She thought of the unknown Angelina—had he once loved her, or had she loved him?—but only for an instant. All at once she wanted to believe he was right—that everything would be fine. She yearned for it with all her heart.

As much for Clint . . . as for herself.

THE DAY wasn't much different from when Colleen manned the reins of the household. Clint had to go into his office in San Diego just after lunch. With rising so early, all three children fell asleep in the living room shortly after he left. Brian lay sprawled facedown on the sofa. Tess and Bonnie were snugly ensconced in the overstuffed rocking chair. Leslie, on the way to the laundry room with a basketful of clothes, shook her head and chuckled.

Brian was so excited about his team's first baseball game that he scarcely touched any of his dinner. Afterward there was a mad scramble as he rushed around getting ready.

"Leslie!" he cried. "I can't find my jersey anywhere! Mom was supposed to wash it but I'll bet she forgot—"

Leslie handed him a neatly folded gray jersey from the basket of laundry she hadn't yet had time to put away. Brian flashed a grateful smile, but he was back five minutes later.

"I can't find my shoes! Has anybody seen 'em? They're white and—"

It was Clint who found them stashed next to the freezer. He tied the ends of the shoelaces together and looped them around Brian's neck. The boy grinned sheepishly.

They were among the first to arrive at the baseball field. Brian rushed from Clint's car, hopping on one foot then the other in his eagerness.

"The coach said he's gonna put me in as starting pitcher."

Tess pursed her lips. "You already told us," she informed him grumpily.

Across the top of the car, the two adults exchanged a look of silent amusement.

There was a set of bleachers along either side of the infield, and it was there that they directed their steps. Mindful of Clint's leg and Bonnie's hip, Leslie took a seat along the bottom row so they wouldn't have to climb. Bonnie and Tess sat between her and Clint.

Sure enough, Brian was the starting pitcher. He glanced over at them as his team took their places on the field; Leslie nearly laughed aloud. He jammed a fist into his glove, his chest puffed out with pride.

The first batter went down swinging; so did the next. Leslie couldn't have been prouder if Brian had been her own son. She was on her feet before she knew it, cupping her hands around her mouth. "Go get 'em, tiger!" she yelled.

Beside her, Bonnie's eyes grew round. "Tiger," she whispered. Her gaze darted from one corner of the field to the other.

Tess began to giggle. "There's a tiger in one of my picture books. I'll bet Bonnie thinks there's a tiger *here*."

"You're probably right," Leslie said dryly. She glanced at Clint with a rueful smile. "Maybe you should explain the only tigers around here are at the zoo."

He nodded and spoke in Spanish to the little girl. Tess jumped to her feet. "Hey, that's a neat idea. Let's go to the zoo! Bonnie would love it, I know she would." She turned to Bonnie and began bouncing up and down, shaking her hands. "You wanna go to the zoo, don't ya, Bonnie?"

It was unlikely that Bonnie understood a word Tess had said, but Bonnie's head bobbed up and down in tempo with Tess's body.

Clint caught her mid-leap. "Whoa!" he laughed, settling her next to him once more. "I'm beginning to think you belong in the zoo with the monkeys."

Bonnie's eyes were as wide as silver dollars. "Monkey," she repeated in awe.

Leslie pulled Bonnie onto her lap, struggling to hold back a laugh. "I suppose there were monkeys in your book, too?"

"There were!" Tess laughed. She turned again to her uncle, not about to be dissuaded. "Can we go to the zoo, Uncle Clint? Can we?"

"I don't see why not," he relented with a grin. "But Leslie and I will have to talk it over and decide what day we should go. Okay?"

Tess clapped her hands. "Okay!" she cried.

The easy way he deferred to her filled Leslie with a golden glow. Their eyes met and something passed between them, a silent current of understanding. He was right, she thought warmly. Things would be just fine ... and the two of *them* would be just fine.

Brian played like the shining star he aspired to be. He and the other pitcher the coach later brought in managed to hold the other team to four runs, while their team chalked up a whopping ten. Brian also managed to hit a double and a home run.

After the game he ran up to them. "Uncle Clint, did you get my home run on tape?"

Clint patted the leather case slung over his shoulder. "You're destined to go down in baseball history, kid. I'd say in another dozen years or so they'll be keeping your seat warm on the Padres' bench."

"Gee," he breathed. "Boy, would that ever be neat." He was clearly halfway to heaven.

"I'd say this calls for a celebration," Leslie put in. "We didn't get to go out for sundaes last night. Why don't we make a pit stop on the way home?"

The decision was unanimous. Half an hour later, they traipsed into an old-fashioned ice cream parlor decorated with candy-striped wallpaper and gaily-colored balloons suspended above each booth. They soon found that Tess had unveiled a kindred spirit in Bonnie, who was the first to finish her sundae. Even Clint laughed when she echoed Tess's plea for more. Brian, however, was more interested in talking than eating. For once he was the one who chattered non-stop—and every other word was about baseball.

Tess and Bonnie went outside to a small play area the restaurant provided. Brian announced his intention to join them, but he hadn't gone more than a few paces when he dashed back to the table.

"Hey, Uncle Clint," he said excitedly. "The coach said if we keep on playing the way we did tonight, we could make it to the regional championships—maybe even state! Wouldn't it be neat if we did?"

Clint clapped a hand on his shoulder. "It sure would."

"If we do, you'll come, won't you? And you, too, Leslie. They're held the last two weeks in August." He gazed at them imploringly.

Leslie reached out and ruffled his hair. "That's a distinct possibility," she told him warmly.

A spasm of regret had crossed Clint's features. He spoke very gently. "You know I wouldn't miss it for the world, Brian. But as soon as the doctor gives me the all-clear—" he patted his injured leg meaningfully "—I'll be heading for Alaska." Brian's expression started to fall, so he quickly added, "But if your team makes it into the finals, I'll do my darnedest to see if I can get back to see you play."

Brian's face brightened, but Leslie's mind was suddenly filled with a yawning bleakness. These last few weeks she had deliberately blinded herself to the fact that Clint would soon be gone....

Darkness was complete by the time the car pulled into the drive. Together Leslie and Clint escorted the children inside; surprisingly, neither Brian nor Tess protested when Clint suggested they head straight for bed. A genuine quirk of amusement pulled at Leslie's lips as she watched Brian disappear into his room. His eyelids were drooping, but his eyes were as bright as the stars. He might be ready for bed, but she suspected it would be a while before he settled down enough to sleep.

Upstairs in Tess's room she helped the girls undress, then sat down on the bed to brush out Bonnie's hair. Tess watched the brush glide through the length of Bonnie's hair, then went to sit cross-legged on the floor in front of them. When Leslie glanced over at her, she was surprised to find Tess looking rather forlorn. Only then did it strike her that Tess had been unusually quiet ever since they left the ice cream parlor—especially for Tess.

The brush stilled. "Tess," Leslie said with a frown. "Do you feel okay?"

Her head ducked down; the child traced an idle pattern on the carpet. "I was just thinkin'," she muttered.

Leslie smiled. "About what?"

"Bonnie."

Leslie blinked and laid aside the brush. She patted the spot beside her. "Come and tell me why thinking about Bonnie has you looking so blue," she invited.

Tess crawled up beside her and looked up into her face. "Brian said Bonnie has to leave pretty soon—that she's gonna go live with somebody else."

Leslie bit her lip and glanced down at Bonnie, whose dark eyes were fixed on Tess. "Bonnie," she said lightly, "can you go brush your teeth? Brush teeth, okay?" She extended her forefinger and made as if she were brushing her teeth.

Bonnie slid obediently off the bed.

When she was gone, Leslie paused uncertainly. "That's true," she admitted slowly. "But not for a while yet, sweetie. Bonnie still has to have the surgery on her hip. And your daddy's agency has to find a set of parents who want to adopt Bonnie."

"But I don't want her to leave! I want her to stay here with us!"

Tess was visibly upset. Her voice quavered. Her chin trembled. She looked ready to burst into tears.

Leslie sympathized completely—because she felt exactly the same as Tess. She wanted desperately to reassure her, yet what could she say?

"I know, sweetie." She pulled her onto her lap and wrapped her arms around her. "You and Bonnie get along so well. And I know Bonnie's going to be lost without you, too."

Tess clung to her. "Then why can't she stay? Bonnie likes it here. Why can't she stay and be my sister?"

Leslie's heart wrenched. "Tess, it's not that simple. Your mom and dad already have a family—you and Brian—and soon you're going to have another baby brother or sister."

Beneath her hands, she felt Tess go still for a moment. Then she pulled her head back slowly and stared up at her. "Bonnie likes you, Leslie. And Mommy said you might move here. If Bonnie can't live with us, can't she live with you? Then we could still play together sometimes."

Her tone was so earnest, so pleading, that Leslie almost hated herself. Still, it would be worse to let Tess look forward to something that would never happen.

"Oh, Tess, I'd like that—you don't know how much!" She could hardly speak for the huge lump in her throat. "I know it's hard for you to understand, but I'm not married, so I don't have a husband. And I'm sure there's someone who'd love to have Bonnie as their daughter as much as Bonnie needs a mommy *and* a daddy.'' *And if you move,* reminded the sometimes bitter voice of reason, *you may not even have a job for a while.*

''I doubt that Bonnie would be allowed to live with me.'' She attempted an encouraging smile. ''But maybe whoever adopts Bonnie will let you two see each other sometimes.''

It was the best she could do. Miraculously Tess appeared to accept her reasoning. She even laughed when Bonnie came back into the room, and Leslie proceeded to tickle them both. Finally she tucked them into bed, then first kissed Tess then Bonnie.

As her arms came around Bonnie's thin body, a surge of fierce protectiveness welled up inside her. For the first time Leslie realized just how thoroughly this dark-haired little sprite had captured her love—but it was a thought that stirred a stark pain in her heart.

It was just as she had told Tess. She had no husband, no warm, stable, family environment to offer a child like Bonnie. Also, she wasn't infertile. No court would ever grant custody to her. Why should they, when there were other couples far more desperate for a child?

Wearily she made her way downstairs. Clint had switched on the television, but he was standing near the window, staring out into the night. As she watched, he shifted his weight slightly, the only sign that he still favored his injured leg.

His brows rose when he spotted her. ''You were a long time,'' he commented. ''Did Tess give you a bad time about going to bed?''

She shook her head listlessly and halted several steps away.

Clint frowned. He searched her face. "Is something wrong?" He reached out and caught her hand.

Her tone was very quiet. "Tess is upset about Bonnie leaving and going to live with someone else."

He said nothing. She resisted his attempt to tug her closer. She also knew he was wondering what had come over her; she wasn't sure she could explain.

She met his eyes squarely. "It's going to hurt Bonnie just as much when she has to leave." She paused, careful to betray no hint of the turmoil in her heart. When she spoke, her words were precise and very deliberate. "She adores you, Clint. Surely you know that."

The words hung between them. Leslie was outwardly calm and composed, but inside she was stretched as taut as a drum. She held her breath and waited, praying she was wrong—that he wasn't as cruel, as insensitive, to Bonnie as he appeared. But whatever she expected—denial or concurrence—never came.

His expression was closed and impassive. His gaze was riveted to her face, yet she had the feeling he looked through her...beyond her. The grip on her hand had tightened to a point just short of pain, but she never even noticed. With every breath, every heartbeat, the storm inside her twisted and churned, struggling to be free.

"See me to the door," he said finally.

The storm broke. She wrenched her hand away. His voice came to her through a red haze of fury.

"That's it?" Her voice sounded high and tight. "*See me to the door?* I've seen Bonnie reach out to you a dozen times—and a dozen times I've seen you look away, pretending you didn't see! And you didn't see the hurt and confusion on her face, either, damn you! You're not a cold man, Clint, or I wouldn't think twice about it! But how can you be so cruel? Why can't you acknowledge her, just once—"

His arms came around her. It was the only thing that stopped her outburst. He pinned her against him, his grip fierce and tight, but there was no help for it. He clamped her head against his shoulder and buried his face in her hair.

"Don't," he whispered. The word came out sounding broken and raw. "Don't say anymore... please."

All at once Leslie sensed that something was very, very wrong. Her head jerked back just far enough to catch a glimpse of his face.

And what she saw rocked her clear to her soul. His expression was riddled with guilt—and an agony that pierced her heart like an arrow. He looked like a man going through hell—and Leslie knew then that he was. Whatever battle was going on inside him, it was still being fought. When he finally spoke, his voice was so hoarse and strained she scarcely recognized it.

"I... it's not the way it looks... it's not what you think. I don't mean to hurt her, I swear. But it's just so damn hard." The breath he drew was deep and jagged. "She reminds me of—of someone I once knew, you see...."

Angelina. He didn't have to say her name, and still Leslie knew.... There was a sharp, knifelike twinge in her chest.

Yet she couldn't be angry, not when he looked like this; not when she could feel his hand trembling in her hair. She couldn't even be jealous.

Her arms slid around him of their own volition.

"Oh, God," she whispered. She was horrified at her thoughtlessness. "I accused you of being cruel, but I'm the one who..." Her voice grew thick with tears. "I'm sorry, Clint. Please believe me."

"Leslie." Her name sounded choked. "I know I should tell you—"

"No," she said, and this time she was the one who begged. "If it hurts you this much, maybe I'm better off not knowing."

Clint pulled her closer yet. God knew he shouldn't have felt so relieved. But there was time enough later to feel guilty. For now, it was enough just to hold her.

How long they stayed locked in that desperate embrace, Leslie never knew. But by the time they drew back, she was glad to note that some of the horrible bleakness had left Clint's features. He even managed a semblance of a smile. "*Now* will you see me to the door?"

His words were not what she expected. "You're sleeping in the bungalow? Not in the house?" The question emerged unthinkingly. The minute it was out, she felt a blush heat her cheeks. "I—I thought maybe you'd take Rob and Colleen's room," she explained hastily.

Clint shook his head. "I know Colleen said you were like one of the family—" that ghost of a smile deepened ever so slightly "—but you don't exactly inspire brotherly feelings in me."

The tension inside her eased. If he could tease, surely he was all right.

His gaze rested on her face, avid and intent. The heat in his eyes conveyed a message that was unmistakable. It was a look that spoke of need and wanting. But there was more in his gaze than just desire, much more. Mingled within was tenderness and caring, and it was that which made her heart catch.

Strong fingers closed around hers. "Does that bother you?"

Her lips curved. "You don't exactly inspire sisterly feelings in me, either."

The words slipped out unbidden. When she realized what she'd said, her blush seemed to spread from head to toe.

He tugged her along with him to the back screen door, then turned to her once more. His fingers remained curled around her own.

Unable to resist, he lifted his free hand and ran his knuckles across her cheek. "You sure you'll be okay alone with the kids?"

She nodded. He seemed strangely reluctant to let her go, and the neglected woman inside her reveled in the knowledge.

Her hand was still tenderly imprisoned within his. The pressure on her fingers increased, easing her closer still. "Good night, Leslie." His mouth came down on hers, so achingly sweet and gentle it reminded her of the healing kiss they had shared on Coronado. He kissed her again—once, twice, yet again.

He released her mouth reluctantly. "Remember," he whispered, "I'm just across the terrace if you need me."

If she needed him. Her heart contracted as she watched him disappear into the night. The words kindled as much pain as pleasure. She suspected she needed him far more than was good for her.

A vague, restless feeling enveloped her. Was she falling in love with Clint? She caught her breath. She was half afraid she was, just as afraid she wasn't. After her disastrous marriage to Dennis, the last thing she needed was another man in her life—or was it the only thing she needed?

Unbidden, unwanted, that disturbing question surfaced once more. *Who was Angelina?*

All at once she was remembering what Clint had said the night he'd first seen Bonnie. *I doubt if you know what it is to lose someone you loved so much it feels like your heart's been ripped out.* And just as suddenly she was almost certain that someone had been Angelina....

She hugged her arms around herself, as if she were chilled to the bone. Her pleasure had turned bittersweet. She reminded herself that the mysterious Angelina was only a shadowy figure from the past; that Clint was here, with her. But Leslie knew with a riveting certainty that Angelina had once held his heart.

Perhaps she still did.

CHAPTER ELEVEN

THERE WAS A SUBTLE CHANGE in their relationship after that night. Neither could deny any longer that they shared a very special kind of closeness, something that went beyond mere kinship. Despite Angelina—despite Bonnie—Leslie was more comfortable with Clint than she'd ever dreamed possible. Nor could she deny that he made her feel good about herself, something she hadn't felt in a long, long time.

The only dark cloud on the horizon was Clint's reaction to Bonnie.

Tess was overjoyed when they made the promised trip to the zoo on Wednesday—but not as thrilled as Bonnie. Bonnie watched the animals. Leslie watched Bonnie. And though Leslie wasn't always aware of it, Clint watched Leslie. They all laughed over Bonnie's rapt absorption with the chattering, cartwheeling monkeys, even Clint.

But Clint's reserve was still there. He was polite and obliging with Bonnie, but the warm affection she knew he was capable of was conspicuously absent with Bonnie. Yet Leslie knew he was trying—just this morning he'd read a story to Tess and Bonnie, with both girls huddled close to his side.

At times Leslie longed to demand why he continued to hold himself at arm's length. The demand burned on her lips, but in the end she said nothing, for several reasons. She didn't want to jeopardize their newfound closeness. And she wanted him to tell her, freely and without reservations. Yet after witnessing the torment on his face the other night, Leslie wasn't always sure she wanted to know.

It made her heart ache to watch Bonnie with Clint. But what gnawed at her the most was the awareness that he still hadn't touched the little girl.

THURSDAY MORNING, just as they'd finished breakfast, the phone rang. Clint answered it, and Leslie knew from the gist of the conversation that it was Colleen. Brian and Tess immediately clamored to talk to their mother. Brian proceeded to give Colleen the play-by-play of the week's two baseball games. Tess started off well enough, but all too soon huge tears welled up in her eyes as she pleaded for Colleen to come home.

Leslie was last on the line. "Don't rush home because of Tess," she said cheerfully into the mouthpiece. "I hate to disappoint your motherly soul, but right now you'd never know she was crying two minutes ago."

She was relieved to hear the smile in Colleen's voice. "Crocodile tears?"

"Only enough to make mothers worry," Leslie observed wryly.

Colleen chuckled but then her tone turned serious. "How are things going? The kids giving you any trouble? Clint said everything was fine, but men have such a tendency to pooh-pooh things, I'd feel better hearing it from you."

Leslie twirled the cord around her finger. "Brian and Tess are fine, Colleen, and so is Bonnie. You'd never know that Clint and I are completely new at this. In fact, I'd say we're doing a bang-up job." She smiled, her eyes veering straight to Clint's. His answering smile sped straight to her heart. It came to her then how easily and naturally she thought of Clint and herself in the same breath—and her use of "we" and "Clint and I" confirmed it. In the back of her mind, an unseen presence whispered that line of thinking was dangerous.

When she asked about Colleen's father, there was a hushed stillness on the other end of the line. Then Colleen said quietly, "There's been no change. But then he—he isn't expected to improve." Leslie's heart wrenched. The tiny break in Colleen's voice said all that words could not.

When she hung up a few minutes later, Leslie gave a silent prayer of thanks that Rob was with Colleen.

Colleen had reminded her of Bonnie's upcoming appointment with Dr. King, though Leslie hadn't forgotten. Bonnie's caseworker Fran also phoned later that day to offer to pick Leslie up and accompany her to Bonnie's appointment.

When Friday afternoon rolled around, Fran was right on time. Leslie was amazed to find herself just a little nervous. Clint had already explained the reasons for the return visit to the doctor, but Bonnie seemed rather apprehensive. On the way out to Fran's car, Tess patted Bonnie's shoulder reassuringly.

"You'll be okay," she announced matter-of-factly. "Besides," she grinned, "I bet you'll get a sucker or a toy afterward."

Bonnie's eyes lit up. "Toy," she echoed.

Leslie found herself stifling a laugh. How quickly they caught on.

Tess leaned closer. "Just don't let that dumb old nurse give you a shot," she warned.

They didn't have to wait long in the doctor's office. When the nurse announced Bonnie's name, Fran rose and held out her hand to Bonnie. Bonnie hesitated. She looked almost fearful, though Fran was smiling warmly. All at once the child's gaze rushed to Leslie. "Come, Lee," she pleaded in a hushed whisper. She seized one of Leslie's hands with both of her own and began to tug. "*Por favor* . . . you come."

"I don't mind," Fran assured her when Leslie glanced uncertainly at her. "If it eases her mind, it's probably better that you're with her."

Leslie flashed a grateful look and got to her feet beside Bonnie. In the examination room, the nurse weighed Bonnie, then Leslie helped Bonnie from her clothes into a paper gown that tied at the back. The nurse had apologized, saying they'd run out of children's gowns. They all chuckled when Bonnie lifted the voluminous folds from her small body and gave a broad, impish smile.

Dr. King was a kindly looking middle-aged man who reminded Leslie of Mr. Magoo. He lifted Bonnie to the examination table, but the little girl immediately stretched out her hand to Leslie. Before she was even aware of it, Leslie was at her side, taking her small hand and smiling down into her wary little face. Bonnie lay still and quiet while Dr. King gently probed her hip joint with his fingertips. Leslie's chest grew tight with emotion. Bonnie was so brave. She had accepted her limp far better than Leslie herself might have.

The doctor was pleased with the weight Bonnie had gained. Going over the X rays, he was guardedly optimistic that a nearly perfect correction could be made, though he warned there could be no certainties until after the surgery. He finished by scheduling her for a pre-op appointment in several weeks.

In the car, Fran glanced over at her. "Do you mind if we stop by my office for a few minutes? We've managed to locate a couple that's expressed an interest in adopting Bonnie. When I spoke to them today I mentioned I'd be seeing Bonnie this afternoon. They suggested this might be a good time to meet her. You're welcome to sit in, if you like. This is just an informal get-acquainted visit. Besides, I think Bonnie might be more at ease if you're there."

Leslie's smile froze.

Fran didn't appear to have noticed anything amiss. "Actually," she went on thoughtfully, "it would work out quite well since they're one of the few who are interested in an older child rather than an infant. I was hoping we'd be through with Bonnie's appointment by three, so I asked them to drop by around three-thirty." She glanced at her watch, her tone cheerful. "Believe it or not, the timing couldn't be better. We should get there just about the same time they do."

Leslie felt she'd been punched in the stomach. Beside her, Bonnie flashed a blindingly sweet grin as she felt her gaze. Leslie smiled back at the child, but inside, her mind was whirling. She didn't want to think about Bonnie's adoption!

She tried telling herself her reaction was stupid. After all, that was why Bonnie had been brought here in the first place—that and the surgery. But it didn't stop the bleakness seeping through her.

Sure enough, the couple was waiting in Fran's office. Jack and Lisa McCall were, Leslie soon learned, the perfect professional twosome—young, successful, extremely well-off. He was a banking executive, while she was the public relations director for a local firm. Leslie experienced an inexplicable spurt of triumph when Bonnie clung to her hand and refused to let go.

When she sat down, Bonnie immediately crawled onto her lap. Her arms around the little girl, Leslie sat quietly.

Bonnie soon slid from her lap. She gazed longingly at the small table in the corner where a box of crayons and several coloring books were stacked. Seeing where her attention lay, Fran stopped and gave an encouraging nod. "It's okay," she told the little girl. "You can color if you want."

Bonnie shyly crossed the few paces to the desk. From across the room, there was a shocked gasp. Leslie had started to follow Bonnie, but at the sound she turned abruptly.

Lisa McCall's meticulously defined red lips were twisted as if in repulsion. "How awful," she blurted. "You didn't tell us she walked like...like *that*."

Leslie's back stiffened. She recalled her own reaction the first time she'd witnessed Bonnie's awkward gait—her heart had gone out to the child. But never—*never*—had she looked upon Bonnie with horror...the way Lisa McCall just had.

Her mouth opened, but before she could say a word, Fran spoke up. "On the contrary," she stated with precise deliberation. "Bonita's limp was one of the first things I mentioned to you. I recall you told me you had no qualms about accepting a child with a problem like Bonita's."

Lisa McCall glanced at her husband. "That's true," she admitted uncomfortably. "Though I understood her surgery will correct the problem."

While Fran explained the details of Bonnie's surgery, Leslie knelt down beside Bonnie, determined to put the McCalls out of her mind. She managed to ignore the couple until she heard Jack McCall's voice.

"She's a nice-enough-looking little girl," he murmured. There was a brief but significant pause. "I suppose, though, considering her background, it's impossible to have any idea how intelligent she is."

It was too much. Leslie's head shot up. "I happen to be a teacher, Mr. McCall—" her eyes flashed fire and her chin tipped "—and I can assure you that Bonnie has no worries there. Her intelligence is much better than average." *Certainly superior to yours,* she thought scathingly. "She's only been here a month, and it's unbelievable how much she's picked up already."

Though Leslie knew it wasn't her place to spout off, she couldn't quite regret her outburst. With an effort, she resumed her place next to Bonnie and tried very hard to shut out the discussion around her.

Fran had risen and walked the McCalls to the door when Leslie raised her head again. "We discovered years ago that we couldn't have children," Lisa McCall was saying. "And now that we've decided to start a family, we're anxious to get on with it. Naturally any child of ours won't lack for anything—especially since we plan to adopt only one child.''

Leslie swallowed. So, she thought with a pang. If the McCalls adopted Bonnie, she would be an only child. She thought of how much Bonnie enjoyed playing with Tess and Brian. Her mind suddenly filled with a bleak vision of Bonnie's future... being scuttled off to a day-care center, and later perhaps a boarding school.

She battled a debilitating frustration. The McCalls were so cold and—sterile, somehow. They hadn't even tried to talk to Bonnie. They'd simply looked her over like a horse at an auction. Bonnie had been deprived of so much already. She needed laughter and warmth and life.

"You've earned quite an admirer.''

Leslie started when she realized Fran was speaking to her. "We're all very fond of Bonnie.'' Quiet as her tone was, there was an element of defensiveness she couldn't withhold. Her hands lingered on Bonnie's silky black hair.

"Especially you?''

There was something in the other woman's tone that brought Leslie's head around immediately. Fran was watching her with an enigmatic expression. Her voice was very gentle, but there was an elusive sadness in her eyes.

Leslie rose to her feet, feeling for all the world like a kid who'd just been caught cheating in class.

"I like working with children,'' she heard herself murmur, "or I wouldn't be a teacher. And Bonnie is—'' there was an almost imperceptible pause ''—an easy child to like." *And an easy child to love,* she amended silently.

"Then I'm sure you'll all miss her when she's gone. But thank heaven Bonnie will finally have a home— and a mother and a father to care for her."

Fran's tone was neutral and even. She was even smiling. Yet it was the unspoken message in the words that made Leslie feel sick. Fran was warning her not to get too attached to Bonnie—only it was too late. Far, far too late.

Her heart had been put through a wringer the last hour. And still it wasn't over.

She thought of what Tess had said the other night. *Why can't Bonnie come and live with you, Leslie?* If only she could, Leslie thought bleakly. If only she could...

But she didn't stand a chance against a couple like the McCalls. They were well-off. Successful. They could give Bonnie everything a child could possibly want.

Leslie said nothing, but suddenly she felt as though she would crack into a thousand pieces. When she and Dennis had been married, children had been her shining hope for the future. Now even that hope was gone. And the future still loomed before her...darker and lonelier than ever.

But she trusted her feeling that the McCalls simply weren't right for Bonnie.

Because Bonnie needed to be held, to be touched...to be loved...as much as she did.

IF LESLIE WAS QUIET that night, she couldn't help it. It was hard to pretend that nothing was wrong, when she suddenly felt that everything was wrong. She tried hard not to show it, and hoped she succeeded. She was secretly thankful that Clint spent much of the evening poring over blueprints spread out on the dining room table. Even Tess didn't chatter on as much as usual.

Later she tossed and turned restlessly in her bed. Her mind simply refused the release it might have found in sleep. Finally she drew a robe over her nightgown and slipped into the kitchen.

Her gaze lit on yesterday's newspaper, carelessly folded and lying on one end of the countertop; on impulse she reached for it.

Ten minutes later she heard a sound and then the back door opened. She started almost guiltily and glanced up from where she'd spread the newspaper out on the table in time to see Clint step inside.

"Hi," he said softly.

"Hi." She withdrew her elbow from the table and folded her hands in her lap.

He pulled out one of the chairs, turned it around and sat down. Crossing his arms atop the back of the chair, he glanced at her inquiringly. "I saw the light in the kitchen. Couldn't sleep?"

A tiny rueful smile curved her lips. She shook her head.

His smile matched hers. "Me, too."

"Why not?" she heard herself ask. It was odd, really. But seeing Clint like this was just what she needed. She hadn't realized how tense she was until she felt herself relax.

"I was thinking of you."

His quick response startled her, but only for a moment. She saw that his eyes were teasing and decided to reply in kind. "That," she murmured, "could be dangerous."

"I know."

Again his vehemence took her by surprise. Leslie saw that he was still smiling, but she wasn't at all sure that he was teasing. And she was suddenly quiveringly aware that while Clint was still fully dressed, she most certainly was not.

Vivid, sensual images tumbled around in her brain. His nearness confused her...and pleased her. He was so close she could clearly see the shadow of beard that darkened his jaw. She wanted to lay her palm against his cheek and discover for herself the raspy firmness of his skin.

He aroused urges in her that were painfully sweet...and just plain painful.

She wanted Clint. She could no longer look at him, talk to him, touch him in the most casual way without wondering how it would feel to lie next to him, with nothing between them; to experience for herself the magic his long-fingered hands could make on her body....

She wasn't sure if she was disappointed or relieved when she realized he was frowning at the open newspaper. "You're reading the want ads?"

She nodded. "I—I was just checking to see if there happened to be any teaching jobs in this area."

His gaze sharpened. "So you've decided to make the move after all?"

She nodded and confined her attention to folding up the newspaper. Clint reached out and pulled the newspaper from her fingers. "I think that's probably the best thing you could do for yourself."

"You do?" She hadn't realized until just then how much she wanted his approval.

"Yes," he said softly. "I do. You're wonderful with kids. And I don't doubt that you're a good teacher, so if that's what you want, you should have no trouble finding a job."

"Thank you." The first genuine smile of the evening crept across her lips. Though neither one said anything, the silence that followed was anything but awkward. It ran through her mind that she couldn't remember when she'd felt so at ease with anyone, even Colleen. But when Clint tipped his head to the side and continued to regard her, she couldn't quite place his expression.

"What is it?" she asked curiously.

"I was just thinking...." He seemed to hesitate.

She propped her elbows on the table. "Come on," she invited laughingly, "spit it out."

"I was just thinking—" he paused for the space of a heartbeat "—that your husband was a fool for walking out on you."

Leslie's smile withered. "He didn't walk out on me." The words were rushed and hurried, instinctively self-protective, but she immediately wished she had stayed silent.

"Then what happened?"

Leslie flinched as if she'd been physically struck. She couldn't tell him. Dear God, she couldn't.

Clint watched her reaction with a growing despair. "Look," he said, his voice very low. "Maybe I shouldn't have said that—maybe I shouldn't ask.

Colleen told me your divorce was tough on you, and somehow I assumed that Dennis walked out on you. But you were the one who pointed out once that I didn't know much about you—or your divorce. Yet every time I've mentioned it, you make it very clear the subject is taboo."

Leslie turned her head away, unable to confront the slight censure in his expression. She silently prayed he'd let the subject drop.

"You said a few weeks ago that you hated all the traveling he did." Clint took a deep, fortifying breath and focused on her tense features. "Was that it? You broke up because you were tired of Dennis being away so much of the time?"

Yes. No. Oh, damn you, Clint, she screamed silently. *Why can't you just let this go?*

His voice came again, doggedly insistent. "Is it, Leslie?"

Her breathing grew jerky. She felt his demanding stare like needles digging into her skin. In all this time, no one had guessed. No one even dreamed... Through a haze she heard her voice, flat and emotionless. "You wouldn't believe me if I told you."

But his tone was infinitely patient. "Try me."

The silence that drifted between them was endless. Clint was fighting a fierce inner battle of his own. He hated himself for putting that stricken look in her eyes, yet he was bitterly frustrated that she refused to talk to him.

He wanted to let the subject drop—damn, but he did! Something told him there was more—much more—than the little Leslie had told him. The last thing he wanted to talk about was either her marriage or her ex-husband. He wanted to talk about . . . what? The two of them? Their future? Yet he couldn't discard the notion that Leslie was hiding something from him. He had to know what—he had to.

His mouth tightened as he watched her push herself from the table, her movements precise. "I think I'll make us some tea," she muttered.

Something snapped inside Clint the instant she turned her back on him. He surged to his feet and shoved the chair aside. "Dammit, Leslie, I don't want tea, I want to know why the hell your marriage went sour!" He grabbed her arm and whirled her around.

The mug Leslie had just reached for slipped from her grasp. It fell from her fingers and crashed to the floor, splintering into dozens of tiny pieces. Leslie stared at the broken shards numbly.

A bitter oath rent the air as she slowly bent to pick up the pieces. "Leave it," Clint ordered brusquely. "We're going to straighten this out once and for all, Leslie. One minute I'm convinced your husband was a bastard who made your life a living hell. The next, I can't help but think maybe you're still in love with him!"

"In love with him . . . !" There was a shocked, startled gasp. Her head jerked up. Their eyes collided. "I could never love Dennis after what he did . . . *never*!" It was a cry of outrage, a cry of pain . . . and Clint knew it for the truth.

"Then tell me, Leslie." The anger was gone from his voice, but not the relentless demand. "Tell me what happened. What did Dennis do that was so awful? Did he lie? Did he drink? Steal? Cheat? Gamble?"

Leslie closed her eyes. If only, she thought desperately. Oh, Lord, if only...

There was a suffocating pressure in her chest, a huge lump in her throat. She didn't think she could breathe, much less speak, but suddenly it was all pouring out.

Her lips snapped open. "Dennis...he wanted someone else," she said jerkily. "He married someone else."

Shaken to the core by the haunting emptiness in her eyes, Clint wondered if he'd heard her right. "He jilted you for someone else?"

Oh, Lord, that was rich. She stifled a bitter laugh. "No! He wanted us both—both of us, Clint!"

"His wife...*and* a mistress?"

"*No!* Didn't you hear what I said?" She felt she was unraveling at the seams, but she couldn't help it. "He married her, Clint. He *married* her long before I ever divorced him!"

"You're not making sense," he said slowly. "If he was married to you, he couldn't possibly be married to someone else—"

"But he was," she cried wildly. "Don't you understand? Dennis had a wife in San Francisco—and another one in Houston."

Clint stared at her in disbelief. He floundered helplessly, his mind grappling with the implication of what Leslie had just told him. Then all at once, comprehension came in a dizzying rush.

"Oh, my God," he whispered.

CHAPTER TWELVE

THE QUIET THAT DESCENDED was almost unbearable. Clint couldn't tear his gaze from Leslie's face. Her eyes were huge and betrayingly moist from unshed tears. He was stung to the core by the naked anguish on her face.

He tried to speak, failed, and tried once more. "Dear God," he said faintly. "Two wives...he had two wives."

Leslie's shoulders slumped. Her lungs burned with the effort it took not to cry. "Yes," she whispered. "Dennis was a—" she heard herself say the words she had never before spoken aloud, "—a bigamist."

Hearing her, seeing her like this, so broken and defeated, something caught in his chest, something that made him hurt as he knew she was hurting. She didn't resist his attempt to draw her close. When his arms closed around her, she turned into his chest as if he were a haven.

Clint didn't say anything. He didn't move. He just held her, his eyes squeezed shut, an unfamiliar tightness closing his throat.

For long moments they clung to each other desperately, until at last Clint eased back. One arm holding her tight against him, he guided her from the kitchen and into the living room. When they reached the sofa, he gently pushed her to the cushions and eased down beside her. Tucking her head against his shoulder, he fitted the rest of her flush against the hardened contours of his body.

His touch was immeasurably gentle as he smoothed the hair from her cheek, marveling at the tenderness that rushed through him.

"How did you find out?" he asked quietly.

She stiffened. *Don't,* he pleaded silently. *You've come this far, don't shut me out now.*

His expression regretful but determined, he slowly hooked his fingers beneath her chin and brought her gaze to his. "Please, Leslie. I have to know."

Leslie's nerves were stretched to the limit. Dear God, if Clint felt sorry for her she didn't think she could bear it! But when she searched his face, there was only compassion—not pity—reflected on his features. Besides, she realized defeatedly, he knew the worst. What did it matter if he knew the rest?

All her resistance abruptly drained from her. She leaned back against the cushions and began to speak.

"How did I find out," she repeated tonelessly. She shrugged, the barest movement of her shoulder. "It was little things mostly. I'd always done most of his packing and unpacking for him. A few times I came across a piece of clothing that I hadn't bought for him, or that I knew he hadn't received as a gift. He said he'd bought it himself on one of his runs, yet Dennis hated to shop, even for himself. But then he brought home a wild Hawaiian shirt that seemed totally out of character for him. He gave me the same excuse, but the very next time I unpacked for him, I noticed his clothes smelled of a different detergent than the one I used."

When she stopped, Clint probed very gently. "He denied it?"

A look of distress crept across her features. Her lashes lowered before she spoke again.

"I didn't say anything," she confessed jerkily. "I think it was then I began to suspect . . . he'd been on a regular run to Houston for years. The next time he was there, I phoned him at his hotel, the hotel he was supposed to be staying at. I usually never called him; he'd always said that the airline's schedule was sometimes delayed, so it was easier if he phoned me. But the hotel claimed Dennis wasn't a guest there—the clerk checked and insisted he'd *never* been a guest there."

Her fingers plucked restlessly at a fold in her robe. "I decided to confront Dennis then, thinking that he was involved with another woman, that he was having an affair. But when I did, Dennis broke down and told me the truth . . . that he wasn't having an affair, he had another *wife* there in Houston.

"God, I couldn't believe it!" Clint felt slashed to ribbons by the anguish in her voice. "I thought he was playing a horrible joke on me. But he wasn't. He showed me their marriage license—" her voice quavered "—and a copy of the birth certificate for their one-year-old son."

All the heartache, the remembered shame and degradation washed through her. For long, tense moments Leslie struggled with herself, wondering if she could go on. When she did, her tone was so flat and wooden that Clint felt a chill inside hearing it.

"It seems Dennis had married her several years after he married me. Nearly half the time *we* were married, he was married to *her*. And they had a baby together—" her voice wobbled traitorously "—they had a baby while *I'd* been wanting one for ages."

Listening to her was like a knife turning inside him. He suddenly understood so many things. Leslie's dislike of travel. The elusive hurt and uncertainty he sometimes sensed in her.

"That's when you divorced him?" he asked quietly. "You didn't file charges against him?"

His hand reached for hers. He slid his palm against hers, weaving their fingers together tightly. Leslie's eyes dropped to take in the movement, watching as he let their clasped hands rest lightly on his thigh. His touch was oddly reassuring.

She let out a shaky breath and shook her head. "I just wanted to forget." She faltered. "There were enough questions as it was. Friends who wondered what went wrong... why it was so sudden.... It was such a nightmare." The words were torn from deep inside her. "How do you explain that your husband decided one wife wasn't enough—he had to have two! God, I wanted to die every time someone mentioned our divorce."

Clint's voice was as unsteady as hers. "Who else knows, Leslie? Anyone?"

"No one, not even Colleen or... or my parents." Her voice was raw, as raw as the storm of emotions churning away inside her. His insides twisted as he thought of all her hurt bottled up within her. He didn't miss her convulsive swallow. Her lips were pressed tightly together, as if she were determined not to show any emotion. He saw her look heavenward and knew she battled tears that were only a heartbeat away.

She hauled in a deep unsteady breath. "Remember the night you said that people today fall out of love as quickly as they fall in love?"

Clint flinched. He still regretted the bitter words he had flung at her that night. "I remember."

"It made me think of Dennis—" her voice caught on a sound that was half laugh, half sob "—only Dennis didn't fall out of love. Can you believe he didn't want the divorce? He claimed he still loved me, that he loved us both. He wanted to go on, just as we had been!"

He could feel the awful tension mounting in her body.

"Afterward, I hated myself for being so blind and—and stupid. I'd think...so what if I was his first choice? I wasn't his last choice, his *only* choice. All the while he claimed to love me, he loved someone else. For months I asked myself why. Had I failed him somehow? Why wasn't he satisfied with me? Was she prettier than me? A better wife? A better *lover*? Why wasn't I *enough* for him? I felt like I was nothing."

Her voice broke; it was like a dam bursting inside her. Burning tears streamed down her cheeks; she tried to choke back a sob that sounded as if it were wrenched from deep in her chest, but it was no use. She was only dimly aware of clutching the front of Clint's shirt, dampening the material with her tears.

His arms tightened around her. He wanted nothing more than to soothe her wounded spirit; to offer the security and warmth and love she silently cried out for.

He yearned to deflect all her pain and restore all that Dennis had taken from her...and more.

So he held her shaking body close, feeling her pain pour into him. His cheek nuzzled the top of her head, his breath filtering through the wispy hair at her temple. His hand trailed slowly up and down the length of her back until he felt her breathing even out. When it was over, he pulled her up beside him. His arm cradling her shoulders, he led her up the stairs and into her room.

Leslie scarcely noticed when Clint untied her robe and pulled it from her body. He dropped it on the end of the bed, lifted the covers and softly commanded she slide in.

Reality seeped in slowly when she saw him unbutton his shirt. Clint glanced over and discovered her expression was faintly startled. He leaned over and cradled her cheek in his palm. The pad of his thumb slid over her lower lip. "I'm not leaving you like this," he stated quietly.

She watched through heavy eyelids while he shed the rest of his clothes. A blessed kind of numbness had overtaken her. His torso was bare and hard...she wanted to reach out and slide her fingers through the furry darkness on his chest, but it would have required too much effort.... It seemed altogether right and natural when Clint climbed in beside her and pulled her close. Seconds after the room was plunged into darkness, she sniffed pitifully. Her throat felt raw. Her eyes stung.

"Oh, God, I—I'm so tired." The words escaped without her knowing it.

"I know." His warm breath trickled over her forehead. His lips brushed the soft skin at her temple. "Just try to relax and go to sleep," he murmured.

Her head came up. He could feel her staring at him through the darkness. "You—you won't leave, will you?"

His heart wrenched. She sounded so frightened and alone. *No*, he thought. *Lord, no.*

He reached out and pillowed her head on his shoulder once more. "I'm not going anywhere," he promised softly.

"It feels so...so good to be held." Her voice was still thready with tears.

Her breathless confession, so simple—so telling— went straight to his heart. Did she know how humble and proud it made him feel to hear her say that?

"Not half as good as it feels to hold you." His throat oddly tight, he pulled her shaking body closer yet, loving the way she melted trustingly against him.

Leslie's eyes closed slowly. She didn't question the way her body craved the warm security of his. She was too exhausted, too dazed to let herself think about whether this was right or wrong. All she knew was that she had never needed anyone as desperately as she needed Clint right now.

For Clint, the moment was just as precious. He loved feeling Leslie's softness, the way she instinctively curled against him as if they'd been sleeping together for years. His hands spoke of comfort, not passion, as he slowly stroked the length of her back and shoulders.

He thought about all that Leslie had said…all that she had suffered. He acknowledged vaguely that if he were wise, he'd get up and leave this very instant.

For so long now, he'd let himself believe that no other woman could ever take Angelina's place in his heart.

He had just discovered how wrong he was. But along with that realization came another…and it was infinitely painful.

Where Leslie was concerned, he was probably the worst man on earth for her…and just when he'd finally discovered that Leslie was the only woman in the world for him.

LESLIE WOKE VERY SLOWLY the next morning. Sunshine painted the room in a pale yellow glow. She had slept heavily; her mind was still dulled with sleep. For a moment she couldn't think why her eyelids felt heavy and swollen…. Remembrances of the past night gripped her mind. Her eyes swung immediately to the empty pillow beside her; her thoughts skipped wildly from one to another.

Dennis. She had told Clint about Dennis.

And then she had cried her heart out. Oh, Lord…what would Clint think of her? She rolled over and clutched her pillow, moaning in shame. Her eyes squeezed shut as a hundred different sensations flooded through her.

Clint had stayed with her the night through…they had slept together. She dimly recalled waking once, disoriented and cold; then he was there again, strong arms pulling her close and tight against him.

The thought made her feel like jelly inside. She could almost feel his lean fingers stroking her shoulder, touching her, soothing her; his body tucked against hers through the long, lonely night.

Only the night hadn't been lonely...and it had passed much too quickly.

Hearing voices downstairs, Leslie reluctantly pushed herself from the bed. She showered quickly and pulled on shorts and a cool cotton top. After securing her damp hair back in a loose ponytail, she headed toward the kitchen.

She was almost there when her steps faltered. Her heart and mind locked in willful battle. She yearned to see Clint again with every breath in her body...she feared facing him again as she had never feared anything in her life. She wanted to run and hide...she wanted nothing more than to feel the warm comfort of his arms around her again.

She could hear his voice just beyond the doorway. He was laughing at something Brian said. Her feet carried her forward unconsciously.

Bonnie was the first to notice Leslie. Her eyes brightened; her mouth full of scrambled egg, she waved her spoon in greeting. Leslie felt her heart turn over. She smiled, and Bonnie pointed at the empty chair beside her.

As she took a deep fortifying breath, her gaze traveled to Clint, who stood over the stove, a spatula in his hand. She was just a little disconcerted to find his dark gaze already upon her.

Their eyes met. The contact was brief...but oh-so-thorough. Her heart skipped a beat. His expression was tender and watchful—and very, very searching.

"Good morning." How she forced the sound past the tightness in her throat, she never knew.

"'Morning," he said with a faint smile. "You're just in time."

"We're havin' breakfast," Tess announced.

"Yeah," Brian chimed in with an ear-splitting grin. "The first toast Uncle Clint made burnt. But we put peanut butter on it, and I thought it tasted great."

"That's 'cause you eat anything," his sister put in disgustedly.

"Uncle Clint seems to have quite a weakness for peanut butter," she murmured.

No, Clint thought with a pang. What he had was a definite weakness for a pretty lady named Leslie with shadows in her eyes and darkness in her heart.

He watched her gaze slide painfully away from his. In a way he couldn't completely define, she was even more vulnerable now than she had been last night, when she lay limp and exhausted against him. He sensed her discomfort and wanted nothing more than to drive it away—for more than just the moment. For more than just the day.

For a lifetime.

He forced a smile and a light tone. "So what'll it be, pretty lady? Burnt toast? Or burnt peanut butter toast?"

Her eyes cut back to his. Miraculously she laughed. It was a shaky, tentative laugh, but it was a laugh nonetheless.

It was a sound that tied his heart in knots.

Breakfast wasn't the ordeal Leslie expected, thanks to the presence of the three children. She even managed to convince herself that this morning was really no different from yesterday morning, or the morning before. As soon as Brian, Tess and Bonnie finished eating, they dashed from the room, leaving the two adults alone.

Panic seized her. Once more she wanted to run and hide. Yet what purpose would running away serve?

They cleared the table together. Without the chattering of the children, the kitchen seemed oppressively quiet. Clint murmured an idle comment here and there, but Leslie scarcely heard. Her misery increased with every second.

She could barely look at Clint. Why was he doing this? she wondered frantically. He was acting as if nothing had happened last night. Was it because he didn't really give a damn...or because he cared enough to spare her? In an anguished kind of way, she was relieved; her terrible secret no longer burned inside her. But now that Clint knew, did he think less of her? Differently, perhaps?

She finished wiping the tabletop. Her movements studiously precise, she rinsed the dishcloth, folded it carefully and draped it over the divider in the sink.

She paused a moment, bolstering her courage in order to face him. When she did, she saw that he had propped his hip against the other end of the counter, taking the weight off his injured leg. There was an air of negligence about his pose. For an instant Leslie experienced a contradictory blend of envy and outrage. How could he look so normal and strong and capable while she felt she was coming apart at the seams?

Clint watched her slowly turn to face him. Her fingers strained against one another. He sensed her nervous tension; he heard the tiny sigh she emitted. He doubted she was even aware of it, but it reflected all her confusion and uncertainty.

Leslie swallowed bravely. "About last night," she began awkwardly. "I—I just wanted to apologize."

His eyes met hers squarely. She flinched and glanced away. "It's all right," she heard him murmur. "In fact, there's really no need for you to—"

"Yes. Yes, there is!" Her vehemence startled them both. Leslie dragged her gaze back to him, feeling her face burn guiltily. "I didn't mean to embarrass you," she said, her voice very low.

"You didn't. And *you* shouldn't be embarrassed, either."

A feeling of utter mortification washed over her. "But I made such a—" to her horror, she began to quaver "—a fool of myself..."

She never got any further. The tortured quiver in her voice stabbed into his chest like a knife blade. Clint's eyes never wavered from hers as he closed the distance between them.

"Don't," he ordered, his tone both tender and rough. "Don't say it. Don't even think it."

Leslie opened her mouth. Whatever she might have said, she never knew. The fierceness burning in his eyes underscored his warning and caused the words to die unuttered in her throat. She held his gaze endlessly, silently battling him . . . and herself.

Clint stared down at her, at dew-soft lips that trembled ever so slightly, at misty blue eyes that refused to meet the silent demand in his.

At last he wove his fingers through hers in a burning handclasp. Bringing their joined hands to his mouth, he kissed the back of her hand, sending a ripple of sensation clear to her toes. Her gaze trickled slowly, inevitably upward, to merge with his.

"I liked being there for you." The pitch of his voice was low but intense. "I liked holding you. But what I liked most of all was being needed...by you. You can trust me, Leslie. You don't need to worry about it going further than the two of us. Nor do I want to hear any more nonsense about feeling embarrassed or foolish. Okay?"

His gentleness completely disarmed her, making her want to cry all over again. There was a strangely husky quality to his voice she'd never heard before, and her heart leapt as she absorbed the tender concern on his dark features. She wanted to believe he cared. She wanted it with all that she possessed, but she wasn't sure she dared. She nodded, but the eyes that clung to his were almost fearful.

"That's my girl," he whispered. He resettled her hand firmly on the muscled plane of his chest, his hand remaining tight and firm over hers. Beneath her fingertips, Leslie could feel the hardness of muscle and bone, the wiry rasp of hair below the thin material of his shirt.

His head dipped slowly. Leslie found she couldn't look away. *Trust me,* he said. She wanted to—Lord, how she wanted to! With a muffled cry deep in her throat, she melted against him at the same instant his lips met hers.

His lips were fleeting and tender, barely skimming hers. Leslie couldn't help herself. She twined her arms around his neck and buried her fingers in the dark hair that grew low on his nape. His mouth moved yearningly over hers; the kiss deepened, growing bolder.

His tongue flirted with the corners of her mouth. Hungry for the sweet sensation, her lips parted, granting him access to the moist interior of her mouth. A tiny little tremor shot through her. She was quiveringly conscious of the steely strength of his thighs bonding with her own. He was so warm. So totally masculine. His kiss kindled a poignant ache inside her, reminding her just how much she needed to be held. To be touched. To be loved...

Slowly, reluctantly, Clint broke the searing contact of their mouths. Just holding her like this again tied him up in knots. Last night, he had wanted nothing more than to make love to her until they both died from the pleasure of finding fulfillment. But he had battled his feelings of desire, knowing she was simply too vulnerable just then.

From the doorway came the sound of a giggle. Two pairs of very startled eyes met a pair of impish green ones.

Clint rested his forehead against Leslie's, rapidly amending his last thought. It appeared that now was not the time, either.

The giggle came again, this time joined by another. They saw that Bonnie had stepped out beside Tess.

"We saw you kiss," Tess informed them matter-of-factly.

Leslie groaned and ducked her head beneath his chin. She felt like a teenager who'd been caught in her first kiss by her parents—only they had been caught by a four- and a five-year-old.

"We noticed." Clint's mouth twitched. Leslie's mortified expression was precious. He stroked a finger alongside her jaw and chuckled. "Chin up, Les," he chided good-naturedly. "It could have been worse."

Tess was suddenly at their side. She tugged at Leslie's sleeve, her eyes sparkling. "You must like Uncle Clint a lot. Are you gonna be his awful wedded wife?"

She nearly choked. "His awful wedded wife..."

The rumble of Clint's laughter echoed beneath her fingertips. "Tess, I think you mean *lawful* wedded wife."

The little girl frowned. "That's what I said." She'd wandered over to the built-in desk next to the refrigerator and began rummaging through the bottom drawer where Colleen kept crayons, coloring books and the like.

Leslie smiled weakly. "I think if it were up to your niece, your bachelor days would be over."

A small blond head bobbed up and around to stare at them once more. "What's a bachelor?" she asked curiously.

"A bachelor is someone who's never been married—like your Uncle Clint here." It was Leslie who answered. Reluctantly withdrawing from Clint's arms, she pulled detergent from the cupboard and started the dishwasher.

She never even saw the odd look that flitted across Clint's features.

He was going to have to tell her, he realized bleakly, and tell her soon. He only hoped that she would understand why he had waited this long, but he wasn't sure that she would.

No, he wasn't sure at all.

THE DAY PASSED far too quickly for Leslie. Brian had
a baseball game that afternoon, and once again, they
all went along to watch. A quick trip to the grocery
store followed, and then it was time to start dinner.

The atmosphere between Leslie and Clint was warm
and comfortable. But there was also a tingling current of awareness that neither could deny, for it was
there in every look, in every casual touch that passed
between them. The knowledge made Leslie feel warm
both inside and out, yet a tiny voice inside warned that
she was a foolish, foolish woman for daring to hope.

She was bushed by the end of the day. She was glad
for Clint's help in putting the three children to bed.
Grinning sheepishly, Brian pronounced himself to be
too old to be tucked into bed, but Tess was adamant.
Leslie read a story about farm animals, while Bonnie
stared with rapt absorption at the pictures. Clint sat at
the foot of the bed, smiling and occasionally shaking
his head.

Finally she snapped the book shut and rose from the
bedside. Clint rose as well and stepped to her side. Tess
was the last to slide between the sheets, and she
promptly demanded a good-night kiss from each of
them.

Leslie quickly kissed both girls' cheeks. To Bonnie
she whispered, "*Buenas noches,* Bonnie. Good
night."

Clint's turn came next. Tess raised her cheek obediently, but just as he began to straighten, she grinned.
"Now Bonnie," she demanded.

His gaze flitted to Bonnie. The child looked like an
angel, her hair spread out over her thin shoulders,

dressed in a white eyelet nightgown and clutching a tiny stuffed dog.

Time stood still. Bonnie gazed up at Clint adoringly. Clint's skin had gone pale beneath his tan. Watching him—watching them both—Leslie battled a painful sense of expectancy. She held her breath and waited . . . waited.

Hands still splayed on the mattress, he leaned forward. Bonnie threw her arms around his neck and hugged him fiercely. Clint's face was hidden from her, but it was as if Leslie could see every muscle in his body tighten, then slowly ease. Bonnie withdrew just as quickly and scuttled under the covers, as if she were embarrassed.

Leslie turned away, an odd tightening in her chest. She wanted desperately to see his face right now, but she was afraid of what she would see—or perhaps afraid of what she *wouldn't* see.

In the living room, she took a deep cleansing breath. Brian had brought out several photo albums, and they had all laughed at the baby pictures of him and Tess. Now she saw that a dozen or so loose photos had fallen from the album, so she busied herself picking them up.

She knew the exact moment Clint entered the room. Her skin prickled; her gaze was drawn as if by a magnet. She was relieved to note some of the color had returned to his skin.

One picture showed a one-year-old Tess, still in diapers, crouched beside a puddle of rainwater, her tiny mouth pursed to get a drink. Leslie chuckled all over again. Over her shoulder, Clint smiled as well.

"A few years from now Tess won't thank Rob for taking that picture," he said.

"I don't doubt it," she agreed.

Their eyes meshed. Again that sizzling heat flashed between them; she felt herself go weak inside.

He bent and began to help her gather up the pictures. She swiveled around on her heel in order to retrieve another.

Perhaps it was because it was bigger than the others; perhaps because it was of the lush, tropical background. Or perhaps it was because Clint was in this photo, looking younger, more alive, more open than she'd ever seen him.

He wasn't alone. There was a woman by his side. He was smiling down directly into her upturned face... She was young. Vibrant. Strikingly beautiful with silky-looking long black hair.

A gnawing pain clutched at Leslie's heart.

Just as suddenly, Clint sensed that something was different. He leaned over to glance at the picture in Leslie's hands. He froze.

Leslie's throat was bone dry. "Clint. This woman... this is Angelina?"

There was a heartbeat of silence. "Yes."

The word sounded hollow and wooden. Staring at the picture, at the two of them, Leslie died a little inside. They both looked so tender, so much in *love*. She had never seen that expression in Clint's eyes... undoubtedly she never would.

"The night that Bonnie came, I heard Colleen mention her name. She said that Angelina spoke Spanish, too." She moistened parched lips, marveling that she could sound so rational. "I've wondered ever since . . . how you knew her. . . ."

Her eyes locked on his face. Seeing the bleakness creep inevitably into his eyes, she wanted to tear her gaze away, but she couldn't.

"Angelina was my wife, Leslie." A sad, poignant smile touched his lips. "I married her."

CHAPTER THIRTEEN

SOMETHING SNAPPED inside Leslie. Past and present meshed in her mind. For an instant they were totally inseparable. She saw Dennis, contrite but sweetly pleading as he sought to keep on using his foolish, gullible wife. And she saw Clint, the same guilt etched between his brows.

"Married...a wife...and you didn't tell me?" She flung the words at him. "Damn you, Clint Stuart. Damn you!"

Guilt forged a burning hole inside him. "I tried to. The night Bonnie came to me with that ribbon. Leslie, I wanted to tell you then...."

It was an excuse and they both knew it.

He stretched out a hand toward her. She jumped up and flew to the other side of the room, as if she sought to get as far away from him as possible.

The wildness he sensed in her disturbed him. He shook his head. "It's not what you think." He tried again. "Listen to me, Leslie. Angelina's gone. She died three years ago."

Leslie heard, and yet she didn't. All she could think was that she had trusted him—she had poured out her soul to him only last night!

Her emotions lay scattered in every direction. The hurt she felt was like fire in her lungs. She felt deceived. Betrayed all over again. Everything she felt lay naked on her face. It was just like Dennis. No, no, that wasn't right. It was different...yet the same. Clint had been married and he hadn't told her. *He hadn't told her.*

"Tell me, Clint," she choked out. "Whenever you've held me and—and kissed me—did you think of Angelina? Did you compare me to her, the way Dennis must have done with *his other wife*?"

He flinched as if she'd struck him. "That's not fair, Leslie."

"Fair! What about the times we talked about my divorce? You could have told me then, Clint, but you didn't. Was that fair? And then last night, when I think of how I confessed every sordid little detail about Dennis—" Her sob was strangled.

This time it was Clint who scarcely heard her words; all he heard were a million layers of hurt. What could he possibly say to ease her pain? Yet he knew he had to try, for both their sakes.

His sigh was an infinitely lonely sound. "I'm sorry," he began, his voice very low. "I know I should have told you. I was wrong for—"

He never got any further. From the darkness behind him came a shrill, aborted cry. A dull, thumping sound followed.

Leslie's eyes locked frantically with his. A sharp cry tore from her throat. "Oh, my God! It's Bonnie!"

She was right behind Clint when they reached the stairs. Bonnie lay sprawled below the last step. Leslie dropped down to her knees beside him with a stricken cry. Halfway up the stairs was Tess, her small body paralyzed.

His face tight with fear, Clint reached for Bonnie. The little girl was sobbing wildly; as he eased her gently to her back, Leslie gasped. "She's bleeding, Clint. There's blood all over the rug . . . !"

"I know. Her head must have caught the corner of the molding when she fell." His long fingers slid into Bonnie's hair, gently probing her scalp.

Leslie rushed to grab a washcloth from the hall. Tess had scrambled down the stairs, and Brian was there as well, his eyes huge in his pale face. When Leslie dropped back down to her knees and thrust the cloth into Clint's hands, Tess pressed close to Leslie's side. Tears streamed down her cheeks.

"I—I just wanted to get a drink," she sobbed. "Bonnie was right next to me...I didn't know she was gonna fall...."

Leslie slipped her arm around her. "Shh," she soothed. "It's not your fault. And Bonnie will be fine, you'll see."

Clint's features were grim. Already the cloth he'd pressed on the back of Bonnie's head was nearly soaked through with blood. "I think she's going to need stitches," he said. Leslie could have sworn there was a tremor in his voice. "I'd better get her to the hospital."

Leslie jumped to her feet. "I'm going with you. I'll call Tim's mother and see if she'll stay with Brian and Tess." Her tone left no room for argument. Clint nodded and rose to his feet. Bonnie's sobs had quieted, but she was still crying. While Leslie was on the phone, he cradled Bonnie to his chest, murmuring to her in Spanish all the while.

They hurried from the house as soon as Maryann stepped inside; she had decided it would be easiest all around if she simply took Brian and Tess home for the night. Once Leslie was settled in Clint's car, she reached automatically for Bonnie. Another time, perhaps, and she might have noticed the torn expression on Clint's features as he relinquished the little girl. But right now all Leslie could focus on was the quietly weeping child.

In the emergency room, Bonnie lay still and limp in her arms. Leslie's nerves were stretched to the limit. There were several other patients before them, and it seemed like they waited forever. Leslie jumped when the huge double doors in front of her burst open and the nurse announced Bonnie's name. Leslie's arms tightened instinctively around the child as she got to her feet.

Next to her, Clint rose as well. The nurse bestowed a kindly smile on them but shook her head, already reaching for Bonnie. "Sorry," she said firmly. "At this age she's better off without either of you there, believe me."

"But she doesn't speak any English," Clint began.

"Then it's a good thing we have a Spanish-speaking nurse, isn't it?" With a breezy smile, she plucked Bonnie from Leslie's arms.

Bonnie burst into tears and stretched out her arms. "Lee!" she cried piteously. *"Papá!"*

The huge doors whisked silently shut.

Leslie's stomach knotted. She never even noticed that Clint looked just as shattered. Sinking down on the vinyl bench, she buried her head in her hands, not caring who saw her. Her thoughts were wild and dis-

jointed. What if Bonnie was seriously hurt? Head in-
juries were dangerous, weren't they?

Clint stared down at her bent head, aware of her
secret fears while trying desperately to curb his own.
More than anything, he wanted to gather her close and
tuck her head against his shoulder. They could share
it together—the pain and the waiting.

"I'm sure she'll be fine, Leslie." Her head jerked up
at the sound of his voice. Low as it was, the words
dropped into the air with the weight of an anchor.

He attempted a smile and reached out to touch her
shoulder. "The nurse was right, you know. This is
probably harder on us than on Bonnie—"

"Just stop it, will you!" she hissed. "We both know
you don't really give a damn about her, so why pretend you do?"

Clint dropped his hand as if he'd been burned. For
the longest time, he said nothing. He simply stood
there, as silent and motionless as a statue, his face shut
down from all expression.

When he finally resumed his seat next to Leslie, his
movements were slow, almost tired. Less than a foot
separated them, but the distance between them had
never been greater.

WHEN THE NURSE carried Bonnie back out, her dark
eyes were red-rimmed and swollen, but she was
beaming—she clutched not one but two lollipops in
her fist. Leslie jumped up with a little cry and hugged
her fiercely the instant the nurse handed her over.
Clint stood slightly apart, surveying them silently
while the nurse gave instructions.

Little was said on the ride home. Leslie confined her attention to Bonnie, and the girl quickly fell asleep. It was a struggle getting out of the car without waking her, but Clint held the door wide and somehow Leslie managed.

The house was still and dark. Breathless from carrying the little girl's dead weight, Leslie paused to shift Bonnie from over her shoulder to her arms. Clint flipped on the light in the living room and strode toward her. "Here," he said. "I'll take her up and put her to bed."

His hands were already sliding under Bonnie's limp form.

"But your leg—"

"Is fine."

For a fleeting instant, their eyes met. Leslie's first instinct was to snatch the girl back, but Clint's expression was set and unyielding.

Her hands fell away from Bonnie the moment he had her firmly in his hands. She hated herself for her possessiveness, but she couldn't help it. She turned away before he was less than halfway up the stairs, feeling cold and hollow inside. She stumbled into the living room and collapsed on the sofa, too tense to sleep, too tired to relax.

Upstairs, Clint pushed aside the rumpled sheets with one hand, holding the little girl in his other arm. Bonnie gave a tiny whimper and tossed her head restlessly. He stood as if paralyzed, not moving a muscle, hoping she wouldn't wake up.

The black fringe of her lashes lifted. She stared straight into his eyes, and smiled a smile so sweet and pure it touched something deep inside him.

"Papá," she sighed. Her lashes drifted closed and she slept once more, nestling her cheek trustingly against him.

Clint began to tremble, inside and out. Dear God, he thought brokenly. He'd known it would be like this. He'd known that if he touched her even once, he'd be lost.

His chin came down on Bonnie's shining head. He clutched the little girl to his chest. This closeness—this feeling of holding a child tight against his heart, was something he'd never known—something he'd been robbed of.... Yet he couldn't deny the deep-seated sense of rightness he felt; he couldn't have let this child go even if he'd wanted to.

He turned and sank down on the bed. Head bent, arms tight around his precious burden, he cried.

He didn't know that near the door, another figure watched—and heard the strangled sound torn from deep in his chest. And her cheeks were just as wet as his as she cried . . . not for herself, but for him.

LESLIE RETURNED to the living room, wiping away her tears with her fingertips. Seeing Clint like that had stunned her. But what really hurt was the knowledge that for a while tonight, she had deliberately turned a blind eye to him. With a stab she remembered the fear in his eyes as he knelt over Bonnie; the way he had cradled her close, refusing to release her until he had to, when she, Leslie, had reached for Bonnie in the car.

She was still standing before the fireplace when he finally came downstairs. She heard a rustle of clothing as he passed by her, then all was silent. Overcome with shame, she could scarcely summon the courage to face him.

He stood before the window, his hands thrust into the pockets of his slacks. The chiseled planes of his face were thrown into stark relief by the lamp glowing in the corner. Staring at him, Leslie couldn't think when she'd seen anyone who looked more lonely.

As if sensing her scrutiny, he slowly turned. She didn't miss the tension in his stance as he faced her.

Silence lay thick and heavy between them. Neither one said anything; neither one moved.

It was Leslie who spoke first. Her fingers knotted together before her. "All this time," she whispered, "you acted as if you didn't care about Bonnie." She swallowed painfully. "But you do, don't you?"

He stared at her oddly. Something flickered in his eyes. "You saw, didn't you?" His voice was as strained as hers.

"You were so long that I wondered if something was wrong." When he said nothing, she regarded him pleadingly. "Tell me, Clint."

He closed his eyes. His voice was low and taut then at last he spoke. "I care."

Leslie wished she could have been relieved. Instead, when he opened his eyes, the pain she glimpsed brought agony to her heart.

"I have to know," she heard herself say. "That first day, you clammed up when I mentioned Central America. It's because of—" she stumbled on, her throat tight and aching "—because of your wife. And the way you've acted around Bonnie...you said she reminded you of someone...it's all connected with Angelina, isn't it?"

She saw his body stiffen. For a moment she didn't think he would say anything. Then, just when she couldn't stand it anymore, he held out his hand. "Come here," he said softly.

She went, on shaky legs. They were the hardest steps she'd ever taken.

His fingers closed around hers, strong and warm. "Will you let me explain? Will you let me tell you about her?"

His quiet entreaty made her ache inside. Suddenly she wished she had remained silent. Right now, the last thing she wanted to hear was how much he'd loved Angelina, how he would always love her, no matter what.

"There's no need," she said unsteadily. "I shouldn't have said what I did earlier. I was hurt and I—I struck out blindly."

"I want to, Leslie. I think I need to—" the look he bestowed on her was deep and intense "—for both of us."

How could she refuse? She squeezed his fingers, wordlessly conveying her assent.

Tugging gently on her hand, he eased to the floor in front of the sofa and pulled her down beside him. Leslie fought a twinge of hurt when he let go of her hand. But her heart went out to him as he rubbed the back of his neck wearily. Then, for the longest time, he said nothing. Leslie had begun to think he'd changed his mind.

She stole a glance at him. "You told me you'd worked in Central America." Her tone was tentative; she was half afraid to say anything. "Is that where you met her?"

She held her breath while the seconds stretched out. At last he nodded slowly. "I was part of a team of engineers sent by our government to help build a cross-country highway system."

The lines etched beside his mouth revealed how difficult this was for him. After a few seconds, he went on.

"Angelina was a nurse. She grew up in the mountains there, so she didn't mind the remoteness—or the fact that our team didn't always stay in one place. Villagers in the area had helped raise the money for her training in the city. As soon as she finished, she came back and started a mobile medical clinic—she got businesses in the city to donate funding and supplies." A sad, wistful smile touched his lips. "In some ways, Angelina was a lot like Colleen."

"How?" Leslie asked softly.

"She had the same strong personality. She was opinionated. Determined." He paused. "When the time came, most of the guys on the team couldn't wait to get home. Angelina and I were married by then, so I volunteered to stay.

"After a while, there was talk about a rebel uprising to overthrow the current government. We were so far from the city that hardly anyone took it seriously. Everyone thought that even if it materialized, we wouldn't be touched by it."

His forearm propped on his upraised knee, Clint stared into the shadowed corner. Watching him, a prickly foreboding crept up Leslie's spine.

"I'd been wanting to come back and visit Rob and Colleen. We had it all planned out, but the rumors were escalating, so I tried to talk Angelina into leaving early and waiting for me here. But she refused. It wasn't just the clinic or her work there. She said she wouldn't leave without me, not with the baby coming—''

A sharp gasp escaped before Leslie could stop it. ''She was pregnant?''

He nodded.

God. Oh, God. Angelina was dead...and their baby along with her? Leslie's stomach gave a sickening churn. She noticed Clint's features had gone taut and rigid, his eyes empty. The ache in her heart turned to an icy chill of dread.

''Things were quiet for a while,'' he went on. ''The baby was due in a month. We'd decided to postpone the trip until after the baby was born. But then the rebels decided to flex a little muscle. They chose our village because they'd heard rumors a high-ranking military official had come to inspect the highway construction. But they'd managed to keep it a secret. One day I was on my way back to the village. I remember thinking there was an odd smell in the air...''

His voice was deep and low; it was so scratchy she hardly recognized it.

''All at once I heard the sound of bullets. Then there was nothing... *nothing*. That was almost worse than hearing the gunfire! I jumped out of the Jeep and started to run. Yet somehow I knew even before I got there that it was too late...and it was. I found Angelina lying face down in the dirt, her arms locked tight around her belly...''

She must have cried out then; she couldn't be sure. The next thing she knew she was gripping Clint's hand tightly between her own, the pressure so intense she was sure she must be hurting him.

But all his pain was on the inside. His features were haunted; his eyes revealed the depths of the emotional scars he had suffered . . . still suffered.

Long painful seconds passed before she was able to say anything. When she did, her tone was as raw as his just moments earlier. "The night that Bonnie came, when I found you sitting in the dark . . . it brought it all back, didn't it?"

He neither agreed nor disagreed. Leaning his head back wearily, he sighed. "I'm not sure I can explain," he said unsteadily. "I know to you I probably seemed callous, maybe even cruel. But Angelina was ecstatic when she found out she was pregnant. All she could talk about was the baby. She wanted a girl, a girl with shiny waist-length black hair that she could tie back with ribbons."

Leslie's mind traveled swiftly back to the night Bonnie had arrived, when she had twined a yellow ribbon through Bonnie's silky black hair. And then later, when Bonnie had extended that very same ribbon to Clint . . .

Leslie almost lost it then. Willpower alone kept her from breaking down. She was heartbreakingly aware of Clint's violent struggle to contain his emotions. When he spoke again, his voice was thick with anguish.

"It hurt to look at Bonnie. I can't deny it. And I don't know if you can ever understand this, but it was easier to look away than to let myself be touched. All I could think of was how much I'd had—and how much I'd lost. That if I'd had a daughter, she might have looked just like Bonnie... *just like Bonnie*."

Through misty eyes, she caught sight of his profile. His face was drawn and strained, full of pain. It was then that she realized...

"You blame yourself," she whispered.

He drew his hand away and stared sightlessly ahead. "I shouldn't have taken any chances," he said tonelessly. "I should have sent her here. I shouldn't have let Angelina talk me into letting her stay. But I did and I lost them both. It was my fault, Leslie, mine—"

"No!" Leslie could stand it no longer. She got down on her knees before him and framed his face with her hands, her eyes beseeching.

"Don't," she begged. "Don't do this to yourself, Clint. You couldn't have known what would happen."

Strong arms wrapped around her and pulled her close. This time it wasn't she who needed Clint, but Clint who needed her. She pressed her face against his and found his lean cheek wet with tears. But it wasn't until their tears joined that she realized she was crying, too.

Clint closed his eyes and gathered her blindly against him, his embrace both fierce and tender. The feel of Leslie's body fused against his unleashed a storm of profound emotion inside him. Holding her like this, heart to heart, cheek to cheek, he experienced a sense of relief so powerful it seemed to rock his soul. It was as if he could feel everything inside him going from dark to light.

He could have stayed like that forever. But all too soon, Leslie drew back. He took quiet note of the regret in her eyes. He heard the deep tremulous breath she took. "Hey," he said softly. "Don't look like that."

Her lips trembled. "I wish now that I hadn't said anything. You shouldn't have had to relive the terrible way that—" she faltered just a little "—that Angelina died. I was wrong to make you tell me, Clint."

"No." There was no mistaking his firm conviction. "I'm glad you did."

She searched his face wonderingly. "You are?"

"I've never been able to talk about Angelina, even to Rob and Colleen." He hesitated. "I won't lie and say this was easy, because it wasn't. But I'm glad it happened, because I think it's finally brought things into focus."

Leslie cringed inside. *Here it comes,* she despaired silently. *He's going to tell me how much he loved Angelina... how he'll always love her.*

"About... Angelina, you mean." Her voice was barely audible. She couldn't look at him.

"Yes."

"I'm glad." She struggled to keep the disappointment from showing on her face. But her smile fell flat. She tried to pull away but he wouldn't let her.

Slipping his knuckles beneath her chin, he guided her eyes to his. "It's also made me come to terms with my feelings for Bonnie," he told her quietly. He paused, and a faint smile lifted his lips as his regard became more penetrating. Leslie sensed he wanted to say more.

She began to tremble, whether from fear or hope, she didn't know. "And?" she whispered.

There was a heartbeat of silence. "And you."

CHAPTER FOURTEEN

"I DON'T KNOW what you mean," Leslie whispered uncertainly.

The pad of Clint's thumb passed over her quivering lips. He feigned a light tone, but it was impossible to keep the edge from his voice. "Remember the other night when I told you you didn't exactly inspire a brotherly reaction in me?"

To his relief, Clint felt her smile tremulously against his thumb. Tenderness and desire washed through him, in equal measure. She hadn't bothered to wipe away her tears, yet she had never looked more beautiful to him.

With his fingertips he swept back the hair from her forehead, savoring the smooth texture of her skin beneath his fingertips. "I want you," he whispered. "I want you so much. I want—" he paused to control the quickening breath evoked by the mere thought "—I want to make love to you."

The throbbing intensity in his voice made her cry all over again. A single tear slid down her cheek. Seeing it, Clint wrapped her tightly in his arms. At the feel of her trembling against him, the storm of emotion inside his heart broke free.

He kissed her then, a gentle, healing kiss that conveyed his feelings far better than words. The salty warmth trapped between their lips sealed the unspoken bond between them.

The instant his mouth claimed hers, everything inside her seemed to weaken. She was tired of fighting the confusion in her heart. Only last night she had lain with this man as intimately as a lover... yet they were not lovers. How would it feel, she wondered giddily, to make love with Clint?

Something gave way deep inside her. She wanted to know, she realized shakily. She wanted it more than she could ever remember wanting anything, and somehow she wasn't surprised by the thought.

His mouth brushed hers again, tentative, flirting and exploring. Their breath mingled. The pressure of the kiss deepened... deepened. A heady desire surged through her. With a breathless cry, she slid her fingers into the midnight darkness of his hair.

Her response was almost unbearably sweet. Clint's heart seemed to swell with the powerful emotion that seized him. She roused protective, possessive, and starkly raw feelings he'd thought were dead and buried. She was so sweet, so vulnerable, yet he'd never wanted anyone more.

Her breasts lay full and ripe against him. He was achingly conscious of the tempting swell. The loose neckline of her top offered tantalizing glimpses of the smooth, honey-colored flesh he yearned to plunder with lips and hands. All that was masculine within him hungered for all that was feminine within her; he ached with the need to bury himself inside her and lose himself in her softness.

"Leslie," he said into her mouth. He dragged his mouth from hers and stared down at her. His fingers slid down the length of her throat.

The urgency of his touch made her breathless. She didn't flinch from it, though. Wordless messages passed between them, communicating the depth of their need, the longing they could no longer deny.

She seized his hand and carried it to her cheek. "Don't leave me," she whispered. "Please don't leave me."

Trembling lips nuzzled the warm roughness of his palm. Clint's heart nearly stopped when he felt the moist heat of her breath, the gentleness of her lips as she pressed a kiss there.

He was lost. The words went through him, inside him, transforming everything from dark to light. The heat rising in his body spoke of a need long denied, but the hunger winding through him was far more than physical. Leslie was the one woman on earth who could cleanse his soul from the demons of the past, and he was never more certain of it than he was at this moment.

He eased back on an elbow and pulled her down beside him, then stretched his length against hers. He loved the way her fingertips slid down his nape, then tugged him closer with gentle insistence.

"How's your leg?" she whispered.

Their lips almost touched, but not quite. Somehow it only heightened the rampage of desire that thundered in his body.

"Never better." His outward calm was deceiving; inside he was trembling.

"Are you sure? I'd hate to think I was causing you any pain."

He watched as she tipped her chin to see him better. The slender column of her neck glowed enticingly. He wanted to dip his tongue into the mysterious hollow there and taste the wild flutter of her pulse...and he promised himself he would.

"If I'm in pain," he found himself teasing, "it's because you won't stop talking long enough for me to kiss you."

An impish light appeared in her eyes. "Is that all you want to do? Kiss me?"

Clint's laugh was husky and breathless. "Among other things."

"Then maybe I'd better stop talking and let you get started."

"That's one of the things I like best about you," he murmured. "The fact that we're on the same wavelength."

His head dipped. Leslie's breath caught when his tongue came out and flicked across the skin stretched across the base of her throat. She felt him smile; he was still smiling when his lips came up to close over hers.

His kiss was sweet and long, both gentle and fierce and breath-stealingly thorough. She never knew where it ended and the next began. She loved the taste of his mouth on hers, the intimate stroke of his tongue curling around hers, the faint woodsy smell that clung to his skin. Most of all, she thrilled to the full, straining evidence of his need nestled tightly against her thighs.

Unable to stop herself, her fingers flitted to the buttons of his shirt. Not until the last slid through its prison did she realize Clint had been pleasurably intent on the same task.

Every nerve ending in her body was screaming as the buttons slipped free. His lips never left hers as the lightweight cotton slowly parted; the front clasp of her bra was found and released. By the time his hands pushed both aside impatiently, her heart had forgotten how to beat.

This time his kiss was tinged with a dark desperation, flooding both of them with a raging heat. She nearly moaned aloud when at last he laid claim to the naked bounty of her breasts. Fireworks burst inside her as his thumbs feathered over and over the straining summit in a tauntingly evocative rhythm.

Unable to stop himself, Clint crushed her tight against his bare chest. Her nipples stabbed into his chest, quivering points of desire. He closed his eyes and dragged his mouth away from hers, battling for a control he was precariously close to losing.

"Oh, Leslie." He released her name on a ragged sigh and rested his forehead against hers. His laugh was shaky. "This is a hell of a time to realize it, but this is something I hadn't planned on...."

The pained tenderness in his voice tugged at her heartstrings. Her mind groped fuzzily for a date only a few days past. "It's...I should be okay," she whispered shyly.

"Are you sure?" He braced himself above her and slipped his knuckles beneath her chin.

Her fingers stole to his cheek, thrilling to the sandpaper roughness of his skin. Her hand slid back and curled around his nape, silently urging him closer. Her breathlessly whispered "yes" was trapped somewhere in the back of his throat as she wordlessly offered her mouth. Their lips never parted as she slowly peeled his shirt away from his shoulders as he had done for her only moments before.

Their kiss caught fire and raged out of control. All too soon they both lay naked, free of the restrictions posed by their clothing.

But with one barrier down, up soared another.

All of a sudden, doubt swelled like a rising tide inside her. Shadows chased in her mind. In her rational mind she knew that Dennis's betrayal was not her fault. But her tormented heart gave her no peace. A part of her couldn't quite banish the thought that Dennis must have found her lacking.... Would Clint as well?

Clint's gaze was riveted to her profile. He stared down at her, at misty blue eyes that refused to meet his, at dewy soft lips that trembled ever so slightly.

She was shaking, he realized as he drew her against him, but not half as much as he was. He kissed her as gently, as tenderly as he possibly could, putting all his tumultuous feelings into that one sweet caress.

"You're so pretty," he whispered when at last he raised his head. "Here." He brushed the velvety fullness of her lips with his. "And here." His knuckles grazed the pouting upthrust of her breasts. "And here." A lazy finger tormented them both as it stole down the concave hollow of her belly, clear to her dimpled navel and beyond.

His voice caused her to tremble all over again. Warmth unfolded like budding sunshine within her. It was just what she wanted to hear. More, it was just what she *needed* to hear.

Time stood still as he pulled back once more to stare at her. His eyes were as warm as whiskey and just as potent as he feasted on the bare body that lay open to him. His gaze was dark and searing; she felt its fiery stroke clear to her soul.

"So pretty," he murmured again.

The air between them grew close and heated. Her doubt evaporated like dew before the blazing morning sun. Her senses climbed to a screaming pitch of awareness as he lowered his head. She clung to his arms as his mouth coasted with slow heat down her neck.

His warm breath fluttered across the pink bareness of her breast. Heat unfurled within her like the showering rays of the sun. She wanted to die of pleasure when his mouth closed over the straining peak. His tongue swirled around the quivering nub, over and over, tasting and teasing until at last he drew the dark center into his mouth and initiated a mind-spinning tugging that threatened to drive her mad. Deep in the pit of her belly, a spiraling heat began to spread.

But suddenly Leslie wanted more than to lie passively and reap the rewards of his hands and mouth on her flesh. She desperately wanted to give Clint the same searing pleasure he was giving her.

Shyly, gently, she stroked her thumbs over the jutting hardness of his collarbone. With growing boldness her fingertips glided over the veins that traced along his arms, savoring the feel of the knotted hardness of muscle and bone. The hair on his chest and abdomen was like a dark shadow; it fascinated her. She splayed her hands wide against his chest and stroked in ever-growing circles, loving the wiry rasp of hair against her palms.

At the first tentative touch of her hands on his flesh, the bonds of restraint surrounding Clint slipped away. It was all he could do to stop from sweeping her beneath him and losing himself in her body. With delicate demand, her taunting palm skimmed the rigid fullness of his manhood. He gritted his teeth against the incredible sensations bombarding him. When he could stand her tormenting touch no more, he gasped out his pleasure and sought her mouth once more.

His lips were fiery, all-consuming, his hands both daring and gentle. His fingertips scaled the inside of her thighs, brushing the secret cove of her womanhood with a maddeningly elusive touch that made her want to pound her fists in frustration. She nearly cried out in relief when at last his fingers slid down to cup her downy thatch, searching out and discovering the honeyed cleft with a breath-stealing rhythm that shattered her senses.

"Clint—" She cried out against his throat.

He rejoiced in the piercing need he heard in his name. The sound filled his heart near to bursting. He wanted to tell her... so much. The words burned like flames deep inside his chest. But he wasn't sure Leslie was ready. Yet when he lifted his head, he knew he couldn't hide the naked honesty of his feelings. "Look at me," he whispered.

Her eyes flickered open. She stared directly into his eyes, entranced by the promise she saw there. Fierce desire rained down on her, but it was tempered with a tenderness that made her feel beautiful and cherished as she'd never felt before.

His fingers skimmed her temple, smoothing the wild tangle of curls. "I want you so much I'm shaking with it," he breathed.

"So am I," she confided breathlessly, and knew it for the truth. She could feel the pulsing heat of him searing the gates of her womanhood. The piercing emptiness inside her was like nothing she'd ever felt before. She needed to be filled. She needed to be made whole.

She needed Clint...as she had never needed anyone before in her life.

She didn't realize she had spoken aloud until the words spilled from her throat in a soft, pleading cry. Then suddenly she couldn't stop.

Her arms encircled his shoulders. "I need you, Clint." Her fingers knotted in his hair. She clung to him desperately. "I need you to hold me...I need you to love me...."

I need you. The words washed through him, inside his soul and out. What little control he had disintegrated in that instant.

"Leslie." His voice was raw; it sounded as if it were wrung from deep inside him. "Oh, God, Leslie, I..." He framed her face in his hands. He had only to turn his head a fraction of an inch...their lips met and clung.

And in that timeless moment between one breath and the next, he claimed her body...at the same instant she claimed him...heart, mind and soul.

It was a joining that shook them both. There was no turning back now, for either of them. His hands slid down to cradle her buttocks, completing the journey and bringing them both home. She loved the weight of his body, heavy with need, tense with desire; she loved the filling strength of him inside her, hotly imbedded in the silken clasp of her body, flexing and tightening now as he began the sinuous motion of love....

His hands wound through her hair, fusing their mouths together even as their bodies were already sealed. Each parting and melding of their bodies was soul-wrenching. His deep, scorching thrusts echoed in the chambers of her heart. Her hips blindly sought his, again and again. Her breath quickened ... and so did the tempo of their loving. Release came in a white-hot explosion of sparks; lightning streaked through her over and over.

And as she drifted back to earth, wrapped in the sheltering security of Clint's arms, for the first time in a long, long while, she was on top of the world. She had never felt closer to Clint, never more a part of him than at this moment. She felt whole, and special. She felt needed.

She even felt ... loved.

EARLY THAT MORNING, Clint lay on his back, one arm tucked behind his head, the other curled loosely around the woman whose body lay heavy and relaxed against his side, her breathing deep and even.

For the second morning in a row, he couldn't take his eyes from her. Watching her like this, he felt a hundred different sensations stir to life inside him. Though long dormant, the storm of emotions sweeping through him was not unfamiliar ... and certainly not unwelcome.

With Leslie beside him like this, he felt contented. Possessive. Fulfilled and satisfied in a way that had very little to do with the incredible physical satiation she had given him last night . . . and everything to do with the love that squeezed his heart to overflowing.

Sunlight winked through the draperies, bathing her face in a glow that was almost ethereal. Drawn by a compelling need to touch her, he trailed his fingers along the sloping line of her jaw. His dark gaze softened, absorbing every detail of her features. The flush on her cheeks exactly matched the rosy tint of her lips; her mouth was damp and parted and looked as if she'd just been well and thoroughly kissed. An almost painful ache tightened his gut. The urge to bend down and sample the sweet enticement of her lips was tempting beyond reason.

But just as he was about to give in, the winged arch of honey-colored brows drew together in a slight frown. Clint found himself overcome by a well of tenderness. Even in sleep, she looked lovely and expressive—and so damned vulnerable it made him hurt inside just thinking about it.

It was sheer agony to drag himself from the bed, but that's exactly what he did. There was no telling when Maryann might show up with Tess and Brian, and the last thing he wanted was to embarrass Leslie. He showered quickly and changed clothes in his bungalow, then returned to the house. Bonnie was still asleep when he checked on her. Across the hall, it appeared Leslie had just slipped into her robe.

Somehow he summoned an offhand air he was far from feeling. "Hi," he said, and stepped into the room.

At his casual greeting, she glanced up hurriedly. He had startled her, he realized. He was both amused and faintly dismayed by her reaction. He adored the rosy blush that crept into her cheeks at his unwavering regard. But she sat on the edge of the bed, poised as if she wanted to leap up and run away.

He advanced closer. "What is it?" he asked.

She glanced in his direction, but her eyes swung from the ceiling to the wall behind his shoulder, everywhere but to him. He saw her lips try to emulate a smile, saw them tremble and fail.

It didn't take much to realize what was on her mind. "Is it last night?"

Eyes lowered to her hands, she nodded.

Clint wanted nothing more than to take her in his arms, but he wasn't sure he dared. Instead he sat down next to her, close but without touching her. "Are you embarrassed?"

She shook her head.

"Ashamed?" He held his breath and waited. He didn't want the passion they had shared to come between them. Damn, but he didn't.

"No," she whispered. She looked at him then, and his heart contracted at the plea he saw there.

The need to touch her was all-consuming. He couldn't fight it anymore. He pulled her into his arms with gentle insistence. She responded by nestling into the musky hollow of his shoulder. The tiny sigh she gave tore at his heart.

"What then?" he asked very gently. A sudden thought struck him and he cringed inside. Yet he knew he had to ask. "Are you sorry it happened?"

His tone wasn't rough, but there was an edge to it that didn't go unnoticed by Leslie. She drew back, her gaze meeting his. They stared at each other, the muscles in the arms that held her suddenly rigid, his jaw locked tight. He didn't regret that they had made love. He couldn't stand the thought that Leslie might feel differently.

At last she shook her head. "No," she whispered. But her expression was shadowed.

There was a moment's silence. He felt the deep, calming breath she took. "At least I don't think I am...." She bit her lip. "Look, I know I'm not making any sense, but last night could...change things between us."

"That doesn't have to be bad," he said with a tiny smile.

"I know," she said quickly. "But it...oh, I don't know. I know this will probably sound crazy to you, but it scares me somehow."

"Do you think I don't feel the same way?" he asked gently. "When we first met, I was drawn to you, but it was because I sensed you had been through hell, too. And it wasn't so much a feeling of attraction as a feeling of—kinship."

With a forefinger he tipped her chin to his, reading all her fears, all her uncertainty. "But something did happen, Leslie. It makes my head spin just thinking about it." His voice went very low. "And yes, it scares the hell out of me to think that you made me feel so much...so quickly. But it hurts a hell of a lot more to think we need an excuse for what happened last night."

Leslie inhaled sharply. She wanted so much...too much? She wanted to believe that Clint cared about her; she wanted it with all her heart. But Dennis's betrayal had robbed her of her faith—and not only in herself, but in others, as well. She was afraid to believe . . . to trust in her feelings . . . and his.

She didn't know what to say—and so she said nothing.

For Clint, it was a poignantly bittersweet moment. Watching her, seeing the fear and doubt that crowded her mind and heart, he was achingly aware of the turmoil inside her.

He tipped her face to his, his look deep and intense, yet so achingly tender she felt a burning rush of tears. "Hey," he chided gently. "Don't look like that. It'll be okay, you'll see. We'll just take it one day at a time."

She buried her face against his chest and clung to him. A scalding tear wet the hollow of his throat; he felt as if it seeped clear to his heart.

He stroked her back, the motion of his hand long and soothing. She was willing to accept his comfort, he realized with a pang, but he wasn't sure she was ready to accept his love. He knew it was connected with the way her ex-husband had hurt and used her. In an anguished kind of way, he could even appreciate her feelings.

But it didn't stop the hollow band of tightness from creeping around his chest. He wondered . . . would his future be as empty as these past three years?

His eyes were cloudy as he stared off across the room. It was then that a slight sound captured his attention. Bonnie stood, in the doorway, a forlorn little figure dressed in white. Her eyes were wide and distressed; she looked as frightened and uncertain as Leslie had only moments ago.

He found himself torn between the trembling woman in his arms and the small figure in the doorway. His hesitation was fractional, but in the second that he took to consider, whatever choice he might have made was taken from him.

Bonnie's bare feet carried her noiselessly across the floor. Leslie's head came up at the same instant the little girl stopped before them.

With a gasp Leslie straightened and withdrew from the shelter of his arms. She lifted a hand toward her face, but Bonnie's small fingers were already there. Her little brow pleated in a frown, Bonnie reached up to touch the moisture on Leslie's cheek.

"No, Lee," she whispered, her eyes huge and dark. "No cry."

Leslie made a sound that was a half sob, half laugh. She pulled Bonnie up into her lap and wrapped the little girl tightly in her arms. "I won't cry anymore," she promised. "See?" She buried her chin in Bonnie's silky black waves and hugged her fiercely.

Her tremulous smile tore into Clint with the force of a lance. At the sight of those two heads nestled together—one dark, the other much fairer—something twisted inside him. How, he wondered helplessly, was it possible to feel so much pleasure along with so much pain?

He rose to his feet, loath to withdraw, just as loath to stay. He couldn't look away as Bonnie slipped her arms around Leslie's neck. "*Te quiero,* Lee," she whispered with shining eyes. "*Te quiero.*"

Leslie's arms tightened around the child. Over the top of Bonnie's head, her eyes sought Clint's. "*Te quiero,*" she repeated softly. "What does it mean?"

Clint paused for the space of a heartbeat. *"Te quiero,"* he said quietly, his voice very low, "it means I love you."

And he wondered, even as he said the words, if Leslie knew that he meant them . . . and he wondered if they would ever be enough.

CHAPTER FIFTEEN

THEY HAD JUST FINISHED dinner later that day when Rob phoned with the news that Colleen's father had passed away. As Rob told Clint, they planned to stay for the funeral, and perhaps a few days after to be with Colleen's mother. But at the latest, they intended to be home by the following Sunday.

The next few days found Leslie caught squarely between heaven and hell. First of all, there was Clint. She loved waking up beside him, though he was always careful to rise before Brian and Tess awoke. She liked seeing his wet towel draped next to hers in the bathroom; she savored the intimacy of tucking Brian, Tess and Bonnie into bed at night.

Most of all, she treasured the long blissful hours that followed. They talked; they laughed. They made love....

But a tiny voice inside insisted that she was sidestepping the truth. Was it wrong to want to seize the moment and hold it close to her heart? Being with Clint like this was...almost heaven. But what they shared was still so new and tenuous. She didn't want to clutter up the precious way he made her feel with whys and wherefores.

She wanted to pretend that this time with Clint would last forever, for it only reaffirmed what she had already known, deep within her soul. She wanted a home. A family. Above all, a husband and children to love and love her in return.

But their time together was measured. Leslie couldn't fool herself any longer, the way she had since the first night they had made love. Clint had spent the last few mornings at his office in San Diego. On Friday he was scheduled for what he hoped would be his last appointment with the doctor.

The thought plunged her into turmoil. Did it really matter whether she stayed here in San Diego, or went back to San Francisco? Clint would not be there; that was unalterable. He would not be with *her*. He would be hundreds of miles away in Alaska. And then God only knew where else. . . .

Then there was Bonnie. It made her heart catch to see Bonnie with Clint. Where Bonnie was concerned, the ice around his heart was melting. He was sweet and tender and gentle with the little girl, but his growing feelings for Bonnie were not without cost. Whenever her gaze chanced to rest upon the two of them in unguarded moments, Leslie knew she didn't imagine the pain in his eyes. He fought a silent battle against bitterness and hurt.

But Leslie was busy fighting her own private battle with regard to Bonnie. Each day that Bonnie crawled into her arms, her small body sweet and warm, her enchantment with the little girl grew by leaps and bounds. She couldn't stand the thought of Bonnie with the McCalls—or any other family, for that matter. Nor did it help when Fran phoned to say that the McCalls had requested another visit with Bonnie. The short time they were there was agonizing for her.

Her mood was pensive late Friday morning. Clint had left a few minutes earlier so that he could stop by his boss's office on his way to the doctor. Brian was at Tim's house. The only thing that kept her melancholy mood at bay was the sound of Tess chattering in the other room. She and Bonnie were busy with their coloring books. Tess was happily reciting shapes and colors to Bonnie, while Bonnie dutifully repeated all that she said.

She was in the laundry room folding towels on the worktable when Tess burst through the door, a wad of papers clutched in her hands. "Me and Bonnie drew some pictures!" she cried. "Wanna see?"

Bonnie's oval face peeked out from behind Tess. Earlier Leslie had parted her gleaming hair down the middle and pulled it into two long braids, as she had yesterday. Bonnie looked adorable, and the style had prompted Brian to announce yesterday that she looked like Laura on *Little House on the Prairie*.

Setting the laundry basket aside, Leslie turned to the two eager faces at her side. They both giggled as she oohed and aahed over each one—mostly flowers and trees. Tess proudly pointed out one that she had done of herself, Brian, her mother and father. Finally Leslie came to the last one. It depicted three stick figures, a wobbly looking house and huge yellow sun in the background.

Biting back a smile, Leslie glanced at Tess. "Aha," she murmured. "I'll bet this is you and Brian and Bonnie."

"Nope." Tess shook her head vehemently. "Bonnie drew that one."

On the verge of sliding it to the rear of the stack, Leslie paused. She pulled Bonnie close to her side. "This is good, Bonnie," she praised warmly. "Very good."

Bonnie's dark eyes sparkled with pleasure.

Drawing in hand, Leslie crouched down beside her. She pointed to one of the larger stick figures. "Who is this?" she asked, enunciating the words carefully.

Bonnie grinned. *"Papá."*

Leslie's heart stood still. All at once it clicked. There were three figures, and one was smaller than the other two. Surely Bonnie hadn't... "And this?" She indicated the next figure.

The little girl poked her playfully in the chest. "Lee!"

All at once Leslie couldn't take her eyes off the third—and smallest—of the three figures. "And what about this one?" Her finger moved slightly; her voice was as unsteady as her smile. "Who is this?"

Her little chest seemed to swell with pride. "Bonnie!" she cried happily. Warm, bare arms slid around her neck. She hugged Leslie as fiercely as her small body would allow.

For a moment all Leslie could do was cling to the little girl, caught up in the sweetness of the moment. Tears misted her vision as the realization poured through her. Bonnie had done the same as Tess. She had drawn the three of them—herself, Clint and Leslie—as a family.

Leslie's heart began to bleed. For herself. For Clint. But mostly for Bonnie. Because a family was the one thing the three of them could never be....

Her throat was so clogged with emotion she could hardly speak. "Bonnie." She whispered her name. She drew back to frame Bonnie's face with hands that weren't entirely steady. *"Te quiero,"* she told her raggedly. "Bonnie, I love you. I love you so much. And I wish you *were* my daughter. God, how I wish you were mine! I'd never let anything hurt you again." It didn't matter that Bonnie couldn't possibly understand all she was saying; what mattered was that she knew she was loved.

It was then that Leslie realized she would never be satisfied if she simply sat back and let the McCalls take Bonnie. And didn't she owe it to herself—and Bonnie—to at least *try* for custody?

Her thoughts were a strange jumble of hope and fear as she went through the afternoon. She didn't know what would happen with her and Clint—if what they had was more than fleeting. But where Bonnie was concerned, if there was any way at all the two of them could be together, then she was willing to give it a chance.

A fighting chance.

LESLIE WAS RINSING a stalk of celery in the sink when the back door slammed later that afternoon. The breeze blew a rush of hot air inside the room; an even hotter glow of anticipation settled in the pit of her stomach. She hid a secret smile, knowing what was about to happen. Footsteps echoed across the floor behind her. Strong fingers closed around her upper arms. She felt herself bodily turned and brought up against a hard male form.

She was still smiling long moments later when Clint finally released her lips. He looked her up and down when he saw that she still clutched the celery stalk in one hand, a paring knife in the other.

"What is this?" he teased. "Assault with a deadly weapon?"

She wrinkled her nose at him. "I was about to start dinner, and the Stuart specialty happens to be the number one request. Besides," she added pertly, "if anything is deadly around here, it's you."

A roguishly arched eyebrow tilted further. "You think so?"

"I know so," he was informed brashly.

"I beg to differ with you then." He pulled the celery and knife from her hand and proceeded to show her exactly what he meant, taking her mouth in a long unbroken kiss that sent her spinning away on a cloud of pleasure.

He pulled back, his features soft and tender. "You see?" He imprisoned her hand with his own where it lay clasped against his chest. Beneath her fingertips, his heart beat as rapid a drumbeat as hers. "Lethal," he murmured, eyes fixed on her mouth. "Absolutely lethal."

Leslie's laugh was husky. Things had been so good these last few days. She wanted it to go on and on. Yet even as her mind filled with wistful imaginings, she couldn't help the faint uneasiness that crept through her. She wasn't looking forward to telling Clint of her decision about Bonnie; the truth was, she wasn't entirely sure of his reaction.

"How did the visit to the doctor go?" Outwardly she was calm, but inside she was a quivering mass of uncertainty.

A faint frown had appeared between Clint's dark eyebrows. His slight smile never made it to his eyes as he watched her pull away from him. "Smooth as butter."

She paused, one hand on the handle of the refrigerator. "So you don't have to go back again?" She marveled that her tone was so even. "He gave you the all-clear to go back on the job full-time?"

He nodded. Their eyes met. Leslie was the first to look away, though she despised herself for doing so. She'd known this was coming, she'd known it for days now. So why did she feel as if everything were breaking loose inside her?

She attempted a smile. "You must be ecstatic—no more cabin fever." Her laugh was falsely bright. "And no more having to play chauffeur—"

His fingers around her upper arm crammed the words back in her throat. "We need to talk, Leslie."

He searched her face, his expression so penetrating and intent she wanted to close her eyes against it.

"I need to start dinner."

She tried to pull away, but he wouldn't let her. "Dinner can wait—"

The back door burst open. Brian rushed in from outside. "They're home!" he shouted. "Mom and Dad are home!"

The house was suddenly buzzing with commotion. Brian flew out again, with Tess right behind him. The sound of laughter and a deep male voice drifted through the open door. Leslie pulled away, almost grateful for the interruption. She didn't see the tight white lines that appeared beside Clint's mouth.

There was no sign of anything out of the ordinary, though, when Rob and Colleen traipsed in from outside. Greetings, hugs and kisses were exchanged. Colleen looked tired but glad to be home. Tess was anxious to show Bonnie's stitches, just as anxious to see if they'd brought back presents, while Brian, his eyes vibrant, was busy relaying every last detail about his baseball games.

Leslie didn't have to bother with dinner after all. Colleen collapsed on the sofa and sent Rob out for hamburgers. Clint's manner was easy and relaxed, but Leslie wasn't fooled. She noticed his eyes, dark and enigmatic, lingering on her more than once during the meal. She wondered what he had wanted to tell her; she sensed it had been important. A part of her was relieved she hadn't had to grapple with whatever he'd been about to reveal. But despite the knot of tension within her, the atmosphere was warm and comfortable.

It was during one of the few lulls that she decided the time was right to tell them about her recent decision. Clearing her throat, she glanced around the table. "In case anyone's interested, I have a little announcement to make."

All eyes turned toward her.

"I've decided it's time I made some changes in my life—" she smiled at Colleen "—and one of those changes involves pulling up roots in San Francisco."

Colleen's eyes widened like a child's at Christmas. "You mean all that talking I did actually did the trick? You've decided to move here after all?"

Leslie nodded.

Her friend jumped to her feet and threw her arms around her. "Leslie, that's great! You won't regret it, I know you won't. Oh, it'll be such fun being together again. Phone calls are fine, but it's just not the same as being *with* someone!"

Leslie laughed shakily, touched by Colleen's excitement. "This hinges on being able to find a teaching job, though. And then, of course, I'll have to find a house...."

Colleen waved airily. "You can stay here while you do all that. In fact, we insist. But you can worry about that when the time comes. The important thing is getting you moved down here."

Leslie's glance conveyed a silent thank you, but her mind was already jumping forward. "There is one other thing, though," she murmured.

Colleen chuckled. "There's more?"

Leslie nodded. Her gaze slid unerringly to Clint. He was watching her, the merest hint of a curious smile on his lips. The flicker of warmth in his eyes was reassuring, especially since his reaction was the one she feared the most. She'd come this far, however. There was no turning back. And, she thought determinedly, there would be no changing her mind.

She slipped her arm around the little girl at her side. Bonnie looked up at her with shining eyes, and Leslie felt her chest swell with love and tenderness.

"I want to be Bonnie's mother," she said softly. "I want to adopt her."

IT WAS A LONG TIME LATER before the four adults left the table. Leslie told Colleen and Rob about the other couple—the McCalls—who had also expressed an interest in Bonnie.

"I don't know if I can explain it." She paused, her voice low and steady. "To me it's not a question of Bonnie being right for the McCalls. It's more a feeling that the McCalls just aren't right for Bonnie. I just can't shake the feeling that Bonnie would be just a convenience, another toy to add to their list of possessions...like a house or a new car. And Bonnie needs so much more than that. Besides—" she bit her lip and glanced around the table "—I felt close to Bonnie right from the start. What I feel now is even more special. More important, it's not one-sided. I know Bonnie feels the same way about me."

Colleen glanced at Rob. "She's right, you know. Bonnie turned to her that very first night we brought her home."

He smiled, shaking his head in remembrance. "That's for sure. She didn't waste any time at all choosing you as her protector."

Leslie felt the excitement mounting within her, but she wasn't sure she dared hope too much for fear of being disappointed. "Will it make any difference that I would be a single mother?"

Rob shook his head. "It might have once, but not anymore."

Leslie took a deep breath. "Tell me the truth," she said evenly. "What are my chances of adopting Bonnie? Do I have any kind of a shot at all?"

Rob's smile faded all too soon. "Placing a child like Bonnie usually isn't easy," he admitted. "Besides the language barrier, we won't know for certain what her physical limitations will be until after her surgery—

and maybe even longer. I'm sure Fran thinks we're lucky to have a couple like the McCalls taking a second look at Bonnie." He paused, running a hand through his dark hair. "That's not to say that you don't have a lot going for you, too," he added quickly. "I'd say your chances are fairly good."

Her expression grew cloudy. It wasn't so much what he had said, as what he didn't say. "But not as good as they might be if the McCalls weren't in the picture," she finished for him.

His quiet tone matched hers. "I'm afraid so."

For an instant she sat very still, fighting to quell her silent despair. Oblivious to Rob and Colleen's sympathetic gaze, she refused to be meekly accepting.

And suddenly Leslie felt very, very determined. She didn't want to let herself down. More, she didn't want to let Bonnie down.

She might yet win custody of Bonnie—or perhaps she might not. But at least she would have the satisfaction of knowing she had given it her all.

Stiffening her spine, she glanced at Rob and Colleen, a grim little smile on her lips. "Then it looks like I'd better get to work and start looking for a job—and a place to live if I'm going to give Bonnie the home she deserves."

Colleen didn't know when she'd been more proud of her friend. She reached over and squeezed her hand. "You know we're behind you on this all the way," she said quietly. "If it means anything, I think you're doing the right thing—" her gaze slipped down the hall where Bonnie lay sleeping "—for both of you."

Leslie did know, and her expression betrayed both her gratitude and her affection. "Thanks," she said softly. "It's nice to know I can count on you."

Clint was another story.

He had been strangely quiet since her announcement—or perhaps it wasn't so strange after all. Nor could Leslie deceive herself. She had been reluctant to look directly at Clint, afraid of what she would see.

After Rob and Colleen had said goodnight, Leslie rose and dumped out the muddy remains of her coffee. She felt the weight of his stare drilling into her back as she carefully rinsed the sink. It took every ounce of courage she possessed to turn and meet his eyes. Oddly he was the first to look away.

He got to his feet a fraction of a second later. "Walk me out," was all he said.

His half smile seemed forced. Leslie wanted to close her eyes and shut out the sight, but she couldn't take her eyes from his face as she moved numbly across the floor to join him. When he wished, Clint had the uncanny ability to school his features so that his expression betrayed no trace of emotion whatsoever. At that moment, she heartily resented him for it.

He didn't take her hand, weaving their fingers warmly together, as she expected...as she wanted. He let her precede him through the door; their bodies never touched.

Dread gathered into a tight, heavy coil in the pit of Leslie's stomach. By the time they reached his bungalow, her insides felt as if they were wired and ready to explode.

At his door, it was she who broke the silence. "You don't approve, do you?" she asked.

His eyes flickered. "Of what? Your decision to try to adopt Bonnie?"

She nodded, wishing she could see him better. His voice, like his expression, gave her no clue to his thoughts. She fought a deep, despairing hurt as the emotional distance between them yawned wider and wider.

She had no way of knowing that Clint was embroiled in a battle that was just as fierce. The taste of self-loathing was like acid in his mouth. He had borne witness to the bond forged between Leslie and Bonnie. He had seen it grow stronger with each passing day. He should have expected Leslie's decision to try to raise Bonnie as her own; he should have seen it coming.

Foolishly... oh, so foolishly, he hadn't.

He didn't know what to say to her. He knew Leslie wanted his blessing, for lack of a better word. He was also aware it cost her no small amount of pride to confront him point-blank, but this was no less difficult for him.

Where Bonnie was concerned, he fought an almost constant tug-of-war. There were so many conflicting feelings rolling away inside him. Her unquestioning surrender made his heart ache. Her blind acceptance of him made him feel guilty as sin. It still tore him up inside to touch Bonnie; Leslie couldn't know how it filled him with nearly as much pain as pleasure.

Perhaps if she hadn't caught him off guard, this might have been easier. But she had, and he just didn't know how to deal with it. And so the words he knew she longed to hear just wouldn't come.

The merest glimmer of a smile touched his lips—but not his eyes. "I'll admit you surprised the heck out of me," he murmured.

Her gaze sharpened. "Why don't you just say it, Clint?" She faced him almost defiantly, her eyes flashing fire. "You just don't approve. You don't think I should try to adopt Bonnie!"

He stared at her, thinking of all the times she had struck him as fragile and vulnerable. She didn't know it, but she was the one who was strong.

"I didn't say that," he began.

"You don't have to!" she cried. "Do you think I can't tell?" She clamped her hands around her arms, hating herself for the stinging rush of tears. She stared at him, her eyes both accusing and pleading. "Damn you, Clint Stuart! Why do you think I dreaded telling you? But I kept hoping I was wrong... I—I just don't understand you! You care for Bonnie, I know you do! How can you not want what's best for her?"

It was not so much a question as an accusation; the words struck a blow so powerful that he flinched. "I *do* want what's best for Bonnie," he said hoarsely, shaken to the core that she could think him so cruel. "But you're putting words in my mouth that don't belong there. I wasn't lying when I said you caught me by surprise. And yes, maybe I should have realized you'd want to adopt Bonnie, but I didn't. I didn't, and it's going to take a little time to get used to the idea."

He reached for her but she stepped back, deliberately avoiding his touch. Clint's jaw tightened. His mood was suddenly vile. All at once he felt like shoving his hand through the wall.

"Look," he said abruptly. "We need to talk, Leslie—really talk. About Bonnie. About us. But this isn't the right time, and it's certainly not the place." He thrust his fingers through the dark hair on his forehead. "Besides, there's something else I need to tell you, and I suspect you're not going to like it."

The screaming pitch of her nerves wound tighter. She stiffened, her body taut with expectancy. "Tell me."

"I have to catch a flight early tomorrow morning."

Shock held her motionless, but only for an instant. "You're leaving?"

"I have to do some last-minute supervision at a site in Washington. The lead engineer was called home on a family emergency. I was available, so I'm being sent in his place."

The night was still and silent. Hundreds of diamond-bright stars glittered against the midnight velvet of the night sky. A warm breeze undulated around their figures, but Leslie suddenly felt cold as death inside.

"Why didn't you tell me?" Her voice was choked. As hard as she tried, she couldn't keep her hurt from showing.

"I was about to when Rob and Colleen came home." His edge of frustration was gone. He stepped closer, wanting to hold her, wanting to touch her. . . .

Unable to stop himself, he lifted his hand and slowly guided a strand of honey-gold behind her ear. He let his fingertips glide across the smoothness of her cheek, loving the downy texture of her skin and wondering how the hell he would get through the next couple of weeks without her.

His voice stole quietly through the silence. "I didn't know before this afternoon, Leslie, I swear. If I had, I would have told you."

Leslie stood as if paralyzed, feeling herself come apart inside at the gentleness of his touch. She wanted to rage and shout, even as she wanted to plead and cry that he stay with her—and not just today. Tomorrow. The next day. For a lifetime ... for always.

There was so much pain swirling around inside her, she didn't know which was worse—the agony of knowing Clint was leaving, or not knowing what, if anything, would happen when he returned.

The weight of his hands came down her shoulders, searing her with his heat. It was a touch that reminded her of long, magical nights spent with his arms locked tightly around her, the sound of his heart echoing strongly beneath her ear. She had felt safe then, safe and sheltered and secure. She'd have given anything to believe they could go on like that forever....

But Leslie wasn't sure she believed in forever. Not anymore ... And so she mourned her silly, childish hopes. She mourned her foolish, foolish heart.

Clint's hands tightened on her shoulders. "Don't look like that," he said roughly. "We'll get all this straightened out when I get back."

"And who knows when that will be!" she flung at him.

"I won't be gone long, Leslie. A week. Two at the most."

When she said nothing, Clint cursed the circumstances that had brought them both to this point. There was so much he wanted to say, yet he wasn't sure

Leslie was ready to hear it. He bitterly regretted that they hadn't had tonight alone, as he had hoped. But he hadn't known that Colleen and Rob would be arriving home, and he hadn't counted on Leslie revealing her plans for Bonnie. That, too, was something he would have to come to grips with . . . and soon.

"Come with me to the airport tomorrow."

Leslie's eyes widened. She drew a sharp breath.

Her reaction wasn't lost on Clint. He increased the pressure on her shoulders. "Please, Leslie. Please…"

His tautly voiced plea cut her deeply. Her thoughts were wild and just a little panicky. Did he really expect her to watch him walk out of her life, not knowing when—if ever—he might appear again?

Speech was beyond her right now. All she could do was shake her head in wordless denial, utterly miserable and unable to keep from showing it.

He didn't ask again, but his eyes never left her face. "Then kiss me goodbye," he whispered.

There was no time to protest, no time for anything at all. She had one glimpse of his face just before his head descended. His features were etched with emotion, his eyes as dark and tormented as she knew her own must be. She had the strangest sensation that Clint was just as confused as she was. Yet she feared that if he touched her—if he kissed her—she would shatter into a million pieces.

Her palms came up to splay against his chest, but whether she intended to resist she never knew. She was suddenly clinging to him, her fingers digging into the taut muscles of his shoulders. There was a kind of wild desperation in his kiss that mirrored her own chaotic response. He held her so tightly she could feel his belt buckle digging into her stomach, the roughness of his pants chafing the tender skin of her thighs. And yet it wasn't close enough, not nearly enough for either of them.

His breathing was as ragged as hers when at last he dragged his mouth away. He buried his face against the soft, scented curve of her neck. His fingers dug almost convulsively into her waist while he fought to curb his runaway desire.

Fingers that weren't entirely steady smoothed the hair from her temple. He lifted her chin so that she was forced to meet his demanding gaze. "I'll be back soon," he whispered.

She didn't believe him. He could see it in the tears that filled her eyes.

"I will, Leslie." His promise was low and fierce. "I'll be back as soon as I can." He caught her to him once more and kissed her cheek, the tip of her nose, the trembling lips she couldn't withhold. Then he turned and walked inside.

BY MORNING, Leslie still hadn't changed her mind. It was Rob who took him to the airport the next day. Instead, she watched from the window while he stowed his suitcase in the trunk of Rob's car. Colleen was there, and all three children, as well. She saw him ruffle Brian's hair, then swing Tess high in the air to plant a kiss on her cheek.

Bonnie was next.

Clint eased down before her, reaching out to tweak a long black curl. Leslie saw him smile and shake his head as he spoke to her. She could almost hear his voice, low and gentle as he explained he was leaving.

The anguish was nearly unbearable, but Leslie couldn't tear her eyes away. She stood rooted to the floor, watching as Bonnie flung her arms around Clint's neck. For a heart-stopping, frozen moment in time, he did nothing. Then slowly, almost tentatively, she saw his arms come out. Leslie almost lost control as he pulled the little girl close, his big hand stroking her hair, over and over.

It wasn't until the car had disappeared from view that Leslie realized she was crying. Slowly, her movements painstakingly resolute, she turned away from the window. With her fingers she wiped the tears from her cheeks until she was dry-eyed once more. She had watched Clint leave this time....

She could never stand to do it again.

CHAPTER SIXTEEN

IN THE DAYS that followed, Leslie was glad for the hectic pace that kept her busy. Now that she had made up her mind, she wasted no time contacting Fran and setting the wheels in motion for Bonnie's adoption. Colleen plunged in with both hands as well, hauling out her typewriter and typing up résumés. Leslie thought her friend also welcomed the chance to take her mind off her father's death. At any rate, between the time spent on the phone and pounding the pavement, she managed to line up a number of job interviews for teaching positions.

She and Colleen also checked out the housing market. With the situation being so rushed, Leslie decided it might be easier to rent a house and look into buying later. They managed to locate a few good possibilities, but Leslie hadn't yet made a final decision.

There was only one dark cloud on the horizon—or perhaps two. One was Bonnie. The stitches in her scalp came out on schedule, but then she caught a cold and ended up with an ear infection, as well. Dr. King thought it best to postpone her surgery until after she had finished the ten-day course of antibiotic treatment.

The other was Clint. Leslie soon discovered that reality was a bitter pill to swallow. Leslie reminded herself she had no right to expect anything from Clint. No words of love had passed his lips. She had no claim on him, no claim whatsoever. She wanted to believe that he cared—that he loved her—but she was also afraid.

She didn't hear a word from him.

Every time the phone rang, she jumped, thinking it might be him. And every time she died a little when it wasn't. She told herself it was for the best, that Clint was all wrong for her. His life-style was too much like Dennis's. She told herself over and over the best thing she could do for herself was to forget him.

If only it were so easy. . . .

The activity was what she needed to keep her from sinking into the doldrums over Clint, though how well she succeeded was questionable. There were times when she couldn't stop herself from thinking of him. Her mind was filled with images: that rare smile that lit up his eyes as he laughed at something silly Tess had said, his dark head bent as he listened in earnest to Bonnie. Leslie remembered every word, every touch they had shared . . . every burning caress.

She didn't realize the telltale loneliness that crept into her eyes whenever she chanced to let her guard down. Every so often, she caught Colleen regarding her with somber intensity. It was at times like this that Leslie suspected Colleen knew what had happened between herself and Clint, down to the last detail. She half expected Colleen to pounce and nail her to the wall, yet her friend never said a word.

The morning of her formal interview with Fran, she was rushing around trying to find her black pumps when Brian let out a yell from the kitchen. "Les-lie!" he howled. "Phone call for ya!"

Her heart lurched. She stood stock-still, but only for an instant. She scampered down the stairs as quickly as she could. Brian stood patiently holding the phone.

She flashed a grateful smile, took the receiver and spoke a rather breathless greeting into the mouthpiece. When the caller identified himself, she wasn't sure if she was disappointed or relieved.

Five minutes later she hung up the phone, still rather stunned from the conversation.

Colleen breezed into the room just as she turned. "Who was that?"

A slow secret smile edged across Leslie's lips. "Wouldn't you like to know?" she teased.

Colleen laughed and plucked an apple from the bowl on the table. "If I didn't before," she said cheerfully, "I certainly do now."

A shuffling and clunking Tess walked into the room, a devilish glow in her green eyes. She was fully decked out in one of her mother's cast-off dresses. Leslie took one look at her feet and whisked her off the floor. "The case of the missing pumps is hereby solved! Hand 'em over, you little thief, or I'll haul you off to jail!"

Tess giggled. Bonnie had appeared as well, her tiny figure hidden beneath the folds of an old paisley skirt so that only her head peeked out. Leslie swooped her into her arms, as well.

Colleen gave an exaggerated sigh. "Maybe you'll get around to telling me who was on the phone sometime next week."

Leslie's lips twitched; she fought a grin. "Oh, that," she murmured, her tone deliberately nonchalant. "It was just the school board president from Del Mar."

Colleen nearly choked on the bite of apple she was chewing. "The school board president—" she swallowed hastily "—what did he want?"

Leslie couldn't stop the silly grin that formed. "What do you think?"

Her friend's jaw dropped. "A job? It was about a teaching position?"

Leslie nodded, unable to hold back any longer. "When I was interviewed on Tuesday, there was only one position open. I called yesterday and found out they had already filled it. But the board found out last night that one of the second-grade teachers is pregnant with her second baby, so she's decided to call it quits."

"And they offered you the job?"

"Yes!"

"I guess I don't have to ask if you accepted it." Colleen's laughter rang out sweet and pure. "That's what I call luck! Now all we have to do is find a house." She snapped her fingers. "I saw several in the classifieds that are in that area. If we call right away, we might have time to check them out before your appointment with Fran."

Leslie nodded. She buried her face in Bonnie's sweet-smelling hair. "We're going to make it," she whispered happily. "We're going to end up just fine, I just know it."

And in that moment, she never doubted it.

LATER THAT AFTERNOON, her doubts resurfaced. She had been on top of the world only an hour earlier; the second house they looked at was an absolute dollhouse. The landlords were a retired couple who clearly kept everything in tip-top shape. Though Leslie wasn't specifically looking for a three-bedroom, she decided the extra bedroom could always be used as a playroom for Bonnie. The yard was small without being too small, and low maintenance; there was even a swing set left behind by the last tenant. She was so entranced with it she wasted no time paying the deposit and first month's rent.

Colleen had left the kids with Maryann so she could come along with her. On Clint's specific instructions, Leslie had used his car for her job-hunting. But Leslie was glad Colleen had driven today. She was so nervous about the upcoming interview with Fran that she wasn't sure she could have found her way around the block right now. To top it off, Fran was late getting back from her last appointment. Nor did it help that the July heat outside was blistering. She felt like a wilted flower.

In the hall outside Fran's office, she paced back and forth until finally Colleen reached out and caught her arm, pulling her down beside her. "You're making *me* nervous," she complained.

Leslie couldn't find it in her to laugh. Colleen gave her hand a sympathetic pat. "Relax, Les. You're worrying for no reason at all."

"That's easy for you to say. You're not the one who has to go in there and face her."

Colleen bit back a smile. "You make it sound like Fran's a dragon lady. Why, she's more of a soft soap than Rob!"

The faint lines between Leslie's eyebrows etched deeper. "But she practically warned me not to get too close to Bonnie."

"So?"

Leslie wanted to scream. How could her friend sound so cool and matter-of-fact? "So obviously I didn't listen or I wouldn't be here!"

"Exactly." Colleen's lips twitched. "But if you take a minute to think about it from Fran's point of view, that's a plus in your favor."

Leslie wasn't convinced. "You think so?"

"I know so," came the smug response. "Now here, read this." Colleen dropped the latest issue of *Parents* magazine into her lap. Leslie opened it, but she was still staring at it five minutes later when Fran came down the hall. There were a few moments of small talk, then Fran ushered her inside. Leslie followed behind, feeling as if she were approaching the hangman's noose.

Fran dropped into the chair behind her desk. "Lord, but it's hot out there." Fanning herself with a notebook, she expelled a weary sigh.

Leslie murmured something polite—ten seconds later, she couldn't recall what she'd said. Fran turned her attention to the matter at hand all too soon. She pushed her chair up to her desk and flipped open a folder. Pen in hand, she directed a smile across the desk top.

"I see you're in the process of moving from San Francisco."

Leslie tried to smile back, but she was sure the effort was an abysmal failure. "As a matter of fact, I just rented a house today."

"You've lived in San Francisco... how long?"

"Most of my life."

"Moving must have been a big decision, then."

"It was." She folded her hands in her lap to keep them from trembling.

"Adopting a child is also a big decision."

Leslie didn't flinch from her directness. "I know that," she said levelly. "But to be perfectly honest, deciding to file for Bonnie's adoption was a much easier one to make."

"I'm not surprised to hear that," the other woman said softly. "Bonnie has certainly blossomed since she came here from Mexico." A slight smile curled her lips. "Frankly I think a lot of that has to do with you."

The praise was unexpected; Leslie realized that Colleen was right. Fran was not a foe. They were on the same side after all—they both wanted what was best for Bonnie. She relaxed after that, and the interview went much easier than she expected. Still, it took all her courage to ask about the McCalls as Fran prepared to see her out.

The other woman sighed. "I have to be honest with you, Leslie. They're looking at another child as well, but they're still interested in Bonnie. I'm afraid I still have to consider them viable candidates."

Leslie dropped her eyes to hide the disappointment she knew she couldn't hide. At the door, she spoke quickly before she could change her mind.

"Fran, I...I know it's probably not my place to say this—and the last thing I want is to make comparisons. I know I can't compete with the McCalls for material goods. But I can still provide for Bonnie without any hardship at all. She'll have everything she needs—and more." Her voice took on a note of intensity. "She'll know she's loved."

She was almost afraid to meet Fran's eyes, but the older woman's expression was warm with understanding. "I know," she said softly. "I'll remember that. And I'll be in touch."

Leslie came out of Fran's office feeling far better than when she had gone in. But as she told Colleen in the car, she was worried about competing with the McCalls. Nonetheless, she felt better just sharing it with someone.

The conversation turned to Colleen and Rob's plan to take the children and spend the weekend at a lodge in the mountains. Leslie reflected that maybe a little time together alone with Rob was just what Colleen needed to cope with the stress of the last few weeks, so she offered to stay with Brian, and Tess and Bonnie at home.

Colleen shook her head and pulled Tess close. "I didn't see them for nearly two weeks. Right now, I don't think I could stand to be away from them for two whole days." Though her eyes were filled with laughter, there was a note of gravity in her voice that Leslie didn't miss. Brian and Tess were also eager for Bonnie to experience her first try at fishing.

When they arrived home, she helped Colleen pack and load the station wagon. They left as soon as Rob came home. Leslie had planned to spend the weekend house-hunting, but since that was already taken care of, she mused wryly that a little quiet time alone was exactly what *she* needed. With Bonnie's surgery approaching, the impending move, and the prospect of starting a new job, her life would soon be overflowing. Monday, she decided, was soon enough to make reservations for a flight back to San Francisco to wrap up her affairs there.

But when darkness dropped its veil, the solitude seemed to close in on her. She sat cross-legged in the middle of the living room, clutching a throw pillow tightly to her breast, aware of a melancholy longing rising inside her. The house was quiet, despite the drone of the television in the background. She missed Tess's incessant chatter, and Colleen's full-blown laughter. She missed Brian's wide grin, and Bonnie's shy sweet smile.

Most of all she missed Clint.

Memories battered her from all sides. How would she ever sleep tonight—in her lonely bed—without remembering the strength and security of his warm male body hard and tight against hers? Without thinking of their sweetly urgent mating, the way their bodies strained and sought the blistering heat of release...and the way their hearts slowed together as one in the blissful aftermath.

The memory of his loving made her feel warm and weak. What they had shared was more than physical; it was a melding of mind and spirit, the most wonderful experience of her life. If she were honest with herself, she would admit she had no regrets about sharing herself with Clint.

But she had doubts—a world of them. And yet the bitter truth buried deep in her heart struggled to be free.

"I love him," she whispered, hating herself for her weakness, for falling in love with the wrong man...again.

She clutched the throw pillow tighter, wishing—perversely, foolishly—that Clint were there with her. But there was no one to listen. No one to hear. No one to care.

Her chest filled with a deep, weary despair. She knew she was feeling sorry for herself. She stared listlessly into the deepening shadows, too tired to move, too tired to think, too tired to care.

Outside a car door slammed; she scarcely noticed. It wasn't until the sound of the doorbell sliced through the air and penetrated her consciousness that she shook off her desolate mood. She rose to her feet and switched on a lamp, then peeked through the drapes in time to spy the orange-red glow of taillights fade into the night. She paused uncertainly, unwilling to open the door to a stranger. Colleen and Rob weren't expecting anyone. It wasn't late, just after ten. Still, it was dark and she was alone....

The decision was taken from her hands.

She heard the unmistakable sound of a key sliding into the lock. With a gasp she stepped instinctively back to avoid being hit when the door swung open. She caught her first glimpse of the unexpected caller.

It was Clint.

For long, breath-stealing moments neither one moved. Neither said a word. She stared at him. He stared at her. Each was obsessed with drinking in the pleasure wrought by the sight of the other.

Her heart began to race; her pulse vied thunderously with its pounding rhythm. She tried to control its frantic throb and failed. It was sinful, the longing his mere presence aroused in her. She drank in the rugged male beauty of his face and body. The pale pinstriped shirt he wore brought out the midnight sheen of his hair. His tailored slacks clung lovingly to lean hips and strong thighs. Never had he looked more handsome—or more dear to her heart—than at this moment.

He stepped inside and dropped his suitcase in the entryway. His eyes never wavered from hers as he shoved the door shut with his heel.

"Hi," he said softly.

She tried to smile and murmur a hello. But her jaw wouldn't work properly. Her lips refused to do her bidding. She blinked rapidly, trying desperately to forestall the burning threat of tears. All she could do was stare at him, wishing she could hide the emotion that lay naked on her face and knowing she couldn't.

The haloed lamplight made her eyes look huge and bright and glistening, but they were overly bright. It was the sight of her quivering lips, though, that made Clint come completely undone. He breached the short distance between them in a single stride, hauling her into his arms and wrapping her fiercely close.

"I missed you." He rubbed his jaw against the soft cloud of honey-colored hair that tickled his chin. "God, I missed you!"

Leslie's eyes squeezed shut. How was it possible to feel such pleasure in the face of such pain? It was impossible. Unfair! His fervor made her heart soar, even while a tiny voice inside reminded her she was playing with fire. She knew it was wrong to prolong this, to let him pretend they could just pick up where they had left off. She had made up her mind that there could be nothing between them—not now, not ever. But the words that would have driven him back just wouldn't come.

Strong fingers slid beneath her chin, the gentle pressure urging her face upward. She met his gaze helplessly, unable to hold back anything. "Oh, Clint, I—I missed you, too." The ragged little cry was torn from deep inside where she couldn't hide from the truth.

Their lips met and clung. The kiss seemed to go on forever, so sweet, so unbearably gentle, she wanted to cry and rage against the bitter ache it roused. She gave a tiny moan, a sound of confusion, a sound of satisfaction.

He was smiling when at last he lifted his head. "Now I know why I broke my neck getting back here," he murmured.

Leslie tried to return his smile; she really did. But she was totally incapable of doing anything but trying to cope with the reality of his presence.

She wasn't ready for this, she realized. The sight of him had kindled a thousand chaotic responses. She longed to sweep back the fringe of hair on his forehead. Her fingers ached with the need to smooth away the lines of exhaustion carved beside his mouth.

A tremor ran through her. Dear God, she thought bleakly. Why had he come? She wasn't up to watching him leave again—the very thought was annihilating.

Her lips parted; the words that emerged weren't at all what she intended. "How long can you stay?"

His smile faded. Leslie steeled herself against the fleeting regret that flashed in his eyes. "Just the weekend, I'm afraid. We finished early in Washington." There was a brief pause. "Monday it's off to Alaska."

Despite the fact that she had known it was coming, the words were like a slap in the face. My, wasn't she lucky! Two whole days—he was home for two whole days! And then how long before he was back again? A week? A month? Six months?

She withdrew slightly, needing to put some distance between them before she came completely apart. She didn't see the shadow that drifted over his features as he watched her retreat into the middle of the living room.

"I thought you'd be glad to see me, Leslie."

Quiet as his tone was, there was an underlying hurt that was unmistakable. "I—I am, Clint...you don't know how much."

With one step he reclaimed the distance she had taken. The weight of his hands settled on her shoulders. "Are you sure?"

Her gaze strayed helplessly to his. "Yes," she whispered, aware that she was baring her soul to him but unable to stop it. "I...it was awful here without you. And I kept wishing you would at least call...."

His expression softened. "I wanted to. God, I had to stop myself a dozen times," he told her fervently. "But I thought maybe we both needed a little time to think—" his voice dropped to a whisper "—about us."

As he spoke, he lifted his hand. Gently...oh, so gently, he ran his thumb over the satin fullness of her lower lip, giving her the time to pull back if she wanted. She closed her eyes and leaned into the fleeting caress, loving him, wanting him so much it hurt inside. His heart soared when her arms slid around his waist, her mouth blindly seeking and finding his.

It was a long time before either one of them resurfaced from the heady bliss of their kiss. Clint sighed and rested his chin atop her head, loath to let her go. His breath stirred the wispy hair at her temple. "You make me forget everything but you," he chided teasingly. "But all of a sudden I'm wondering why on earth it's so god-awful quiet in here. Is everyone asleep?"

Leslie drew a deep tremulous breath, just as reluctant to let him go. His hand trailed up and down her spine, the touch comfortably familiar. She wanted to capture this moment—this melting feeling of closeness—snatch it fiercely to her breast and hoard it deep within her heart to make up for all the lonely days she knew would follow.

Her head was nested cozily into the hollow of his shoulder. "They're spending the weekend in the mountains." She pressed her lips against his neck, loving the slightly abrasive texture of his skin. "Bonnie will be disappointed she missed you," she murmured unthinkingly.

The soothing motion of his hand stopped. Leslie went very still inside. Uncertain of his reaction, every nerve in her body heightened to an almost painful pitch of awareness.

She heard his voice above her head. "Has her surgery been scheduled yet?"

"The Thursday after next. I'm going back to San Francisco on Monday or Tuesday to see about having my things moved so I can be back before then."

She slipped from his arms and turned away. He didn't try to stop her. She couldn't look at him, afraid of what she would see—or perhaps what she wouldn't see—on his face. She couldn't stop the chill of resentment that seeped through her veins. Frustration and anger followed in close succession. Neither voiced the thought that was foremost in their minds. It really didn't matter when Bonnie's surgery was scheduled....

Because Clint wouldn't be there. He would be thousands of miles away in Alaska.

"Leslie." Her name was deep and low. "Leslie, if there's any way at all I can be here, I will." He reached out and caught her by the hand, pulling her around to face him. "You know that, don't you?"

There was a note in his voice she had never heard before. Her eyes bore into his. She couldn't look away as his gaze searched her face. She had hurt him, she realized. She hadn't meant to, but she had.

"You will?" The tip of her tongue came out to moisten her lips.

Yes, he thought. *God, yes.* "I promise I'll try my damnedest," he said quietly. "I'd do anything for you—" there was a brief but significant pause "—for you *and* Bonnie."

For a heart-stopping moment she said nothing. "Thank you," she whispered. She smiled, a blindingly sweet smile that stole his breath and crashed straight through to his heart.

With a muffled sound deep in his throat he caught her to him, his hold both tender and fierce. The rush of emotion that seized him clamored for release—demanded it. His eyes delved deeply into hers; all that was in his heart spilled free.

"I love you," he whispered urgently. "Marry me, Leslie . . . please marry me."

CHAPTER SEVENTEEN

THE ROUGH THREAD of need in his voice made her mind reel. The golden glow of the lamplight etched his features in stark relief. But even as he spoke the sweetest words she had ever heard, she was filled with a burning despair.

She could only stare at him helplessly, her gaze welded to his by a force beyond her control. She began to tremble, both inside and out. These last few days without Clint had opened her eyes as nothing else could have. What they had before was no more than an illusion . . . they had been play-acting at something that could never be. Clint was back in his world, a world that involved hopping planes, living out of a suitcase and snatching an occasional weekend at home.

Her knees were suddenly too weak to hold her. She stumbled to the sofa and dropped down numbly. Only dimly did she realize Clint had followed her down.

Clint's entire being was focused on the woman at his side. He wanted desperately to touch her, but he didn't dare. Yet he sensed the moment she withdrew from him; he witnessed the tremor in her hands as she clasped them together before her. And he knew the exact instant he lost her. . . .

"Oh, Clint, I...I want to...you don't know how much..." She looked at him, and there was a world of torment churning inside her. "But I can't...I just can't!"

The silence that followed was nearly unbearable for both of them.

Clint felt every muscle in his body grow tense and rigid. "Why not?" The edge in his voice revealed his frustration. "Dammit, Leslie, why not?"

Her eyes clung to his. He saw the muscles in her throat work convulsively as she battled and won control.

"What about Bonnie?" She swallowed, knowing these were the hardest words she had ever said. "There's not just the two of us to consider, Clint. Bonnie has no one. At least you have Rob and Colleen and the kids. Besides, I—I love her. I want to adopt her. I can't just walk away from her—I *won't* walk away from her!"

His eyes narrowed. "What are you saying? That you have to choose between me and Bonnie? You don't, Leslie. You can have us both—"

"Can I?" she cried. "Do you think I don't know what will happen if I marry you? If I get custody of Bonnie? You'll look at her and see Angelina!" The pain in her heart brought agony to her voice. "Maybe I'm being selfish, but I want to be loved for myself. I don't want to come in second-best next to Angelina!"

She started to lurch to her feet, but he wouldn't let her. His hands caught hers, his grip relentless. He stared at her, his jaw bunched and knotted.

Then all at once he released her. His hand stole up to cradle her cheek. "No. No! Do you think I don't know what I feel for you?" His voice caught raggedly. "Yes, I loved Angelina, but she belongs in the past. I know that now."

"Do you?" It was a cry of anguish, a cry of sheer pain. She thrust his hand from her cheek and jumped to her feet. "I wonder, Clint. Remember the night before you left for Washington—when I announced I wanted to adopt Bonnie? You intended to ask me to marry you then, didn't you?"

She caught him wholly off guard. Stunned, it took him an instant to catch his breath. "Leslie, I—"

"Didn't you?"

He hated himself for the dull red flush creeping up his neck. "Yes."

"But you didn't because of Bonnie. Isn't that right?"

Clint fought a deep, gut-wrenching despair, forcing himself to meet the relentless demand in her eyes.

"What do you want me to say, Leslie? At the time it was true. I told you that night you shocked the hell out of me and I wasn't lying. My God," he said hoarsely, "you alone knew how it tore me up inside to be with her. And yes, I wanted you, but I hadn't counted on Bonnie. I know now that I was blind not to realize how you felt about her—that Bonnie might be part of the package."

Seeing him, listening to him, Leslie experienced a shameful prick of conscience. Had she wrongly accused him? She couldn't tear her gaze away from his face, taut and gaunt. Guilt shadowed the depths of his eyes, but mingled within was a depth of emotion she'd never glimpsed before.

Each word he spoke was brutally honest. "Since that night, I've thought of nothing else, of nothing but you and Bonnie." His voice turned hoarse. "I didn't want to fall in love with you, but I did. And I didn't want to feel anything for Bonnie, but I fell for her just as hard as you did. I *love* her as much as you do. I came here tonight with my eyes wide open. And by God, I don't regret any of it." His gaze locked fiercely with hers. "You are my future, Leslie. You and Bonnie."

With every breath, every heartbeat, his voice took on an intensity she'd never heard before. Never had she loved him more, she realized. But Leslie suddenly felt she was being ripped apart inside. She feared loving him; she feared losing him; she feared never having him.

Her eyes held a wealth of sadness. "Oh, Clint, how can I explain? It's not just Bonnie." Her head lowered, but not before he saw the leap of fear in her eyes.

He was at her side in an instant, his tone imploring. "What then?"

Her lips parted. She had to struggle to find the courage to speak. "These past weeks when you were gone," she said, her voice very low, "it happened all over again, just like with Dennis...waiting for the phone to ring...waiting for his plane...waiting for him to come home. Clint, I could never live like that again."

She paused for the space of a heartbeat. "Clint, I—I'd give anything to say yes," she confessed unevenly. "But if I ever marry again, it's going to be everything it never was with Dennis."

"It will be, Leslie." His tone was low and urgent. "If you'll just give us a chance."

"You don't understand." Her lips trembled. "I want a lifetime. I don't want to be someone you fit into your life. I want to be part of it, to share it."

His eyes darkened. "I want that, too, Leslie, believe me." He hesitated. "It won't always be possible, but I'll be in Alaska nearly a year. You can come with me—"

"And then what?" A bitter smile touched her lips. "Where will your next job take you? A hundred miles away? Or a thousand?"

A shadow flickered across his features. "I have no idea, Leslie. You know that as well as I do."

"Yes." The word was pained. "I do. And I also know that's no way to bring up a child. Bonnie needs a home. Security and roots." The breath she took was tremulous. "But it's not just Bonnie. Remember when you said I was the staunch, reliable type? Dennis was there one week, gone the next. I knew what I was getting into when I married him. But I found out that I needed stability more than I ever knew."

His eyes narrowed. "And that's it? If we can't be together some of the time, we might as well just chuck it all?" His lips twisted. "Forgive me if I'm having trouble understanding your logic."

His long, hard look made her cringe inside. He was waiting for her to explain, yet how could she? She felt trapped, trapped by her own feelings of inadequacy, trapped by the confusion that beat at her in wave after wave. Her emotions were a hopeless tangle, and every one was tinged with contradiction. He said he loved her...but what if he was like Dennis? What if he didn't love her enough? She was afraid of losing him...but what if he was never hers to begin with? Weakened by her own doubt, she could only stare at him helplessly.

For long, tension-filled moments Clint said nothing. He saw her eyes flit away and wondered at the whirlwind of emotions that chased across her face. A half-formed suspicion winged through his mind.

He spoke slowly, almost disbelievingly. "It's just an excuse, isn't it? All of it..." A strange note crept into his voice. "You don't trust me, do you?"

Her mind reeled. Stricken, she stared at him, feeling as if the wind had been knocked out of her. And for a heartwrenching instant, she wondered if Clint were right.... If she married him, and time and distance kept them parted for days at a time, would he be like Dennis? Would he take his love elsewhere?

Her breath came jerkily. "Oh, God, Clint, don't ask me that! It's me, don't you see? What if I'm...not enough for you? What if I'm not all that you want, all that you need, all that you *expect*?"

His heart contracted at the tiny break in her voice. Lifting a hand, he rubbed his knuckles over the curve of her cheek. "But you are," he whispered, "And I promise that will never change."

She thought she would break from the gentleness of his touch. "But I'm scared," she cried raggedly. "I couldn't stand it if I lost you the way I lost Dennis. I—I couldn't take it, not with you, Clint...never with you. And maybe it's better not to have you at all than to end up losing you!"

It hurt to say the words aloud. But they held all the honesty in her soul...and all the fear in her heart.

Exerting a gentle pressure with his thumb, he forced her gaze to his.

"Do you love me?"

She couldn't lie. Dear God, she couldn't. "Yes," she whispered helplessly—hopelessly.

"Then trust me. Don't you think I know this all goes back to Dennis? Do you think I don't know what that bastard did to you? But just forget about him and think about me."

Leslie began to tremble. Her lungs burned with the effort it took to hold back her tears.

"I love you," he said, his voice low and taut and vibrating with all that he felt for her. "I love you enough to believe that we can work through anything that comes our way. If you can't believe in yourself, then believe in me. Trust me. What we have is too precious to throw away. Don't give up now. Give me a chance—give *us* a chance." There was a heartbeat of silence. "Marry me."

His eyes bored into hers, deep and intense, wordlessly beseeching.

If only, she thought brokenly. If only her tears could wash away her deepest fear....

I love you, he said. But she was desperately afraid the words were only words.

"I can't," she whispered. "Oh, God, I just can't." Her voice caught on a trembling broken sound. "I—I love you. You don't know how much. But I won't take the risk of marrying you and—and losing you."

His hand fell away from her. He closed his eyes against the pain pouring through his veins. When he opened them, he was almost grateful for the stab of anger that pierced the hurt.

"I think you're right, Leslie. I think you *are* being selfish. Because I don't see how you can do this to me. Or maybe you just don't love me the way you say you do." His tone was quiet, thoughtful. "Maybe you just don't love me *enough* to believe we can make it."

He stepped back, the stark emptiness in his eyes terrible to behold. An ominous darkness gripped her soul. *No,* she wanted to cry. Didn't he understand? Hadn't he listened? It wasn't at all like he had said. It wasn't because she loved him too little . . . but because she loved him too much.

Time hung suspended. There was a dull roaring in her ears. Eyes wide and unblinking, she saw him turn. His face expressionless, his posture coldly dignified, she watched him pick up his suitcase and walk out the door. . . .

He took her heart along with him.

DAWN SEEPED THROUGH the curtains in Leslie's bedroom, casting spears of hazy sunshine across the floor. Her bed had not been slept in. Her two suitcases lay open across the spread, neatly packed.

In the kitchen, Leslie first called the airline, then a cab. When the cab picked her up a short time later, she left without a backward glance. A blessed kind of numbness had slipped over her. Whether or not Clint was in his bungalow—or on his way to Alaska—she had no idea.

At the airport, she recalled how she had felt the day of her arrival in San Diego. So alone, so out of step and out of place, as if she had been abandoned.

She felt the same way when she walked into her apartment in San Francisco. She collapsed onto the sofa, and all at once the tears she'd managed to with-hold flowed fast and furious.

By Monday there were no more tears left.

She had barely crawled out of bed when the phone rang bright and early that morning. Tired and bleary-eyed, she reached for the receiver and put it to her ear.

"Some friend you are," complained a familiar female voice. "Slinking off in the middle of the night without even letting us know."

"Colleen." Her shoulders slumped, but then she chided herself harshly. Who else had she expected? She dropped down on the bed and ran her fingers through her hair. "I didn't slink off, and it was noon Saturday when I left, not the middle of the night. And I left you a note. Did you explain to Bonnie that I had to go? Did she understand?"

"Don't worry, Bonnie's fine," Colleen assured her, then said accusingly, "You said you weren't going back to San Francisco until this week."

"I—changed my mind." She faltered, her mind groping for excuses. She finally settled for the most logical. "I thought of all the work ahead of me this week and decided to get a head start."

"And the fact that Clint showed up here this week-end had nothing to do with your vanishing act?"

Her heart lurched. "What makes you say that?" she asked quickly.

Colleen's voice was dry. "You'd know if you'd seen Clint's face. I was suspicious when I found Clint here and you gone. And Clint was just as evasive as you. When he left with Rob for the airport this morning, I think he was overjoyed to get me out of his hair."

So he was gone. If there was a tiny ember of hope inside her, it died a lonely, gasping death. "I'm not being evasive," she said faintly.

"Aren't you? Oh, you put up a good front. But I've known you a little too long, and I know when something is wrong."

She looked down at her hands. She didn't know what to say, and so she said nothing.

"It is Clint, isn't it?" Across the miles, she heard Colleen sigh. "Don't bother to answer that. I know it is. I think I knew something was happening before the two of you did."

Leslie squeezed her eyes shut. "Something did," she whispered. "But it's over."

"Your choice or his?"

"Mine." Her voice was barely perceptible.

There was a heavy silence on the other end of the line. "I don't mean to prv," Colleen said finally. "But I really thought you and Clint were good for each other, that you two were just what the other one needed...." Her voice trailed off. There was a stifling pause, then Colleen asked quietly, "You know about Angelina, don't you?"

It required a monumental effort to make her voice steady. Even then, she wasn't sure she succeeded. "Yes."

For the longest time Colleen was at a rare loss for words. "Is that what's wrong?" Her tone was low but earnest. "I know her death haunted him for a long time. But that doesn't mean—"

"I—I know." Leslie rubbed her aching temples. "But maybe there's just too much history behind both of us ... and then there's Bonnie—" she was suddenly babbling, but she couldn't seem to stop "—and we both need stability and a home and . . . and God, I hate myself for feeling he should be here with me instead of some damned job in Alaska!"

There was a shocked silence at the other end of the line. "Well," Colleen murmured with a faint trace of humor, "I'm glad that's settled."

The sound Leslie made was half laugh, half sob. "You see?" she said shakily. "I love the way he makes me feel when we're together. It feels so—so right. And yet I know there are at least a dozen reasons why it would never work."

Colleen wasted no time giving her reply. "And I," she said softly, "could give you just one reason why it will." There was a pulse beat of silence. "He loves you, Les. And I don't think I need to ask if you love him."

The air grew very still. Her throat was so raw she could hardly speak. "Colleen, please, can we just drop this? I don't want to talk about Clint. Okay?"

"Then let's just talk about you for a second. After that, I won't say another word, I promise." There was a brief pause. "Remember when I told you my father was an alcoholic?"

Puzzled, Leslie frowned. "I remember."

Colleen's voice was very quiet. "I know I told you then that my mother stayed with him all those years because she loved him. It's something I've never understood—I still don't. But when Rob and I were there for his funeral, my mother said something that started me thinking. . . ."

Her voice went very low. "She said she did what was right for her—for the two of them. Because when he wasn't drinking, he made her the happiest woman on earth, and that made up for everything else." She drew a deep tremulous breath. "I could never have stuck with my father the way my mother did, Leslie. I don't think there are many women who could. But if there's a chance to be happy, at least give it a shot. It's okay to look ahead. But don't let yourself get too caught up in what *might* go wrong. Think about what's right, too."

Her message wasn't lost on Leslie. Colleen was telling her to listen to her heart.

Their conversation stayed with Leslie throughout the week, much to her dismay.

She thought about Clint constantly. Unendingly. Even while her hands were busy and her mind occupied with Bonnie and the move.

That last horrible scene with Clint replayed over and over in her mind, in stark, vivid clarity. She remembered his expression just before he walked out, his face etched in harsh, bitter lines, lines she had hoped never to see again. He had looked so desolate and empty... as empty as she was now.

She recalled the pained tenderness in his voice. *If you can't believe in yourself, then believe in me. Trust me. What we have is too precious to throw away.*

A tiny voice inside reminded her that she had asked nothing of him. She had made no demands; she hadn't asked him to change his way of life to accommodate her fears. Still another voice took the opposite stand. It unflinchingly told her she wanted too much...all or nothing. Never once had Leslie thought of herself as rigid or uncompromising.

She did so now. And it was then that she began to understand. Clint hadn't walked out of her life. She had *pushed* him out.

The realization had a gut-wrenching impact. She found herself reliving the empty hours alone that characterized her life with Dennis; the shattering moment when she discovered Dennis was a bigamist.

But Clint was a far different man from Dennis. In a matter of weeks, he had given her far more than Dennis ever had. Clint had made her feel cherished, and needed, and oh, so much a woman.

Most of all—best of all—he had made her feel loved.

If she married him, what was the worst that could happen? His work might take him away for weeks at a time; that didn't mean she had lost him. He had asked her to trust him. Was that so terrible? If he missed her, if he missed the warmth of her female body close to his at night, would he find someone else? Somehow she couldn't picture Clint with another woman. He was too strong, too intense and too unwavering in his beliefs. Any commitment he made would be absolute.

She knew he would try to come home whenever he could, even if it were only on weekends. Deep inside where it counted the most, Leslie realized that wherever he was, a part of him would always be hers.

And wasn't that better than nothing at all? Because that's what she had right now...nothing.

In the end, it boiled down to just one question. Did she trust Clint enough to place her love in his hands? It was just as Colleen had said, Leslie realized.

The answer was buried deep in her heart.

THE FOLLOWING MONDAY, the moving company picked up Leslie's furniture and the rest of her belongings. She spent the night with a friend, and very early the next morning climbed into her car and said a last goodbye to San Francisco.

It was nearly four in the afternoon when she pulled into the drive at Rob and Colleen's house. It was with a mingled sense of apprehension and excitement that her gaze veered straight toward Clint's bungalow, which unfortunately told her nothing. Throughout the long drive south, she had tried to prepare herself for the chance she might encounter Clint. Today was Tuesday. Bonnie's surgery was scheduled for Thursday. He'd said he would try to be here; in fact, he had promised he'd try his damnedest. And in spite of the ugliness of their last parting, she prayed he wouldn't let Bonnie down.

At the sound of the car door slamming, Tess peeked around the side of the house. Her eyes lit up when she spotted Leslie. She flipped the lock on the fence gate and bolted toward her.

"Leslie!"

Leslie caught her up in her arms. "Hi, squirt! Are you staying out of trouble?"

Her impish green eyes sparkled. "I guess not, 'cause Daddy made me come out and play in the sandbox while he fixes supper."

Leslie's brows shot up as she lowered Tess to the ground. Rob was home early. Come to think of it, she was surprised that Bonnie wasn't right behind Tess. Maybe Colleen had taken her in to Dr. King for her pre-op appointment.

Rob had apparently heard voices in the back yard. He stepped up to them with a crooked smile. "Hi," Leslie greeted. "I've come to beg the use of your spare room for one last night. The moving van should be here with my furniture tomorrow, and then I'll be out of your hair for good, I promise." She crossed her fingers then glanced toward the house. "Tess said Colleen stuck you with kitchen duty. Did Bonnie have her pre-op appointment?"

"Actually you're just the person we wanted to see." Rob's smile faded. "Bonnie had her surgery this morning."

Leslie's jaw dropped. "This morning! She wasn't supposed to have it until Thurs—"

"Dr. King had an unexpected opening in his surgical schedule, so he decided to work her in ahead. His office phoned Monday, and Leslie's been trying to call you ever since."

Leslie groaned. "Monday! That's when my phone was disconnected." She looked up at him frantically. "Is that where Colleen is? At the hospital?"

His expression was sympathetic. "She's been there all day. She thought she'd be home around dinnertime, but if you hurry you might catch her before she leaves. Do you think you can find the hospital from here?"

"I think I can find my way to Dr. King's office. Isn't the hospital just a block away?"

He nodded. "Let me give you directions just in case." They hurried into the kitchen.

Leslie took the hastily scrawled instructions, then paused. Against her will, against all odds, she heard herself ask, "Clint isn't here, is he?"

Rob appeared to hesitate, then shook his head. Leslie experienced a cold sinking sensation. Clint hadn't come back for Bonnie's surgery. He knew how much it would have meant to her, maybe even more than it meant to Bonnie. To Leslie, it meant only one thing.

It was over between them.

FIFTEEN MINUTES LATER, Leslie ran through the hospital entrance. She hurriedly checked with the receptionist to find out Bonnie's room number then ducked into the elevator. When she stepped out onto the third floor, the ominous hush and antiseptic smell made her stomach tighten into a cold, hard knot.

She had started down the long, dismal corridor when the whoosh of a door opening caught her attention. A smile sprang to her lips as she spied Colleen.

"It's about time you showed up." Colleen rolled her eyes with an exaggerated sigh of relief then hugged her impulsively. "I must have tried to call you a hundred times the last few days."

"So I heard. I stopped at the house and Rob told me." Leslie pulled a face. "Monday was when my phone was disconnected." Her anxious gaze flitted to the door Colleen had just come through. "How did Bonnie's surgery go?"

"Dr. King thought it went pretty well. There's a chance she might need surgery again in a few years, though it probably wouldn't be as extensive. And he stressed that she'll need some pretty intense physical therapy. But he's optimistic about the results."

Leslie held her breath. "Her limp?"

"If there's any at all, it should be very slight." Colleen's grin was purely devilish. "Tess has a bike all picked out for her next birthday."

Leslie felt her heart zip skyward; only seconds ago she wouldn't have thought it possible. A part of her wanted desperately to ask if Rob had brought home any news about her petition to adopt Bonnie, but she wanted nothing to spoil the joy of knowing Bonnie's prognosis was so good.

This time she was the one who hugged her friend fiercely; they both had moist eyes when she finally drew back. "Rob said you've been here with Bonnie all day." She squeezed her friend's hands. "Thank you, Colleen. I don't think I could stand knowing Bonnie had to go through this alone."

An odd, almost secretive smile flirted at her friend's lips. The next second Colleen gave her a gentle push toward the door. "It was nothing," she said lightly. "But now that you're here I think I'll scoot home. Rob's supposed to be fixing dinner." She rolled her eyes. "We'll probably end up at McDonald's."

"I'll see you later then." Leslie flashed a grateful smile, then turned and stepped into Bonnie's room.

A rush of dizziness assailed her at her first sight of the little girl. A tangle of tubes and bottles hung near the head of the bed. Bonnie's hair lay in a fat braid across her chest. Her eyes were closed. She appeared tiny and vulnerable in the big bed, her skin nearly as pale as the pristine white sheets.

Taking a deep fortifying breath, Leslie skirted the foot of the bed and moved to the side closest to the window. She stretched out a hand hesitantly, wanting to assure herself that she really was all right. But

Bonnie looked so fragile and weak she was half afraid to touch her. Her heart aching, she pushed a wisp of hair from Bonnie's forehead.

Bonnie's lashes fluttered slowly open. When she saw Leslie, her dark eyes grew bigger yet, filling with tears. "Lee!" She cried her name weakly.

Leslie leaned over the metal railing and pressed her lips against her forehead. Bonnie slipped the arm that wasn't connected to the IV tubing around her neck.

"Don't cry, sweetheart," she whispered, perilously close to tears herself. "I'm here now and I won't leave you again, I promise."

She drew back with a tremulous smile just as she heard the creak of the door. Pleasurably intent on the sweetness of Bonnie's welcome, she ran the back of her knuckles over Bonnie's thin cheek. Thinking it was Colleen, she smiled slightly, not bothering to look up.

"That was quick. Did the thought of Rob's cooking drive you back here already?"

There was an empty silence. No sooner did the realization that something was not right trickle through her mind, than she heard a voice....

"Hello, Leslie."

CHAPTER EIGHTEEN

"CLINT." She heard herself speak his name, though she'd have sworn her lips never moved.

He was here. *Here!* Her body turned to stone. Her ability to think was lost.

He looked more attractive than ever, dressed in slacks and a pale knit shirt that revealed the dark tangle of hairs at the base of his throat. Her pulse struck up an uneven rhythm as she remembered the feel of that musky hollow against her lips.

She stared at him, her fingers twisted tightly around the bedrail for support. Their last few meetings had been so heartbreaking. She didn't dare speculate how this one might end.

At the sound of his voice, Bonnie had turned liquid brown eyes in his direction.

Leslie couldn't look away as two long strides carried him to Bonnie's side. They stood directly across from each other. He bent and whispered something in Spanish. Bonnie nodded, her eyes drooping.

Leslie found herself bombarded by a hundred different sensations. Her blood was singing joyously in her veins. Clint was here, standing right across from her! He hadn't let her down—he hadn't let Bonnie down! Did he still care? Did he still love her! *Yes, please, yes!* Or had she shattered those feelings forever when she refused to marry him?

Clint's gaze leveled with hers. "You don't have to leave," he said quickly. "I know you just got here." He nodded at the child between them. Bonnie's lashes shadowed her cheeks. Her tiny rosebud mouth was slightly open. "She woke up from the anesthetic asking for you. She's been drifting in and out most of the time since then."

"You've been with her all day?"

Lowering his gaze, he nodded. One lean hand skimmed the hair from Bonnie's pale cheeks. Watching the soothing, hypnotic stroke of his fingertips, Leslie felt her heart turn over. His fingers were so lean and strong-looking. How was it possible for a man's touch to encompass such tenderness? Yet she knew from experience that his hands were infinitely gentle, infinitely patient. . . .

"But I stopped at Rob and Colleen's before I came here," she said finally. "Rob said you weren't there."

He glanced up at her, a glimmer of amusement suddenly appearing. One corner of his mouth slid up in a crooked smile. "That's because I was here."

Leslie blinked. Rob had known what she meant, and Colleen had obviously been here at the hospital with Clint. Maybe they had both figured if she knew Clint was here, she might decide not to come. . . . Apparently Colleen hadn't ceased her matchmaking efforts; now it seemed her husband had joined forces with her.

"When did you get back from Alaska?" she asked.

There was a slight pause. "I never went."

"But Colleen said Rob took you to the airport—"

"I couldn't get on that plane, Leslie."

His tone was quiet. She couldn't look away from him. His expression was as guarded and tentative as she knew her own must be. She was afraid to read too much into it, just as afraid not to.

Her lips parted. "Why not? Why did you stay?" She swallowed the dryness in her throat, her voice scarcely audible. "Because of Bonnie's surgery?"

He shook his head. "I had intended to fly back today."

She had to know why he hadn't left. She just had to. "Then why didn't you leave?" she asked again.

He gave her a look that was deep and penetrating, and countered her question with one of his own. "Don't you know?" he asked quietly.

She shook her head. She was perilously close to losing control.

To her horror, her vision blurred. The next thing she knew she was being bodily turned. His hands settled on her shoulders, warm and reassuring. But Leslie felt anything but reassured. It was as if she were poised on the fringes of some distant, frightening world. She didn't know if she should turn and run back the way she had come, or rush blindly forward. She blinked and tried to focus her swimming vision, looking everywhere but at him.

"Look at me, Leslie."

The low, melting way he said her name made her quiver even more. She felt the gentle pressure of his fingers at her chin, guiding her eyes to his.

His hands stole up to cradle her face, his expression so scorching and intense it penetrated clear to her soul. "I didn't leave," he stated with quiet deliberation, "because of you. I love you, Leslie. I love you too damned much to leave you."

Leslie stared at him. The seconds ticked by. Both his look and his voice were charged with emotion. Everything was going to be all right, she realized numbly. She didn't know how or why she knew, she just did. The relief that poured through her almost brought her to her knees.

Her eyes glistened with tears both shed and unshed. "Clint." She choked out his name, wanting to say more but unable to. "Oh, Clint, I—"

His heart wrenched at the tiny break in her voice. With a low groan he pulled her against him, his hands both tender and urgent. She was trembling, he realized, but so was he.

"Shh," he whispered above the honey-colored cloud of her hair. The hoarseness in his voice revealed the strain he'd been under. "Don't cry, sweetheart. It tears me up inside when you cry."

She gave a muffled half sob and clutched the front of his shirt. "It's all right, babe. Everything's going to be fine, I promise." His arms locked tighter around her. The gentle brush of his lips across her temple was in direct contrast to the almost desperate strength of his embrace.

She sagged against him, burying her face in the hollow between his neck and shoulder, her breathing as torn and labored as his. At her mute acceptance, his eyes squeezed shut, every fiber of his body caught in the torrent of raw emotion that swept through him. He'd almost lost her once, he thought raggedly. He wouldn't lose her again.

It was a long, long time before he reluctantly drew back. Imprisoning both her hands within his, he regarded her intently, his dark features grave.

"We need to talk," he said gently. She began to protest, but he stopped whatever she might have said with a tiny shake of his head. "I need to say this, sweetheart. Not just for you, but for me."

He paused. A fleeting look of pain darkened his eyes, and Leslie knew then how difficult this was for him.

"The night I asked you to marry me," he began. "Do you remember what you told me? That if you adopted Bonnie, you were afraid I'd look at her and see Angelina?"

How could she forget? She nodded.

"You know I've had a hell of a time dealing with my feelings for Bonnie. I—I know I've told you this before, but we have to get this behind us once and for all. It's haunted me ever since that night."

Her heart went out to him. She gave a tiny nod, her eyes encouraging.

"I've always known how Bonnie felt about me. I knew it, and while a part of me was elated at the knowledge, another part cried out that it was all wrong." His gaze slipped to the sleeping child at their side. His expression softened, and Leslie felt an overwhelming tenderness pour through her chest.

His voice stole through the silence, low and fervent. "But it wasn't wrong, Leslie. I realized it the night she fell and cut her head, the night I first held her. Because when I touched her, it felt so—so right. And I knew then how wrong I had been to keep reminding myself that if Angelina hadn't died, I could have had a little girl just like her. But you showed me that Bonnie is . . . special. She's just . . . just Bonnie.''

Leslie saw that his gaze had returned to her face. ''But you were wrong when you said I'd look at her and see Angelina,'' he chided gently. He lifted her hands and brushed his lips over her knuckles, his eyes never wavering from hers. ''Remember the morning after the night we made love?''

Leslie's smile was as shaky as she felt inside. ''The infamous morning after?'' she tried to joke.

One hand slipped around her waist; he pulled her close. ''Bonnie came in and saw you'd been crying. She crawled up on your lap, and wiped the tears from your cheek.'' He lifted a hand and touched her cheek, in much the same way that Bonnie had done. His smile faded.

''Whenever I think of Bonnie, I think of you—and that moment,'' he whispered. ''I think I'll carry that image around with me forever. The two of you, hanging onto each other for dear life, your hair like a sun-kissed morning, and hers so shiny and dark. . . . Something happened to me then, Leslie, something so powerful I can't begin to describe it. I knew then how much I loved you. And I knew then I'd never be able to let you go.''

Her heart was so swollen with emotion, her voice trembled and overflowed with the love she felt. ''Clint, I—I love you so much. I thought I'd die this past week without you.'' Her arms lifted blindly. Tears streamed from her eyes. She clung to him, whispering his name over and over.

The tone that soothed her was one of melting tenderness. ''God, Leslie, so did I.'' He groaned and buried his mouth in her hair. "I should never have accused you of being selfish. Because I'm the one who's being selfish. That's why I quit my job."

She eased back and stared at him. "You what?"

Clint laughed at her dazed expression. "That's why I didn't get on that plane to Alaska." He ran a finger down the tip of her nose. Then, unable to stop himself, he kissed her breathlessly parted lips.

Her eyes were still wide open, gazing at him blankly. He sighed and decided an explanation might be in order. "It didn't occur to me until after you refused to marry me that maybe I was asking too much of you."

She shook her head. "No, Clint," she said quickly. "I should never have doubted you, about Bonnie or anything else. I should have known I could trust you. I *do* trust you—"

Warm fingers against her lips stifled the rest of her admission. He shook his head and smiled crookedly. "To tell you the truth," he murmured, "I don't think I could stand to be separated from you for days at a time, even if I came home every weekend. Besides, it worked out better than I ever expected."

She smiled mistily. "How?"

"When I told Paul, my boss, that I was quitting, he told me he'd been thinking about leaving as well. It turns out he wants to start his own consulting firm here in San Diego." He stopped, his eyes taking on an unholy gleam.

"Well?" Leslie waited breathlessly. "What happened? Did he offer you a job?"

His smile widened. "No," he said mildly. "He offered me a partnership. But you know what the best part is? Since we'll be consulting on engineering projects rather than working on the actual sites, there won't be nearly as much travel involved or as much time away from home. Maybe a few days a month—'' he rested his forehead against hers ''—but not weeks and weeks like it was before.''

Her fingers crept up to touch his lean cheek. ''And you did that for me?''

His eyes darkened. ''I did it for *us*.'' His tone turned husky. ''Now that I think we've managed to get rid of all the obstacles, there's only one left.'' His eyes searched hers. His head lowered so that their lips were only a breath apart.

''I want you,'' he whispered against her mouth. ''Never doubt that I need you, because I need you more than I've ever needed anyone in my entire life. And never doubt that I love you, because I love you in a thousand different ways I could never express.'' He paused. ''Marry me.''

Clint caught his breath at the sweetness of her smile. She was laughing; she was crying. She was in his arms, and nothing had ever felt so right. ''Yes,'' she cried softly. ''Oh, yes!''

The gentleness of his lips on hers said all that words could not. His touch was so achingly tender; it touched her heart, it touched her soul. Only one thing kept the moment from being utterly perfect, and that was not knowing if Bonnie would ever truly be their daughter.

They were so caught up in each other that neither heard the whisper of the door as it opened.

Behind them, someone cleared her throat.

Leslie's eyes snapped open, but Clint made no move to release her. Instead, he pressed her head against his chest and spoke over her head. There was even a smile in his voice as he informed the newcomer, "It's all right. We're getting married."

Leslie twisted slightly and risked a peek at the intruder. She nearly moaned her distress. Of all the people to walk in . . . it was Fran!

Leslie pulled away, even though one of Clint's hands remained insistently anchored at her waist. She was relieved to find Fran's expression one of tolerant indulgence. The smile Leslie managed was a sickly one.

Fran tipped her head to the side and regarded Clint. "You're Rob's brother, aren't you? I know we've met several times before, but I'm afraid I can't recall your name."

"It's Clint. And I think you already know Leslie." The smile he supplied was devastating. Leslie hoped it would have a positive effect on Fran; she still wasn't sure what Fran thought of catching her and Clint wrapped in each other's arms. At least Bonnie wasn't awake, thank heaven.

Fran's gaze slid to Leslie. "I thought I'd drop by to see how Bonnie was doing, but I was hoping you might be here." She was smiling, but unfortunately, neither her smile nor her tone revealed anything. She moved to the opposite side of the bed and laid a hand on Bonnie's forehead. "Poor little angel," she murmured.

Leslie held her breath when Fran glanced up again. "I talked to Dr. King after surgery." She stepped back, her manner brisk. "He said Bonnie will need some long-term physical therapy, possibly another surgery at a later time. How do you feel about that?"

"I expected it," Leslie said, squaring her shoulders. "I knew before Bonnie even went into surgery that there were no guarantees." She met the other woman's gaze head-on, her chin tipped proudly. "I love Bonnie because of who she is. Frankly it doesn't make any difference to me how she talks or doesn't talk, whether she limps or doesn't limp. I love her," she finished quietly, "no matter what."

Fran didn't say anything, but the merest ghost of a smile crept across her lips. Behind her glasses, a sparkle brightened her eyes. "Somehow I thought you'd say that," she murmured.

Clint's hand had slid down to clasp hers. He gave her fingers a reassuring squeeze. "Fran." Her voice was pitched very low. By now she scarcely dared to hope, to even breathe. "Have you decided to recommend for or against my petition to adopt Bonnie?"

Fran's eyes flitted to the child in question. "Bonnie," she said softly, "is a special little girl, with very special needs." There was a heartbeat of silence. "That's why we've decided in your favor."

Leslie stood stock-still. "The McCalls?"

Fran threw up her hands. "Believe it or not, they've decided they're not ready to adopt after all." She must have glimpsed the silent question in Leslie's eyes. "But that had nothing to do with our final decision. They phoned yesterday with the news that they had changed their minds, but we already knew they just weren't the right parents for Bonnie. Which reminds me—" her eyes settled on Clint "—how do you feel about taking on a wife and a child?"

An incredible tenderness flooded his expression as he glanced down at Bonnie. At that precise instant,

Bonnie's eyes fluttered open. *"Papá,"* she murmured, and stretched out a tiny hand.

His fingers curled around her hand. He had to swallow the tightness in his throat before he could speak. His eyes sought Leslie's, his voice suspiciously husky. "I couldn't be more proud to have Bonnie as my daughter... *our* daughter," he corrected himself.

For the second time in just a few short minutes, tears of joy spilled down Leslie's cheeks. When Fran left a few minutes later, Clint brushed away the lingering traces of dampness. "You haven't changed your mind about marrying me, have you?"

She gazed up at him with shining eyes. "Never," she promised.

"I'm going to make you my wife so fast it'll make your head spin, just to make sure," he teased.

"The sooner the better," she started to quip. Suddenly her eyes grew wide. She bit her lip, but a rueful chuckle escaped nonetheless. "I haven't even told you about the house I rented. And I've got a moving van full of furniture due tomorrow."

Clint frowned thoughtfully. "The bungalow's too small for the three of us." He paused. "I've been thinking. How would you feel about building a house? I've been playing around with a few plans this past week—we could live in the house you rented while it was being built."

She touched his lips with hers. "I don't care where we live, as long as we're together."

He kissed her slowly, lingeringly, his lips warm and infinitely gentle. When at last they parted, he smiled, a silly, sentimental smile, the kind only lovers shared.

Seeing the love that blazed warm and tender in his eyes, Leslie felt as if she were glowing inside and out.

Knowing he was watching, she laid her hand atop his where his fingers still curled loosely around Bonnie's, linking the three of them together.

"You know," she whispered tremulously, "we're going to make one heck of a family."

His gaze traveled from her radiant face, to the sleeping child, and back again. "We already are," he said softly.

LESLIE DIDN'T THINK it was possible to be happier than she was at that moment, but it appeared she was wrong. Less than a month later, four adults and three small children filed out of a San Diego county courtroom. Feeling weak-kneed and utterly dazed, the woman leading the group dropped onto the nearest long bench pushed against the wall.

"She's ours," Leslie murmured numbly. "She's really ours."

Clint eased down next to her. His smile was heady as he repeated his wife's words, as though he craved the reassurance as much as she.

"Yeah," he muttered. "She's really ours."

Tess hopped up next to Leslie, her pixie features bright and hopeful. "Now that you and Uncle Clint 'dopted Bonnie, does that make her my sister?"

Brian snorted. "'Course not, silly. If Bonnie was gonna be our sister, Mom and Dad would have had to adopt her."

Tess's face fell. She looked so disappointed Leslie gave her a quick hug. "Bonnie's your cousin now, Tess. That's almost as good, isn't it?"

Tess still looked crushed. "But I wanted Bonnie for my sister. And I know Bonnie wanted me for her sister."

Leslie dropped a kiss onto her blond head. "I know, sweetie. But you and Bonnie are just as close as sisters, and that's what counts. Besides, if Mommy and Daddy's new baby is a girl, then you'll have a sister."

Tess brightened immediately. "What about Bonnie? Will she get a sister?"

Leslie's lips twitched as her gaze met her husband's. Clint chuckled. "That's a definite possibility."

"How?" Tess was fairly bouncing up and down. "How can we make sure Bonnie gets a sister, too?"

Leslie blinked and cast a pleading look at Clint. His eyes were dancing, his shoulders shaking with mirth. Clearly she'd find no help there. Rob had turned his face to hide a grin. "Oh . . . I think you'll have to ask your mom and dad about that," she told Tess hastily.

Colleen chuckled. "See what you're in for?" The next instant she was scrambling for her daughter, who had spotted a drinking fountain down the hall.

"I'll say," Rob put in. "Especially since you two seemed destined to do things in a big way." He shook his head. "My head's still reeling from the two of you married and becoming parents in less than a month."

"Oh, I'm not complaining." The laughter in Clint's eyes turned to melting tenderness. He pressed his lips against Bonnie's forehead. Bonnie responded by laying both small hands against his lean cheeks. "Daddy," she giggled. She still called him *Papá* most of the time, and he wasn't sure he ever wanted her to stop. That one word never failed to flood his entire being with a feeling of incredible pleasure.

The next instant Bonnie's liquid brown eyes turned to Leslie. *"Mama,"* she whispered happily and reached for her. Clint eased the child into her lap, smiling slightly as her face softened with glowing sweetness. She hugged Bonnie as tightly as the cast would allow, her cheek pressed against the little girl's temple. As always, the sight of the two of them—one dark, one so fair—moved him deeply.

Sensing his gaze, knowing they shared the same blinding rush of emotion—Leslie experienced a feeling too intense for words. She smiled, and Clint knew the purity of that smile would remain etched on his soul forever.

It was a long time later, after they'd said their goodbyes to Rob and Colleen, that he lingeringly traced that very same smile with his fingertips. The air between them was close and heated, his heartbeat only now beginning to calm beneath the furious winds of passion that had claimed him only a moment earlier.

He kissed the vulnerable spot below her ear. "Why are you smiling?" he murmured.

"Does there have to be a reason?" She laughed.

"Yes," he whispered, gently nipping the lobe of her ear.

"I could give you a dozen reasons." Leslie thought of the time not so long ago when she had said something very similar to Colleen, something about all the reasons why Clint was all wrong for her. How foolish she had been then—how blind.

And how lucky she was now.

"Or," she added huskily, "I could give you just one."

"Scrap the dozen and just give me the one." She shivered as a lean finger traced a lazy erotic pattern over her full breasts. Yet the next second he had propped himself on his elbows above her, awaiting her answer with a patience he hadn't yet learned to master.

Her eyes darkened. It never failed to thrill her that Clint needed to hear the words as much as she did. Her fingers tangled in the silky roughness of his hair.

"Because I love you," she said. "Because I love you, and you've made me the happiest woman on earth."

This time he was the one who smiled. "That's two, Mrs. Stuart. But I'll let it pass, because I happen to have a very good reason...."

"And what might that be?" She gazed up at him through love-misted eyes.

He reached for the hand that lay curled against his chest, slowly bringing it to his mouth, where he kissed the plain gold band circling her finger with a reverence that brought tears to her eyes.

"Because I love you," he said softly, showering her with the sweetest words she had ever heard.

"I know," she whispered.

And she did.

COMING IN 1991 FROM HARLEQUIN SUPERROMANCE:

Three abandoned orphans,
one missing heiress!

Dying millionaire Owen Byrnside receives an
anonymous letter informing him that twenty-six years
ago, his son, Christopher, fathered a daughter. The
infant was abandoned at a foundling home that
subsequently burned to the ground, destroying all
records. Three young women could be Owen's long-
lost granddaughter, and Owen is determined to track
down each of them! Read their stories in

#434 HIGH STAKES (available January 1991)
#438 DARK WATERS (available February 1991)
#442 BRIGHT SECRETS (available March 1991)

Three exciting stories of intrigue and romance by
veteran Superromance author Jane Silverwood.

**Don't miss one exciting moment of you next vacation
with Harlequin's**

FREE
FIRST CLASS TRAVEL ALARM CLOCK

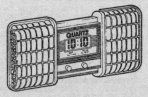

Actual Size
3 ¼ ″ × 1 ¼ ″h

By reading FIRST CLASS—Harlequin Romance's armchair travel plan for the incurably romantic—you'll not only visit a different dreamy destination every month, but you'll also receive a FREE TRAVEL ALARM CLOCK!

All you have to do is collect 2 proofs-of-purchase from FIRST CLASS Harlequin Romance books. FIRST CLASS is a one title per month series, available from January to December 1991.

For further details, see FIRST CLASS premium ads in FIRST CLASS Harlequin Romance books. Look for these books with the special FIRST CLASS cover flash!

JTLOOK

HARLEQUIN'S "BIG WIN"
SWEEPSTAKES RULES & REGULATIONS
NO PURCHASE NECESSARY TO ENTER OR RECEIVE A PRIZE

1. To enter and join the Reader Service, scratch off the metallic strips on all your BIG WIN tickets #1-#6. This will reveal the values for each sweepstakes entry number, the number of free book(s) you will receive and your free bonus gift as part of our Reader Service. If you do not wish to take advantage of our Reader Service but wish to enter the Sweepstakes only, scratch off the metallic strips on your BIG WIN tickets #1-#4. Return your entire sheet of tickets intact. Incomplete and/or inaccurate entries are ineligible for that section or sections of prizes. Not responsible for mutilated or unreadable entries or inadvertent printing errors. Mechanically reproduced entries are null and void.

2. Whether you take advantage of this offer or not, your Sweepstakes numbers will be compared against the list of winning numbers generated at random by the computer. In the event that all prizes are not claimed by March 31, 1992, a random drawing will be held from all qualified entries received from March 30, 1990 to March 31, 1992, to award all unclaimed prizes. All cash prizes (Grand to Sixth), will be mailed to the winners and are payable by check in U.S. funds. Seventh prize will be shipped to winners via third-class mail. These prizes are in addition to any free, surprise or mystery gifts that might be offered. Versions of this sweepstakes with different prizes of approximate equal value may appear at retail outlets or in other mailings by Torstar Corp. and its affiliates.

3. The following prizes are awarded in this sweepstakes: ★ Grand Prize (1) $1,000,000; First Prize (1) $25,000; Second Prize (1) $10,000; Third Prize (5) $5,000; Fourth Prize (10) $1,000; Fifth Prize (100) $250; Sixth Prize (2,500) $10; ★ ★ Seventh Prize (6,000) $12.95 ARV.

   ★ This presentation offers a Grand Prize of a $1,000,000 annuity. Winner will receive $33,333.33 a year for 30 years without interest totalling $1,000,000.

   ★ ★ Seventh Prize: A fully illustrated hardcover book published by Torstar Corp. Approximate retail value of the book is $12.95.

   Entrants may cancel the Reader Service at anytime without cost or obligation to buy (see details in center insert card).

4. This Sweepstakes is being conducted under the supervision of an independent judging organization. By entering this Sweepstakes, each entrant accepts and agrees to be bound by these rules and the decisions of the judges, which shall be final and binding. Odds of winning in the random drawing are dependent upon the total number of entries received. Taxes, if any, are the sole responsibility of the winners. Prizes are nontransferable. All entries must be received at the address printed on the reply card and must be postmarked no later than 12:00 MIDNIGHT on March 31, 1992. The drawing for all unclaimed sweepstakes prizes will take place May 30, 1992, at 12:00 NOON, at the offices of Marden-Kane, Inc., Lake Success, New York.

5. This offer is open to residents of the U.S., the United Kingdom, France and Canada, 18 years or older, except employees and their immediate family members of Torstar Corp., its affiliates, subsidiaries, and all other agencies and persons connected with the use, marketing or conduct of this sweepstakes. All Federal, State, Provincial and local laws apply. Void wherever prohibited or restricted by law. Any litigation within the Province of Quebec respecting the conduct and awarding of a prize in this publicity contest must be submitted to the Régie des loteries et courses du Québec.

6. Winners will be notified by mail and may be required to execute an affidavit of eligibility and release, which must be returned within 14 days after notification or an alternative winner will be selected. Canadian winners will be required to correctly answer an arithmetical skill-testing question administered by mail, which must be returned within a limited time. Winners consent to the use of their names, photographs and/or likenesses for advertising and publicity in conjunction with this and similar promotions without additional compensation. For a list of major winners, send a stamped, self-addressed envelope to: WINNERS LIST, c/o Harlequin Reader Service, 3010 Walden Ave., P.O. Box 1396, Buffalo, NY 14269-1396. Winners Lists will be fulfilled after the May 30, 1992 drawing date.

If Sweepstakes entry form is missing, please print your name and address on a 3″ ×5″ piece of plain paper and send to:

In the U.S.
Harlequin's "BIG WIN" Sweepstakes
3010 Walden Ave.
P.O. Box 1867
Buffalo, NY 14269-1867

In Canada
Harlequin's "BIG WIN" Sweepstakes
P.O. Box 609
Fort Erie, Ontario
L2A 5X3

Offer limited to one per household.
© 1991 Harlequin Enterprises Limited   Printed in the U.S.A.

LTY-H191R

Harlequin romances are now available in stores at these convenient times each month.

Harlequin Presents
Harlequin American Romance
Harlequin Historical
Harlequin Intrigue

These series will be in stores on the 4th of every month.

Harlequin Romance
Harlequin Temptation
Harlequin Superromance
Harlequin Regency Romance

New titles for these series will be in stores on the 16th of every month.

We hope this new schedule is convenient for you. With only two trips each month to your local bookseller, you will always be sure not to miss any of your favorite authors!

Happy reading!

Please note there may be slight variations in on-sale dates in your area due to differences in shipping and handling.